To Alan,

This is an attempt by a veteran poet to communicate "afglovada"!

J. Duff.

CALLED TO SERVE

A ministry of Presence

An Historical Novel

By

[signature: L R Coleman]

Lt Col (ret) Reverend Lyman R Coleman
Honorary Chaplain to the Royal Canadian Regiment

Order this book online at www.trafford.com
or email orders@trafford.com

Most Trafford titles are also available at major online book retailers.

© Copyright 2010 Lyman Coleman.
All rights reserved. No part of this publication may be reproduced, stored in a retrieval system, or transmitted, in any form or by any means, electronic, mechanical, photocopying, recording, or otherwise, without the written prior permission of the author.

Printed in Victoria, BC, Canada.

ISBN: 978-1-4269-3036-2 (soft)
ISBN: 978-1-4269-3037-9 (hard)

Library of Congress Control Number: 2010904061

Our mission is to efficiently provide the world's finest, most comprehensive book publishing service, enabling every author to experience success. To find out how to publish your book, your way, and have it available worldwide, visit us online at www.trafford.com

Trafford rev. 3/30/2010

   www.trafford.com

North America & international
toll-free: 1 888 232 4444 (USA & Canada)
phone: 250 383 6864 ♦ fax: 812 355 4082

Also by this author

Death of Dreams
ISBN 1-4120-9135-7 C$24.95
Trafford.com

IN THIS SIGN
ISBN1-897113-04-8 C$24.95
General Store Publishing House
www.gsph.com

I dedicate this story to the men and women of the Canadian Forces and their Allies who served the cause of humanity during the Afghan conflict. Some gave their lives while others were grievously wounded. They will not be forgotten.

To the chaplains of many countries, you did your jobs valiantly. God Bless you all.

Forward

From the Office of the Chaplain General to the Canadian Forces

When I joined the Canadian Forces in 1981 Lt Col (Ret) Lyman Coleman was a staff officer in the Office of the Chaplain General. He had bags of operational experience and I immediately liked his no nonsense style. Although he was abundantly kind and had a warm compassionate heart you knew that he was as hard as nails and that he probably lived on a diet of them. You knew intuitively that he was the kind of chaplain soldiers, sailors, and aircrew would flock to. He wore jump wings and I admired that he loved the troops so much that he was willing to take any mode of transport to be with them. It became apparent to me that he 'wrote the book' on what being a soldier's padre was all about. I decided right then and there that I wanted to be a chaplain just like Lyman Coleman and I truly believe I succeeded in doing just that.

Lt Col (Ret) Lyman Coleman, one of my heroes, has blessed us with a third wonderful novel. In his first novel, *In This Sign,* he told the compelling and thoroughly entertaining story of a young Canadian Forces chaplain during WWII. In his second novel, *Death of Dreams*, he told the captivating story of the Coleman clan, focusing on a brother lost overseas in 1943. In this latest novel, *Called To Serve,* Lyman Coleman tells the story of chaplains serving in Afghanistan. He has done much research and interviewed a number of chaplains who have been there, done that, and have the t-shirt to prove it. The chaplaincy in the military context is an exciting vocation and Lt Col (Ret) Lyman Coleman will bring this home to you in living colour. You will find yourself in Afghanistan, on the high seas, and in other exciting environments and settings. You will not only get a taste of what is it like to be a chaplain, but how important it is for military personnel to have chaplains performing their ministry of presence in the good times and the bad times and everywhere in between. You will come away from this magnificent story with heightened respect for those who chose to serve their nation, armed only with their faith in God, and their abiding love for soldiers, sailors, air crew and their families.

I recommend this book to anyone who wants to know more about the Canadian Forces in the first decade of the 21st century and to those who wish to know more about the chaplaincy specifically. It is a great read!

D.C. Kettle CD, CMM
BGen/Bgén
Chaplain General/Aumônier général

From the Colonel of the Royal Canadian Regiment

I am honoured to have been asked by Lyman to write this forward to his latest work, *"Called to Serve"*. While a tale of fiction, his story is one that will be all too familiar to those who have served, or will serve, in Afghanistan. Building his plot on the 2007 deployment of a battle group led by the 2nd Battalion, The Royal Canadian Regiment into the Kandahar region, he well captures the bitter sweet experience of an Afghan tour.

Lyman's primary character is Michael Russell, a reserve chaplain who has volunteered and been accepted for a tour of duty in Afghanistan. He walks us through the rigorous process that one must follow in order to be accepted for the very important role of ministering to today's soldier. Russell fits the bill admirably being described by his wife Angie as a "keen warrior". He is a team player who effortlessly bonds with his fellow chaplains and with the soldiers he is there to serve. The anxiety of an operational tour on family is brought home effectively through regular exchanges between Mike and Angie.

Lyman's writing has benefited from the superb research that he undertook while compiling this volume. His description of operations and conditions in Afghanistan is spot on. His collaboration with soldiers and leaders who have been in action in Afghanistan shows in his realistic portrayal of the grind and challenges of their daily routine. With a little imagination the reader is able to taste the dust, feel the heat and experience the tension and exhilaration of a firefight. Through his vivid word pictures the uninitiated are able to appreciate the consequences of tragic events, which are an inevitable result of combat operations.

More important, Lyman shines a light on the critical importance of chaplains to mission success. This is a constant theme in all three of his books, but it is a theme that is rarely mentioned in the modern military context. Lyman serves us all well by reminding us of the fundamental role that chaplains play in ministering to our soldiers and to their families, particularly the families of our fallen and our wounded. This is where the true value of *"Called to Serve"* lay.

Calling upon his 28 years of uniformed service, and his 25 years of exemplary service as the Honorary Chaplain to The Royal Canadian Regiment, Lyman shows chaplains to be like the rest of us, with both strengths and weaknesses on display. His characters are real and believable built as they are on the life experiences of today's front line chaplains. I am confident that most will find *"Called to Serve"* to be a very enjoyable and compelling read and I heartily recommend it to all.

Pro Patria,
Walter Holmes, MBE, OStJ, CD
Major General (Ret'd)
Colonel, The Royal Canadian Regiment

Preface

In preparation for writing this book I wanted to get a better insight into the people of Afghanistan. I found three amazing books to help me up that steep learning curve. *The Kite Runner* by Khaled Hosseini, and his second book, *A Thousand Splendid Suns*, was my starters, and then I found *Three Cups Of Tea* by Greg Mortenson and David Oliver Relin, which enlightened me on a much broader spectrum of that part of our world.

It is not easy for a Canadian to get a clear understanding why we find ourselves in the middle of this conflict. As a nation we mourn for the loss of every life and the growing injury list. We must understand that we are not there primarily to fight; rather we are there to help the Afghan people re-construct their war-torn country. It is a nation made up of many tribes and religious groups, mainly Muslim. Strife appears to be a part of the national culture. For centuries internal clashes and foreign armies have raped the land and people. So why are we there? To assist in establishing a democracy like those we have in the West seems to be an impossible goal in a land where democracy, as a form of government, is totally unknown.

In the recent past Canada has been known as a nation of Peace Keepers. I spent my 28 years in the CF as one of those soldiers and I am proud of our accomplishments in that area. However, times change, and we must change with them, now we find ourselves in a conflict where Canadians place their lives on the line for a cause. Our soldiers are there to protect and defend the men and women who are rebuilding a ravished country. Road builders, bridge builders, irrigation reconstruction, school builders…all working together to give a nation a new start. Are we succeeding? Depends who you talk to. Should we be there? How can we not, when fellow human beings find themselves in such dire jeopardy, when they face death and domination by a demonic regime that has vowed to enslave them. It is a very complex situation, but I believe it is our duty to stand and serve. It's what Canadians have done in the past. It's what we have believed in as a country. It is a part of our heritage and a corner stone of our foundation.

I want to make it quite clear to my reader's right from the start that this story is neither fiction nor non-fiction. The threads woven together come from historical fact. Most of the incidents happened to real people in real time. I have only used 'poetic licence' as a device in the connecting process to make the story more vivid for the reader. Some events and persons may appear chronologically out of order, but I claim the storyteller's prerogative for relating the story as best I can within the limits of believability. Under the title of acknowledgements, I will record the names of those chaplains and others who have contributed to the story. Many padres who served in theatre graciously shared the material in the narrative with me. Some of them found it difficult to reveal their inner most feelings as the events to which they allude are very personal, still running raw deep within their psyche. In many ways a chaplain is a very private person. He or she is a listener who holds in trust the confidence of a soldier, sailor or airman/airwoman who is hurting in one way or another. Military members can be injured in many ways…some are physically wounded, some bleed from their spirit, some experience trauma to the mind, some lose their life; others suffer from events far from the field of battle. The chaplain listens to them all and tries to free the individual from their worries, ease their pain, so that they can apply themselves fully to their professional standards.

The chaplain's most effective role is that of 'being there', or as we call it in the military, providing a Ministry of Presence. The chaplain serves his people in a variety of ways; spiritually by providing opportunities for sacrament and worship, physically by sharing day to day life and hardships, mentally by keeping in tune with the individual as they plod through the horrors and ugliness of war. Never doubt it; war is a journey through Hell. One only has to read Christy Blatchford's book, *Fifteen Days*, for that to become self-evident. The chaplain is the one who confronts Hell with God's Word, as a weapon for the Word is mightier than the sword. Since the story line dictated that I had to zero in on a specific period of time, I have chosen that phase to be from February to July 2007. The Canadian Battle Group was cantered on the Second Battalion of the Royal Canadian Regiment with Lt Col Rob Walker in Command. Captain Steele Lazerte was their designated chaplain. He was supported by other chaplains of

Rotation 5 who took turns with the Battle Group when Steele was "outside the wire" or otherwise deployed. Major Malcolm Berry, a Reserve chaplain, was the Team Leader. Both Steele and Malcolm have made a significant contributions to the story as it developed.

Major the Reverend Jim Short, a Reserve Chaplain had a profound influence on the manuscript by clearly and openly sharing the experiences of his Afghanistan tour of duty in 2008, even to the point of delving into his diary where he enshrined his most personal and delicate feelings.

Therine Ell has been a solid support in reading and editing the manuscript and offering insightful suggestions for the story line. Her perspective, as one who kept the home fires burning, was most helpful.

I am grateful to a number of chaplains who have shared their Afghan tour experiences with me. I also wish to thank those who read the manuscript and provided line editing as well as offering suggestions to help improve the story.

I must confess that I had an ulterior motive for selecting a period when the RCR were in the line. I served with the First Battalion for almost six years (1960-65) and since my retirement in 1985; I have been an Honorary Chaplain to the Regiment. I have served with pride every unit to which I have been attached; HQ Quebec Command, 25 Canadian Ordinance Depot with its attached Apprentice Training School, the Canadian Guards, the Royal Canadian Signals, the Royal Canadian Electrical and Mechanical School, Combat Arms School, three Helicopter Squadrons: 422 and 403 in Gagetown and 442 in Comox, the Royal Twenty-Second Regiment and the Lord Strathcona Horse in Cyprus, Base Chaplain in Gagetown and Comox, Director of Chaplains Administration (2) in Ottawa and on my last posting as Senior Chaplain of the Army in the position of Command Chaplain Mobile Command. I am a military parachutist with 93 jumps logged. Needless to say, the initiation into my first field unit, 1 RCR, branded me for life. Bless the Royals! Pro Patria.

Lyman Coleman

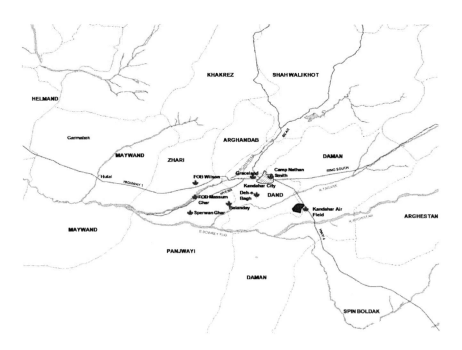

Prologue

Michael Russell, chaplain to the Battle Group, gazed with awe and wonder into the star- spangled sky of the Afghan night. It was crystal clear. There was no moon, but on the celestial stage, light seemed to be magnified to an intense degree. The landscape around the Royal Canadian Regiment's Strong Point at FOB Sperwan Ghar glowed. The shadows were few as the brightness from above beamed straight down. Mike pondered the moment and prayed inwardly, 'Thank you, Lord, for this glorious display of your Universe around us. We seem so insignificant in comparison. The heavens speak… no shout, of Your original powers… from dust You created us… and to dust we shall return. It is the cycle of life.' Mike gazed around him at the sleeping soldiers, heard their night sounds, some breathing evenly, others snoring, and an occasional moan. "Be with these men and women as they answer the great humanitarian cause before them. Many don't understand why they are here. Why lives must be sacrificed and bodies broken. I, too, have questions, but my faith does not bend for I know You are the answer to all problems…all questions, if all men would but turn to You and walk the way of Peace. But this rarely seems to happen as in this poor land violence and terrorism go hand in hand assaulting innocent people. Help us to help them, Lord. Let our people know we are making a difference. Amen."

It is after midnight and half the section is at rest. The chaplain is in his sleeping bag fascinated by the brilliant starry night. On his left, Corporal Ann Kowamoto, aged 30, married with two children back home lays half awake waiting for her turn at stand to. On Mike's right a young Private soldier sits up in his sleeping bag and without thought, lights a cigarette.

"Douse that goddam flame, idiot, you wanna hole between your eyes?" came a sharp order from the dark… an awkward silence.

Private Scotty Martin.
"Are you awake, Padre?" Corporal Ann Kowamoto, comes alert and listens in.

Chaplain:
"Yes, I was just drinking in the beauty of the Universe above. Glorious, isn't it?"

Private Martin:
"What are we doing over here? I mean I can't see much sense in it. And what are you doing here unarmed in this violent, unpredictable God forsaken place?"

Chaplain:
"Oh boy, Scotty, you've asked the main question. First of all, it's not God forsaken. If anything, its man-forsaken…a killing ground for internal and external strife for thousands of years. It's like Guerrilla warfare has become a National sport over here. Let me begin by answering your second question. I am unarmed because I'm a man of Peace.

I believe mankind should learn how to settle conflict by peaceable means as Jesus would have us do…no, that is not a cliché. I'm not some Holy Joe going around pasting hasty notes in convenient places to distract the passers-by.

What I do is help erect signposts to guide people along that unknown highway we call Life. If people watched for these there would be less carnage along the Way. I like that line from the hymn Amazing Grace…

"Tis grace that brought me safe thus far, and grace will lead me home."

I need no weapons to do that! If you think I'm nuts… so be it.

I am a man of unmoveable faith and uncompromising hope… and I believe in the possibility of a new direction forward that would eliminate the need for war. Two thousand years ago the Man of Peace taught us that approach, but there's those who don't listen and still don't. One of the reasons we are here is to try and enlist better methods of communication…that's why the meetings with the locals, the *shuras*, are being held in the villages.

I won't evade your first question, but there are no easy answers. It's a very complex situation. First of all, there are many answers. There is the military answer that we all know. Each one of us chose to join the CF unconditionally; in simple terms, that is why we are here. Then there is the political answer. Canada committed troops to Afghanistan in 2002 as a part of the coalition ground forces to help Afghans to rebuild their country as a stable, democratic and self-sufficient society after the Taliban control was denied. The ultimate goal is to leave Afghanistan to Afghans in a state better governed, more peaceful and secure. To do this, our focus is on not only governance, but on the progressive development of the infrastructure needs of the people and the training of an Afghan National Security Force. It's important to remember that we are here with over 60 other nations and international organizations at the request of the democratically elected Afghan government, and as a part of a United Nations-mandated, NATO-led mission. All to say, this is a humanitarian undertaking to relieve a shattered people. See what I mean by a complicated mix of things. I hope that helps you get a better picture of things?

Private Martin:
"A lot to think about, Padre. Thanks for the larger picture."

Chaplain:
"I have already given a part of my answer and would be happy to go on, but we'd better try and get some rest.

Might need it as dawn breaks. Any time you'd like to talk, just collar me. Back at base would be good, and if you have buddies who would like to share in a chat about this we can have a get-to-gether. OK?"

Corporal Kowamoto:
"I want to get in on this! Would that be all right, Padre?"

Chaplain:
"More the merrier, Ann."

Chapter One

Bishops Court

Kingston, Ontario
April 20th, 2006

Reverend Michael Russell
Land of Lakes Parish
Plevna, Ontario

Dear Michael,

Please find enclosed the formal papers for a Leave of Absence covering your term of service with the Canadian Forces. This will allow you to accept a chaplaincy posting to Afghanistan as a Reserve chaplain during which time you will come under the jurisdiction of the Bishop Ordinary. I am delighted that your grandfather, Canon Ralph Russell, will be able to assume parish duties during your absence. I understand he will work primarily from the family cottage located in the heart of the parish. He is a man of amazing health and ability for his age and the people of the area know him well, for as this is where he started his ministry those many years ago.

On a closing note, Michael, be assured that you and those whom you serve will be in my prayers daily. May God bless you.

+George
Bishop of Ontario

* * * * *

Mike Russell shuffled the papers on his desk in an attempt to find the correspondence he had with the military concerning his enquiry to serve as a chaplain in Afghanistan. He was unsuccessful.

"Angie, have you seen my military letters." He called out to his wife in the kitchen.

"The last time I saw them they were on your desk. Look there!"

"I have been. Can't see them."

"If you'd clean off your desk once in a while, you'd be able to find what you're looking for! I keep telling you, I'll sort things out for you."

"Don't you dare disturb my desk; I know exactly where my stuff is!"

"Right, go find the papers then."

Mike couldn't remember how often this exchange had taken place. He was prone to leave his correspondence in piles, and most of the time could instantly retrieve what he was searching for. He smiled. Angie was a very organized person. She held degrees in Nursing and her training was specific where orderliness was concerned.

"Did you put them in a folder in your filing cabinet?" She offered this suggestion in a more conciliatory tone.

He turned to the cabinet and as soon as he opened the drawer; there were the papers he had filed. "OK. I found them."

Angie joined him in his study. She put her arms around his waist and gave him a hug. "Oh my absent-minded husband," she crooned in his ear. Mike turned and embraced his wife.

"What are you ever going to do without me for six months or more?" she asked.

"That's the question of the day," he replied.

They had dealt with many scenarios in the preceding days since they had come to an agreement on Mike's heart-felt need to offer his services as a chaplain for a tour of duty in Afghanistan. Reserve personnel put themselves forward for active duty voluntarily, unlike the Regular Force where the posting was obligatory.

Angie's heart had missed a beat when he had first discussed his desire to volunteer. He was devoted to the soldiers of the North Country Highland Regiment, as was his grandfather before him, and when members of his unit began to apply for active duty, he felt called to offer his services. His thoughts and prayers had turned more and more to the idea of seeking permission from his bishop for a leave of absence in order to serve with the Regular Force for a tour of duty. Together, he and Angie had been very deliberate in thinking this decision through. Her thoughts and feelings were a significant influence in the decision making process, for Mike would not allow his own wishes to supersede her sincere reasoning, indeed, he could not successfully pass through the screening process if Angie did not sign an agreement of her support for him to go. In the end, as Angie herself expressed it, "I support your wishes for going. I will miss you and can't imagine most of a year without you and hope and pray I am up to the task of living with my own loss, while giving you to the world's gain."

* * * * *

With the bishop's Leave of Absence in hand, Mike proceeded with the next step. He spoke with his parish council and sought their support for an extended period of leave for military service. He told them that his grandfather, whom they knew and respected, would be acting minister during his absence. He had already sounded out the viability of deployment to Afghanistan within the chaplain chain of command and now the formal steps were required. His request was made through his Commanding Officer to the Reserve Brigade and Area Headquarters, thence up to National Defence HQ where it was passed to the Chaplain General for his approval. The process went through the usual bureaucratic steps and in due course, Mike was nominated for one of the number of Chaplaincy positions available for the next rotation to Afghanistan, provided he passed all the physical and psychological tests required for overseas service. He was in top physical condition, as he worked out every week with the NCHR, plus he had his own fitness regime at home. At age 31, he stood a slim six feet tall and was muscular. He wore his hair short in military fashion and had opted for a pencil thin moustache that was traditionally worn by the officers of the NCHR. He passed his fitness tests with flying colours and waited for confirmatory details of his mission report dates to come back down the line. It was a time of reflection for him and Angie and they reminisced over their years together, and how the future might be affected by this time apart and by his service in a place of danger.

Prior to their marriage, Angie had been in training as a psychological nurse in the Veterans wing of St. Joseph's hospital in London, Ontario, while Mike attended Huron Theological College. She was a beguiling, elfin creature with curly red hair that glowed like fire. Her grey green eyes sparkled with energy. She was bright and chatty, a person who enjoyed learning about others, finding out who they really were. Two years later, Mike attended her graduation ceremony and immediately after the event proposed marriage. He still had two years to go toward his Master of Divinity and following his ordination in Anglican Orders they planned to wed. Angie continued on at St Joe's working with veterans who required her specialized skills.

In the spring of 2000 Mike was ordained in the Diocese of Huron on Ascension Day. In June, he and Angie were married with his grandfather as officiating clergy. It was a storybook wedding by all accounts… except for an incident occasioned by Angie's father who initially refused to enter an Anglican Church. "This will be no marriage," he proclaimed loudly before attending the rehearsal dinner the evening before the wedding. He had promised his wife he would behave, but after several pre-dinner drinks, he abandoned his reserve and made several loud derogatory remarks about the Anglican Church. Angie was embarrassed and ran from the room, with her mother, Colleen, trailing.

Brooding, her father moved to a corner of the room with a freshly charged glass of whiskey. Mike headed toward the man he barely knew. Henri LeClaire had not warmed to Mike from the beginning of his relationship with Angie and had discouraged his daughter from bringing her fiancé to his home at Quebec City after their first visit. He had hoped she would eventually break off with Mike and 'find a nice Catholic boy to marry.' Henri recalls Angie flaring, her eyes flashing, 'Father, I love you but you are out of line. I am at an age and live in a time when women can make their own decisions and I choose Michael. If he isn't welcome here, than neither am I.'

While Henri brooded over this memory and Mike came towards him, Ralph Russell stepped in to intervene, and signalled for Mike to wait aside. The old padre had noticed Henri wore the lapel pin of a veteran of the Royal Twenty-Second Regiment, the famous Van Doos of Quebec. Ralph went over to the festering father and succeeded in calming him down enough to learn that the man was opposed to a Protestant wedding.

"You needn't feel that way," soothed Ralph. "Didn't you know that Father Patrick Kelly is sharing the ceremony? He's the Roman Catholic chaplain at the university." Henri sat down crest-fallen. At that moment his red-faced wife, Colleen, came charging back into the room with fire flashing in her green Irish eyes.

"*Tu stupide…tu homme inbicile*…you know you can't hold your liquor. How could you do this to your only daughter?"

Padre Ralph reached for her hand.

"It's OK Mrs. Le Claire; I believe things are in hand. There was a misunderstanding… Ah, here comes Father Kelly now! By the way, M. LeClaire, I see you wear the R22R pin. I was in Sicily at the same time as your unit. Let's find an opportunity to talk sometime."

Later it was learned that Henri Le Claire was an alcoholic. He had come home from WW2 a gaunt and haunted human being who found relief from his anxieties and nightmares in a bottle. The reason Angie chose her field of nursing related back to her father's condition. She wanted to help him and because of him, she found her calling in a Veterans Hospital.

In the end, Mike and Angie were married in a beautiful ceremony conducted by Ralph and Father Patrick, a very ecumenical minded priest…a person devoted to finding friendly relations between Christian churches, as Pope John the Twenty-third had wished in his encyclical Pacem in Terris. Indeed, Mike and Angie had debated the theology of John XXIII and their religious beliefs and she had agreed to attend church services with him as his wife with an open mind. They noted that the life of John XXIII was commemorated in the Anglican Church of Canada each year on 4 June. Instead of separating them, their strong religious beliefs became a bond between them and they were able to share a healthy spiritual relationship respecting the other's deep convictions. As Angie said, "Once a Catholic, always a Catholic."

Mike's reply was, "We say the same thing…Once an Anglican, always an Anglican. Sounds like we may end up Anglo-Catholic!"

"However," cautioned the grandfather when he had heard of their dialogue, "should you two decide upon marriage, it is a clergyman's wife's duty to support her husband in all things." Ralph Russell was very much "old school" and rather out of touch with the day-to-day convolutions of this new generation who were working to find their own identity. Life as he knew it was not as straightforward as he would like it to be. For the university crowd, life was in a constant state of flux…and that created social tensions the aging cleric could not fully comprehend.

And so, on the eve of his Grandson's wedding Ralph could relate somewhat to Angie's father, and Henri and he had a heart to heart visit and ended up roaring with laughter over incidents they had experienced with their units in the Italian campaign. Ralph told Henri that he had met his unit chaplain, Father Leo Gratton, and had liked him very much… indeed, the two chaplains had been kindred spirits. At this point, Father Kelly had joined the conversation.

"I want to congratulate you on such a fine grandson, Reverend Russell. I have had long talks with Angie and Michael. They are exceptional young people with sound vision."

Henri's eyes widened at the priests observations and one could almost hear the wheels turning. "But the boy is not of our persuasion, Father," he said.

"That is so, my friend, but surely we are all on the same journey with God. Do not doubt for one moment that Michael is not a devout Christian. He will make an outstanding clergyman. Mark my words."

The conversation moved into other areas. Toward the end of their tete-a-tete Henri confessed to Ralph that he had been unfair to Michael.

"Father Russell, do forgive my earlier emotional outburst. I can see that Michael appears to be a fine young man and that he comes from a good Christian family. It took my wife's censorship to open my eyes to how blind and self-centred I have been. I saw Michael as an intruder into my self-contained world. I saw him as one who came to break-up our family. How uncharitable I have been. One only has to look at them to see how they compliment each other. Please forgive me. I more than welcome him, and you, into my family."

"And you to ours, Henri. May the Good Lord bless us all."

* * * * *

As they recollected these and other memories while standing in Mike's office, Angie looked lovingly into her husband's eyes and said, "It seems that time has flown past so quickly. We've had so many adventures along the way. I dread being separated from you even for a few weeks, let alone six months or more."

"I know, my love. Let us pray the time will continue to fly. Our loneliness will bridge the miles and when we come together in mid tour on my leave, we'll have a great celebration. Let's plan to meet in Rome. You've always wanted to visit there. Perhaps in that special place we may finally conceive a child. If we do and should it be a boy, we could call him Peter or perhaps John."

"And if it is a girl, may I suggest Marie, after my beloved grandmother. She was my rock, my special place of comfort whenever terror swept over me. My parents both had fiery tempers, would frequently rage and I would run and put my head under the covers, but when my grandmother was there, I would flee to her like a frightened bird. When I was small, she would take me on her knee, circle her arms about me and hold me tight. As I grew older and faced more of life's troubles, I would seek her out and she would see the look on my face and say, 'Child, come sit beside me.' And we would talk for hours. She was my total sanctuary. I miss her so much."

Mike took her hand in his and simply said, "Marie, it will be. It sounds perfect…Marie Russell…a name that sings. I think your Grandmother and my Granddad might be kindred spirits."

* * * * *

In early September, Mike received orders to proceed to CFB Wainwright for pre-deployment training. He flew from Ottawa to Edmonton where he transferred to a military bus enroute to Wainwright, Alberta…a distance of 322 km. Light rain was falling and the temperature hovered near one degree Celsius. The ride across eastern Alberta was on the bleak side. The countryside was mainly featureless farmland on lightly rolling prairie stretching into the distance from every side.

Mike struck up a conversation with the young soldier sitting beside him. "Where are you from, friend?

"I'm from 1 RCR in Petawawa, sir."

"I'd be more comfortable if you called me Padre."

"Yes sir…I mean Padre," the lad replied.

"How long have you been in the Forces?"

"Just over two years. I joined in January 2004."

"You like it so far?"

"You bet. Once over recruit training, it's been a breeze. I really like army life. It's real challenging."

"Are you going on the next rotation? I thought it was to be a 2 RCR Battle Group."

"It is, sir—uh Padre. I've been posted from the First and Finest to the Second to None, as they say in the Regiment."

"You seem to be pretty fond of your Regiment!"

"You're not kidding, sir. It's the best in Canada." The young soldier beamed.

Mike smiled. "Good for you! I'll be joining you in theatre as one of the padres on rotation. No doubt we'll see each other from time to time."

The soldier, now at ease beside a man wearing a Captain's insignia, settled into the journey. Mike opened the book Angie had given him. It was by the novelist Wilber Smith, entitled *The Triumph of the Sun*. The story was about the rescue of British citizens, both military and civilian, trapped in Khartoum on the Nile during an uprising in 1884. Mike enjoyed this author and had several of his books. As he read, his head began to nod and with the rhythm of the bus's motion he drifted off. He had this knack and was grateful, for it provided him with much needed rest in times following strenuous or stressful activity.

Before they knew it, the transport rolled through the main gate of CFB Wainwright. It was a sprawling base and for training purposes had become known as KAF, Kandahar Air Field. Upon off loading, Mike gathered his gear and was directed to a forty-foot tent in the bivouac area. It was used as both quarters and an office for chaplains. It had a dirt floor and in places it was covered with floorboards. In the office area were several folding chairs and tables. The sleeping area contained cots and ample space for barrack boxes, plus a hanging rack for clothes.

As he stood looking about, he heard a voice behind him.

"You must be Michael Russell?"

Mike turned and faced a well-groomed, wiry built man in his mid-fifties who stretched out his hand in welcome and said, "I'm Malcolm Berry, I'll be your Chaplain Team Leader. Welcome aboard! Let's get you settled and then we can go over to the Mess where you can meet some others before the evening meal." Malcolm was the Reserve Chaplain to the fabled 8th Canadian Hussars (Princess Louise) and was called to duty with the Regular Force.

Mike's gear was placed in the tent, which he would call 'home' for the duration of the training exercise. There were other kits beside other cots in the sleeping area. As Mike got a few things organized, Malcolm dropped hints about the upcoming training,

"We are here primarily to meet the men and women with whom we will be deployed. It is an opportunity for them to get to see and know us. Find ways to do this. The experience can be quite sacramental with a handshake here, a smile there, a question or a thought, a kind word. You are establishing a Ministry of Presence. Watch for and seek out those individuals who are returning for their third or fourth tour in Afghanistan, some even on their sixth. These people can be a valuable resource for you as they have first hand experience and know the ins and outs of a very different life situation. Give them your time and listen carefully to their stories. It will help you gain a deeper insight into what lies ahead.

"Each day the Commander convenes a CUB, (Commanders Update Brief) and key members of his team gather to bring him up to speed on things he and the others need to know. Your role in this gathering is basically to listen, and if asked, make a comment. Most of your primary task is dealing with confidential and personal matters related to people or issues on morale and welfare. These things are related to the Commander on a one-to-one basis unless told otherwise.

"But let's head over to the Mess and you'll meet the other members of our chaplain team. I imagine they're ahead of us already with getting to know people," said Malcolm as he nodded toward the tent flaps.

They crossed the field where a large tent stood, set slightly apart. It was the all, ranks dining facility. Upon entering Malcolm was hailed from a corner table where Padre Robert Morin, a Roman Catholic chaplain, and Captain Felix Tachie, a Pentecostal pastor, sat with a tall, athletic looking man with closely shaven head. He was Captain Steele Lazerte, an Anglican by denomination.

"Come join us," one of the men beckoned.

Malcolm and Mike made their way to the table where the Senior Chaplain introduced the newest member to the team. Soon they were chatting away like old friends.

"Felix will be with the PRT (Provincial Reconstruction Team)", said Malcolm, "and Robert will be located with the NRE (National Support Element.) You, Mike, will work primarily with Steele in the Battle Group; that is as long as two Anglicans can get along… ha ha! It is my plan that we will support each other and rotate by turns, "outside the wire". Tomorrow morning at 0800 we will meet to outline a plan of action for the team. It's critical that we get our act together as quickly as possible, for time waits for no one, and our deployment date is fast approaching."

* * * * *

The Wainwright Training area was set up like Afghanistan, complete with villages and Afghan actors, and everything was replicated as much as is possible to simulate the Kandahar region of Afghanistan including cultural realities. The Battle Group was battling insurgents, the National Support Element was doing supply and convoy echelons, the Provincial Reconstruction Team was doing reconstructive and support work with the Afghan people, working with non-governmental agencies. Liaison Teams were undertaking the very important task of training and mentoring the Afghan National Army battalions that now carried the brunt of operations in the Canadian Operational sector. The Military Police, along with their partners from the RCMP and other civilian police forces, were practicing mentoring the Afghan National Police, the Public Affairs people were busy with press releases and the Civil Military Cooperation folks in conjunction with their CIDA counterparts were conducting Shuras (meetings with village elders.) The Chaplains were honing their own skills. Calls concerning simulated casualties and deaths to test their ability to respond, to be where they needed to be, to follow through the various protocols and acts of ministry they would be expected to conduct in such conditions. This included planning for pastoral care, casualty notification to rear party Chaplains, conducting memorials and ramp ceremonies.

Mike's first morning began with a 0530 wake-up call followed by ablutions and shaving. The chaplains stretched and warmed up as a team before a three-mile run, had quick showers, and then headed for the mess tent for a hearty breakfast. At precisely 0800 hrs, the team gathered together for morning prayers in the chapel beside the living quarters/office. The enclosure was a modular tent named "Fraise Chapel". A different chaplain would lead daily devotions. Coffee was kept brewing in the office area and ready to be served when prayers were over.

After a short break, Malcolm, as the Chaplain Team Leader, chaired the session. "Gentlemen, we soon begin another phase of training…an Exercise called Maple Guardian. In the next few days we will practice convoy drills where we will travel beyond the wire. We will be in a convoy that is attacked or hits an IED (Improvised Explosive Device.) We will be exposed to the various sounds and sights of battle and get used to wearing our entire battle rattle. There will be briefings on various military subjects and where the situation currently stands in Afghanistan. We will re-qualify in basic first aid skills and the donning of protective gear in the event of a chemical or biological threat. We will be a part of a mass casualty exercises both at the field hospital level and in the field, which will find us in the midst of a battle, treating injured soldiers, comforting those who are dying, and loading stretchers with people for evacuation by helicopters.

"But before that takes place we will conduct an Exercise of our own which I have dubbed, 'Operation Bible'". The Canadian bible Society has sent us 1900 special edition Bibles for use by our soldiers in Afghanistan. On Saturday, at the beginning of Exercise Maple guardian, we will have a ceremony of Bible Blessings and distribute them. It will be first come, first served, to any who wish a personal copy. Any left over will be available from our tent office.

"I remind you that our chapel is not only a place to conduct services, but also a place for quiet reflection. At the back we have been able to stock a small lending library and other spiritual accessories for personal use; devotional pamphlets, crucifix, and rosary beads, and some multi-faith symbols. I have no doubt that once people become acquainted with the space, we will have personnel wanting to see a chaplain. Make yourselves available, especially in the quiet hours, if there be such a time in a busy 24/7 hour location.

"Pastoral Care in a military setting, as you know, is an interesting and exciting ministry. It is practiced and expressed in many different ways. People are often referred to the chaplains by their chain of command because they have specific problems or difficulties. We play an important role in both engaging in pastoral listening and helping people problem solve. We help them devise a way to deal with everything from difficulties in their workplace to crisis at home that are often aggravated by long periods of time away for training and deployment."

At this point Malcolm wiped his brow with his handkerchief and said, "OK fellows, let's take a break. Steele will you start a fresh coffee perk, please?"

During the lull the men confirmed their understanding of military protocol and reminded each other that chaplains are the only officers in the military that soldiers can talk to without going through their chain of command and that information shared is considered (within the bounds of the law) to be held in confidence.

Padre Morin spoke up. "I expect during meal times, and often in the evenings, we might have a steady stream of people seeking us out and asking if we've got a few minutes to listen. No doubt these encounters will prove to be fruitful. I suppose we could call these sessions a Ministry of Interruption. They will cover a range of life issues: loneliness, problems at home, a death in the family or of a friend, ethical questions about killing and war, spirituality and faith, fears about the upcoming deployment, and so forth. Our people know that the Chaplain's office is a place to vent, to cry and to be heard…a place of healing."

As the conversations passed back and forth, the chaplains felt a cohesiveness building between them. They were feeling each other out and testing each other's knowledge. It had the beginning of a strong effective team. Trust in each other was the common denominator, and when things got tough, as inevitably they would, trust would be the glue that would bind them together.

At the conclusion of that first meeting, the chaplains spread out across Wainwright to the units to which they were assigned. Steele and Mike were taken to the 2 RCR Battle Group lines where Lt Col Rob Walker was about to conclude an 'O' group with his Company Commanders and key advisors. He noted the padres' arrival.

"Well, now," he greeted them with his infectious smile, "our Holy Men have arrived and now we can really get on with our business. First, you all know Padre Steele Lazerte who has been with us these past two years. (A whoha rose from the crowd.) With him is the newest man to join our happy band…Padre Mike Russell. In a sense he is no stranger to the Regiment as his grandfather was well acquainted with our First Battalion during the Italian Campaign in WW2. He and our revered chaplain, Rusty Wilkes, were best of friends. So officially I welcome Mike to the Royal Canadian Regiment. (More whohas.)

"People, we now enter that final phase of training that determines our fitness for deployment to Afghanistan. Don't doubt for a moment that Observer Controllers will scrutinize your movements and tactics with sharp eyes. I expect you to come up to those high standards, which we have worked so diligently to achieve. Pro Patria."

The group disbanded and the Commanding Officer came over to the two chaplains, extending his hand in greeting to Mike. "I expect Steele has informed you of how things work in 2 RCR lines. First and foremost I want you to know my door is always open to my chaplains. You Padres are key to the assessment of Unit morale…in a sense you will be my conscience. I would equate you to thermometers, a good metaphor, I would suggest. I know you must respect a confidence shared, especially if it is in the form of a confession, but let us be clear, the welfare of this Battle Group rests on my shoulders. I expect your total loyalty. I trust you understand my point?"

In unison the two padres responded as one, "Very clear, Sir."

* * * * *

In short order the 2000 plus men and women at Camp Wainwright received the green light to proceed overseas. Personnel returned to their home bases in preparation for disembarkation leave. They anticipated "Warning Orders" that would provide timings for their departure to Afghanistan. It was an anxious time for all concerned…for the soldier, for the spouse and for the children who did not fully understand what the electricity in the air was all about. They only knew that Daddy or Mummy was off again on some military Exercise…their gear stacked in basements or hallways…a sense of immanent expectation spilled over into family gatherings…a dramatic shift was taking place in their lives and they were caught up in the swift current of events.

Chapter Two

Email from Angeline Russell
To Michael Russell
15/12/2006 8:00am
Dearest Mike

Your email arrived this morning indicating your move to CFB Gagetown. Sorry I was out when you called. I had to "baby sit" for Myra, our neighbour for a couple of hours while she took her youngest to a clinic. No great problem, just a spiked temperature, probably due to teething, but with the flu bug around, Myra didn't want to take any chances with her husband away.

I'm beginning to dread that expression... husband away. Do you have any clue as to when your departure will take place? Even more importantly for the moment, when you will get home on embarkation leave? Christmas is just around the corner, so I just presume you will be home for that? Sometimes the military frustrates me to no end! It's always, hurry up and wait.

Sorry, honey, it's just one of those days. I do miss you so much. I've really got to stop saying that even tho' it will always be true. You are the heart that beats within me. I promise from here on I will be more sensitive. I want to be uplifting for you, not a drag.

Hurry home. We have so much to catch up on. I ache to hold you in the middle of the night like we do so often. Come to me soon...

All my love, yours always,
Angie

* * * * *

With the major pre-deployment exercises behind them, the chaplains had one more seminar to attend at Sunnybrook Hospital in Toronto, the city's trauma centre. Here, Malcolm's band of Task Force chaplains gathered to work with a Trauma Team. It was embedded with a number of CF medical personnel. The idea was to prepare those attending for the worst possible scenario in dealing with pain and distress. It was here they would explore methods in dealing with injuries sustained in battle for the pastoral and spiritual care givers. The symposium included lectures from specialists; observing complicated injury operations; viewing an autopsy; and being on call for pastoral care in the wards in the post-operative period; this followed by debriefings and discussion sessions with medical staff and hospital chaplains. The lessons were intensive, dramatic and provided invaluable information on a scale never before experienced by the average parish minister. At the conclusion of the course, Mike felt drained, somewhat intimidated by the skills learned, while at the same time having gained understanding and confidence that would see him through the difficult days ahead.

The five days at Sunnybrook were demanding. The team under Malcolm's leadership had to build a meaningful relationship with the Task Force Surgeon who was a true sceptic of the chaplaincy. He had no church affiliations of his own and had experienced several instances where clergy had interfered with the medical services in theatre to the detriment of patient care. Malcolm had his job cut out for him. He was thoroughly trained in the holistic approach to patient care and knew precisely where a minister belonged in that concept. In due course, he won the respect of the Task Force Surgeon, and integrated his chaplain team into the Role 3 Hospital care for potential casualties. Validation for this responsibility continued at CFB Petawawa where they became the first chaplain team to undergo this training. Here they learned the fundamentals of stretcher bearing, runners and recorders for the medical staff. Time would prove their skills and acceptance as an integral part of the Task Force Care Givers.

On December the twenty-second, the chaplains returned to their homes for the Christmas and embarkation leave period. In Plevna, Angie greeted Mike by nearly bowling him over as he came through the door.

"Darling," she screamed, as she rushed into his arms.

"Hey, take it easy woman; I'm only a poor soldier home for a few days!"

"Oh you tease," she tittered as she covered his face with kisses.

"If you keep that up, I won't ever leave!"

"Hey there, Michael," called his grandfather from the living room. "It's about time you found your way home. This woman's been plaguing the life out of me."

"Hi Gramps. Thanks for holding down the fort. I gather all is going well in the parish? I see Trinity is still standing. All geared up for the Christmas festivities?"

Ralph nodded. "Well, now that you're here, at least the people will hear a good sermon for a change. I've got you on deck for Christmas Eve… trust that's OK?"

"More than OK. Will you be here too?"

"I wouldn't miss it for the world… unless, of course, you want me to make myself scarce? By the way, Grams and I will be staying at the cottage while you're here. It's nice and snug since we had it winterized. Your Grandma loves it as long as the snow doesn't get too deep. But then, we've got good neighbours to keep the lane ploughed out. I don't have to lift a finger. Jimmy even shovels out the doorway." Jim Brash's family were long time members of the Land of Lakes Parish. The cottage overlooked the lake. It was situated on a piece of property formerly a parcel of the Brash family farm that Ralph Russell had purchased those many years ago. "So I'll be off for now… to give you young folks some space, but I'll be back tomorrow, and we'll go over the plans for the Christmas services. Great to see you, grandson," said Ralph. He hugged the two young people he loved so dearly. They waved at him through the doorway as his car pulled out of the yard.

"Alone at last," cried Angie as she tugged her husband along the hallway, his luggage forgotten in the car.

* * * * *

The celebrations of Christmas were an earnest affair for the people of Plevna. Traditions had been built over the years since the earliest settlers had cleared the primal forest and set up their crude homesteads. These structures gradually changed as time passed into solid family homes where large families were raised. In the late 1800's many the pioneer Lutheran families who were unable to support a pastor, joined with the Anglican community where they became a group known as the Mission of North Frontenac. It was a blessed union and Trinity Church thrived.

The German influence brought all the delights of a European Christmas festival. The church windows were cheerfully decorated with boughs of cedar sprayed with artificial snow and hung with glittering Christmas tree balls. A graceful eight-foot spruce stood in one corner of the sanctuary where lights glowed through the covering of angel hair. The top most branch was the resting place of a tattered, but beautiful angel. A child made it from the Sunday school who had won the prize for the best-made heavenly host. In addition to that honour, the child and his family were seated in the front pew closest to the tree.

There were two services held on Christmas Eve at Trinity. An early one, designed especially for the youngest members of the congregation, took the form of a carol singsong and a pageant starring the Junior Sunday School children. They dressed as angels and cherubs, with the Senior Classes reluctantly, and self-consciously, arranged as shepherds and oriental kings around the Christ-child's manger crib…and as always there was standing room only in the church.

Later that night, the Christmas Eucharist was celebrated at midnight. It was a star filled night as Mike and Angie treaded arm in arm up the slight incline toward the church, their shoes crunching in the snow. Smoke curled from the roof chimney emanating from the airtight stove that heated the building. A low chatter of voices could be heard from inside the church as the country folk took time to greet one another and share tidbits of information prior to the service. "Did you know that Billy Gorr had a tree branch fall on his head as he was cutting down that old oak in his lane? He's all right though!"

Reverend Ralph Russell stood at the entranceway to greet his 'sometime' flock as they made their way toward him. He was ensuring them that their Rector, currently on a leave of absence to the military, would be with them this night and would deliver the homily.

As Michael and Angie entered the church the chatting parishioners fell silent, until Merle Lemke, the Rector's warden, stood and began to applaud. All rose to join in the welcome.

To calm things down, Mike held up his hand and said, "Thank you all so much. It's good to be home, even if it's only for a short while. Now let's spend the next few minutes in quiet as we prepare to worship Almighty God."

Angie joined Grandma Russell in her pew as Ralph and Mike went into the small vestry to robe. Moments later the first hymn was announced, and as in the days of old, the carol "O Come all ye faithful" rang out loud and clear. The men's deep voices underscored and uplifted those softer tones of the womens present until the Holy Night was filled with the sounds of Christmas past uniting with Christmas present and the hope of years to come.

Clergy and people in the celebration of the Christ-child's birth joined the Communion liturgy. The hymn before the homily was appropriately "It came upon the midnight clear". Michael knelt in prayer before entering the pulpit, and quietly to himself asked God to give him strength and convincing words to share with his people. He was feeling emotional and feared his voice would become somewhat shaky.

"Good people of Trinity, dear friends, I stand before you tonight with trembling in my heart for I have come to say good bye, at least for a spell. I go to a place as barren as the hills of Judea where shepherds watched their flocks by night." Mike paused and looked at a young smiling face in the third row. "No, Billy, they did not wash their socks." A rumble of amusement passed through the congregation breaking the thread of tension. "No," continued Mike, "They looked after their animals, just like many of you do here in the highlands of North Frontenac. You watch for prowling predators that would prey upon your sheep and tiny calves...and you would do anything to protect the lost and the vulnerable ones.

"Well, in a way, that's what I am about to do. I am going to a land that has a lot of barren, wind swept, waterless places. To a land where people live in extreme poverty...where there is no welfare net to catch them when they fall...where good water is often more precious than gold...where children are deprived of an education. Yes, little girls like you, Annie, are not permitted to go to school even if there was one near your home. Cruel people have forbidden it. These cruel people, whom I would call predators, are responsible for all kinds of evil things in a land called Afghanistan. They have deprived the population of that war-torn country of even the most basic privileges and freedoms we take so much for granted here in Canada. If the people talk against the cruel ones, they are punished with the most brutal form of torture, and often lose all their possessions, even their lives. And that is why I must go over there to be with our soldiers who are trying to help bring peace and justice to a ravished nation...who are doing their best to help the Afghan people re-build that land ravished by untold years of conflict...who are trying to share with them some of the benefits we share together here. But why do our soldiers have to die for them, you might ask? I might put the same question of you...why did

Jesus have to die for us? Why did God come to earth in the form of a wee babe, only to have Him suffer death upon the cross? WHY?

"Why indeed! There are so many whys. There are so many unanswered questions. It all seems so mind-boggling. Suffice it to say, on this Eve of Christmas, that Canadian military and civilian personnel are needed to help the suffering and the lost people of Afghanistan. And they, in turn, need our prayers to uplift them and sustain them in their time of danger and peril.

"But this is not the traditional kind of sermon you come to hear at this Holy Time of year. You normally hear the story of heavenly choirs praising God in the Highest…of shepherds in the fields struck with awe by the magnificent Star that hovered over a simple stable in Bethlehem…of Magi bearing precious gifts for the newborn. That's what you typically hear. Right? Well, that still holds true. Those ancient stories are still valid. Keep them deep within you as you celebrate Christmas with hope and joy in your hearts, but remember there are places in this world where deep darkness lies over the land…where Evil strikes down the innocent and the lowly who are without hope. Let us pray for them and for our service men and women who are trying to sweep the sinister clouds aside. Let your lights so shine before all that they may see your good works and glorify God who is the Source of all Light.

"In closing, I want to comment on what my grandfather has told me. Many of you have asked what you can do to support me while I am gone. First and foremost pray for me and those whom I serve. Second, I plan to seek out ways while I am over there to help the children. I am aware from what I have learned during pre-deployment training that school supplies are almost non-existent. So if you want to offer special gifts…call it an ongoing Christmas gift, I suggest that Trinity, and anyone else in the community who might wish to participate, gather together practical school supplies to be sent over to the children of Afghanistan. It is estimated that less than half the children in Afghanistan are able to attend school, of this number only 20% are girls. Our own Lucy Kellar, good student that she is, has volunteered to co-ordinate this project. Her father Rick, at the hardware store, has pledged assistance in ensuring that the cost of shipping would be found.

God be with you all, now and forever, Amen"

* * * * *

The days were passing quickly, but Mike took time to visit many families of his parish, often with Angie accompanying him. Invariably, they would be invited for lunch or dinner and share many memories. The children were all over Mike, urging him to play with them; showing him their new toys from under the Christmas tree; the men eager to tell their stories of the recent hunting season, and the women, sharing family and work news, offered treats made from new recipes and updating them on friendly community happenings. Mike had a couple of sessions with Lucy who was gathering a team together to head up the School Supplies Project for Afghan children. The idea was catching on big time, with the churches of all denominations in the Township eager to share.

The one thing the couple made sure to do was to be home for the evenings together. They loved to curl up on the chesterfield to watch a TV program or just to cuddle and whisper loving thoughts to each other before bedtime.

All too soon the Christmas festivities were over. Mike had one more week of embarkation leave left. He and Angie took several days to drive to Oromocto, New Brunswick. They spent two nights in Quebec City with Angie's parents and took in all the winter sights that old town had to offer, including the many ice and snow sculptures. On their last night they shared a delightful dinner with her parents, Colleen and Henri, at a restaurant over looking the mighty St Lawrence River. It had been a fun day, as the young couple had spent it visiting many old shops and boutiques of the Old City.

Early the next morning they were New Brunswick bound. At CFB Gagetown, Angie looked forward to meeting the team of chaplains who were gathered prior to deployment. Angie and Mike booked into a room at the Oromocto Hotel.

That evening, Malcolm Berry, the Senior Chaplain, opened his home to entertain the Task Force chaplains. They were a compatible bunch and soon lively stories were being shared and enjoyed. It was a time for those who were being left behind to get acquainted…for the wives to meet their husband's confreres. To look them in the eye and convey the silent thought…please look after my loved one!

During those last days, Angie and Mike would attend various functions where Family Briefings and Farewell ceremonies were taking place. At these gatherings, one felt a different sense of energy in the air – anticipation, excitement and anxiety. All knew they were facing the final goodbyes and the long stretch of parting that lay ahead. People would soon find it would not be as easy to pick up the phone and call family and friends. E-mail wouldn't always be available over there. Posted mail would take longer. As much as individuals cursed the cold now, they would find during the summer months in Afghanistan, they would remember these times fondly and long for snow and cold again. The one thought on everyone's mind was… "We are now facing the "lean and lonely" months. We are quickly moving towards deployment"…before leave, soldiers thought training was like climbing a great mountain and wondered if they would ever get to the top. Since Christmas, immanent departure came like a speeding train, hell bound for the unknown.

Family Briefings were conducted by the various elements of the Task Force. Normally, the Rear Party organized them, those military personnel who remain in Gagetown, and support the home front while the main body of the unit is deployed. All family members and friends were invited to come to these gatherings. After the rituals of hospitality – coffee and sweets, it began with the Commanding Officer introducing the team and sharing their thoughts about the upcoming mission and its risk.

The Military Family Resource Centre, located at each base, described the variety of services it would offer for families of deploying member's… ranging from social events, counselling, to emergency childcare.

Families came to these briefings looking anxious, tentative and apprehensive…no wonder, especially considering the numbers of Canadian soldiers killed or injured in previous deployments. It is, of course, the proverbial 2000-pound elephant in the room that is hard to ignore, but difficult to address. No one wants to be pessimistic, but the topic needs to be addressed. This is one of the gifts the chaplain brings. One tries, by whatever means possible, to be sensitive and honestly address the question that is in the heart of every wife, husband, mom or dad, – "If something serious happens to my love one, how will I be told?"

Thankfully the military had come a long way from the Casualty Lists of World War 1 that were posted outside newspaper or telegraph offices for anxious family members to scan. Perhaps many people watched the war movie *We Were Young and Soldiers Once*, and have an image of a cab driver that delivers telegrams to the family doors of soldiers killed in Vietnam.

The Canadian policy when a military member dies or is seriously wounded overseas, is that the Chain of Command assumes responsibility to notify whatever family member the service person has designated on their next of kin form…following the directions the soldier gave for notification.

A Senior Military officer either from the rear party or a nearby Base or unit in Canada accompanied by a chaplain does that notification in person.

A trained Assisting Officer is appointed for the family, and that person will support them through the next days, weeks or months if required. Assisting Officers are there to help, to offer advice and support, and to explain benefits and policies. It is always touching to observe the sensitivity and compassion of those who are tasked to do this difficult work. In the case of death, the deceased soldier is always accompanied from Theatre by a close mate or friend, who remains with the body until it is interred. The soldier, who is usually known by the family, is a great source of comfort and assistance to the fallen soldier's family and friends.

If soldiers are slightly wounded and still conscious, that soldier, again with the support of the padre, phones home himself or herself and talks directly to their family. When something happens on the home front and needs to be relayed to a member in Afghanistan, the military moves as quickly as operational realities will allow in getting that information to the person affected and provides support for them.

The possibility of being killed or injured is never easy to address. Strangely though, people will often express their thanks for the information, saying that it has eased their minds a wee bit. They are thankful not to hear bad news through a radio or TV broadcast, or by a detached phone call, or through some other form of media. It also creates the acceptable climate for soldiers to explore with their padres their thoughts and fears about dying, as well as questions they or their families may have about the next steps to be taken, be it medical care or a funeral, and the involvement of the military in it all.

If spouses look distracted and tired in these pre-deployment days, they are after all, also on "tour". They will face different challenges than the ones soldiers have trained for. They will hold down the "home front". It is often a time of intense worry, of deep longing for any form of communication, a constant sense of being on edge, and a fear of seeing a padre and a senior officer walk up the driveway to knock on the door. The children present at Departure Ceremonies have an incredible energy, and by Victorian standards, are not well behaved. They find it hard to sit and be quiet. No matter how young or how old, they sense that a change is taking place. They may not be able to express it verbally, but they are feeling the reality of deployment as much as the adults. Some are glued to mother's bosom or father's legs…some sit very quietly in their own world, others wander, some turning cartwheels, others pushing and tussling as children are want to do. Thankfully today, there is an openness to let these children express their feelings.

There's an added burden to these ceremonies. Some troops have families unable to be there because they are living in other parts of Canada, and the soldier finds these ceremonies especially lonely. They are reminded that they are already far from home. As if eating in the mess each day and sitting in rooms alone at night is not enough, this is the last dreg in their cup of sadness, their families and friends are not here to share this farewell moment together.

In the final few days prior to departure, the troops of Taskforce 1/07 were briefed on Cultural Awareness situations. The speakers were well-informed individuals who had lived or worked in Afghanistan. The lectures covered a wide variety of topics dealing with the country and its people, such as, where Afghanistan and its history fit within the global realty; the devastating effect decades upon decades of war has had on the people; the diverse tribal structure of a nation fractured by eons of uncertainty and strife. The customs and protocols of the common people were made clear down to the daily habits of life…such as never point the soles of your feet toward anyone while sitting on the floor of an Afghan home as it is considered extremely rude. The list of 'do nots' underline the cultural differences.

* * * * *

Now it had come down to the day before the Task Force departed. Angie had elected to leave by bus to spend some time with her parents in Quebec City. Mike borrowed Steele's car to drive her into the bus station in Fredericton

"Darling, you know how I hate goodbyes! It seems ever since I got here we have been saying 'goodbye'," said Angie. "I don't want to be left here alone when you go. Please say you understand."

"I do understand, my love. I hate goodbyes, too. So give me one last hug and a big kiss, then get on the damn bus or the tears will come for both of us," Mike whispered.

And indeed they did. Parting tears rolled down their cheeks as the bus pulled out of the terminal. Then she was gone. Mike returned to the base, his heart heavy, but uttering a stern resolve. "I'll be back, sweetheart, just you wait and see!" With his face set, he headed toward the future, clutching an abiding Faith. "Yes, Lord, with your help, I will return."

Chapter Three

Captain the Reverend M. Russell
c/o The Senior Chaplain's Office
CFB Gagetown N.B.
E2V 1C8

5 January 07

My dearest Mike

Soon you will be boarding your flight to Afghanistan. I can well imagine the excitement building in you. You are such a keen warrior for a chaplain. While your adrenalin is being pumped up mine is feeling so low. I try to smile and carry everything off in a light manner, but you know me so well, I would never be able to hide anything from you…other people, yes, but you NEVER.

People are constantly asking? Do you miss him yet? Dammit! I missed you as soon as you waved goodbye…and I will miss you every minute until you return. Thank God I can vent to you. You know so well how it helps me.

As you know, I plan to visit *Mere et Pere* in Quebec City for the next couple of weeks. I will let you know when I plan to leave there. With the *Bonne Homme* Carnival Days starting, it should be a helpful diversion. Papa will no doubt keep me entertained. You have their telephone number and their email address. I will look forward to hearing from you when I get there.

Be sure to call me as soon as you can when you arrive in Kandahar. I can't wait to hear your voice…you'd think I was a giddy girl instead of a seasoned psychiatric nurse.

I hold you in my arms every night in my dreams, my darling,
Take care of yourself… hugs and kisses always
You are my heart, Angie

* * * * *

Aboard HMCS Iroquois
The Dockyard
Halifax N.S.

Dear Mike, old Buddy

At last I have my ship! IROQUOIS is the fairest lady afloat and I am totally taken with her. Definitely a different weather climate from the desert-like geography you will be set in. I came aboard three days ago and was briefed by the Captain, Commander James Glenn. He appears to be a great guy and by all accounts is stern, but supportive of the work of the chaplain. I have a feeling we will get along well together as he has that twinkle in his eye that belies a roughshod skipper. Time will tell.

On my first day aboard, the ship's Chief Petty Officer Sweeny took me to the Captain. He looked me over very carefully and with a nod seemed to approve of my dress and deportment.

The Captain wants to get to know me and outlined his expectations of our mission. He supports my practice to not wear rank indicators, as it sets a tone of accessibility to me for anyone aboard. He was glad I am here while we are still in 'Slackers' so that the crew can get to know me. I guess this is a bit like your pre-training time Mike.

We will be carrying the Squadron Staff (Flag) for part of the deployment, as well as an air detachment. We also expect to be in company with other ships for most of the tour—Canadians and others—who will not be carrying a padre. So, I am it.

When he asked what part of the religious mob I spring from, I told him, I'm a catholic trained, Anglican who can preach like Billy Graham and have read the *Qur'an*. He chuckled, and thought I understood the intent and hope behind his question. I'm guessing Mike that you have a few other denominations represented on your Chaplain team. It's good that we are schooled in multi-denominational service in the Chaplains branch, which holds both of us in good stead, eh?

The Captain wants a service each Sunday, which will be held in the Wardroom (no Chapel here with space at a premium), I have to book a flexible timing through the Executive Officer, as 'ops' will trump it.

Also, he wants to be at the services, which encourages me in his commitment to his own spiritual life, but also in his being there with the crew. The other ships we sail with might have expectations of me as well, so apparently a 'holy helo' is available if required, or I will transfer by boat or jackstay. I have never done a jackstay before, but I'm told it's a knee-knocker. I like the idea of the adventure of it, but will wait to see what the reality is like.

Already I have met a number of my shipmates. They seem to be a cheerful lot who know their business thoroughly. So far they have been very kind to this landsman whose only experience on water has been a fourteen-foot bass boat. They assure me I will come up to Neptune's standards in jig time.

We are soon off to the Gulf for a seven-month tour. (I'm not sure if I should mention that in a letter. Security is pretty tight on board, but since it is going from one CFPO to another, it should pass muster.)

Our days at Huron College seem such a long time ago Mike. I remember them fondly. How is Angie, and does she have any special activities planned while you are in Afghanistan?

Let's keep in touch as time allows.

Blessings, Tim

* * * * *

Tim Tucker and Mike Russell were close friends from their days in theological seminary at London, Ontario. They had enjoyed a variety of sports together, cheered for the same hockey team, the Toronto Maple Leafs, and double dated until things became more serious between Mike and Angie. Tim had been best man at their wedding. When they graduated Mike went to the Diocese of Ontario, while Tim remained in the Diocese of Huron where he stayed in a parish for five years before entering the CF Chaplaincy as a Naval Chaplain. It was about the time Mike had approached his bishop for a leave of absence to serve as a Reserve Chaplain in Afghanistan.

* * * * *

The powerful throb of the aircraft's engines increased as the Airbus 310 edged its way out toward the main runway of the Fredericton, New Brunswick airport…around the terminal, stood groups of people waving wildly at the departing jet.

The date was Sunday, 7 Jan 07. The flight would take a total of 24 hours for it would set down for a four or five hour stop over in Germany, thence to Camp Mirage where personnel and equipment would transfer to Hercules 130 aircraft for the final run to KAF, Kandahar Air Field.

* * * * *

"Wow – I am finally here," thought Mike as he walked down the ramp of the Herc. He made his way to the reception area at Canada House at "zero dark stupid", an expression often heard in the military during the night hours. Recalling a line from the Wizard of Oz when Dorothy says to her dog Toto "I've got a feeling we are not in Kansas anymore". Mike felt a deep feeling of strangeness and anticipation, finally after all this training, he thought, "I am here".

Things became instantly clear to him. The sound of constant activity filled the air – this is a 24/7 operation – vehicles, people, planes, helicopters, convoys, generators and lights – the place buzzed with constant action. The uniforms were a sea of different patterns and colours representing the countries that are in the ISAF (International Security Assistance Force) NATO Coalition.

The winter rains were lashing down as they disembarked the plane. For the people of Afghanistan, this was a blessing. For the past several years a severe drought had plagued the land causing major problems in the agricultural districts of Kandahar Province. Many of the canals that distributed water to irrigate the farmer's fields had dried up and much of the irrigation system was broken down and in varying degrees of disrepair. Now, the area that in the dry season was a dust bowl appeared more like a muddy bog. Huge puddles dotted the landscape creating challenging mud holes for personnel and vehicles to manoeuvre through and around.

Though vehicles were driven on the same side of the road as in Canada, all the vehicles are built with the steering wheel on the right hand side. It produced a double take when a truck was coming towards Mike, and had no one in the usual driver's spot…spooky! No wonder Mike kept getting into the vehicle on the wrong side and had to get out again, and occasionally, he activated the windshield wipers instead of the directional signals. Some differences!

Familiar faces started to appear as the Canadian soldiers that had trained together in Wainright last fall came in, and the soldiers from the previous tour were lining up to leave the theatre on their way home. It was especially great to see soldiers Mike had trained with. It was like greeting long lost friends and people were pleased to see a familiar face.

It didn't take long for Mike to plunge into the reality of the Afghan mission. He was standing in line on the boardwalk leading to the Tim Hortons outlet when a call came in from the Battle Group Adjutant.

"Padre Russell, could you come to my office ASP?"

Mike slipped away from the line up and headed for the Battle Group Command Centre and went directly to the Adjutant's office space.

"We have a notification of a death in Canada for one of our lads. Will you handle it, please? Steele is already involved with another soldier."

He handed Mike the information, which he studied and then headed for Hotel Company lines where he promptly found Master Corporal Peter Thompson. He had met him several times when they were in Wainright, so knew him by sight. He was a strongly built soldier and devoted to the soldiers in his section. He eyed Mike cautiously as Mike called out his name and indicated he wanted to see him outside the quarters. There are no convenient private places in the centre of a Battle Group concentration, so they moved to a space between the two rows of steel container billets.

"Peter," Mike said. "I have some sad news from home."

"I've been expecting it, Padre. It's my Dad, right?"

"Yes, I'm afraid he's had a fatal heart attack."

The soldier's shoulders slumped and his head dropped to his chest.

"Sorry to be the bearer of this sad news, Peter. Would you like to go someplace where we could talk? Perhaps have a prayer together."

"I'd appreciate that, Padre. Let me just tell my buddies I'll be gone for a few minutes." He slipped into his room…then re-appeared a moment later. The two men made their way to Fraise Chapel some distance away. They talked as they walked…Peter shared with his chaplain stories about growing up on a farm in southern Ontario. Explaining how his Dad and he did chores side by side during his schoolboy years. It became obvious that father and son were close. He told how his Dad was disappointed when Peter informed him he wouldn't be taking over the farm…that he didn't want to be chained to a dairy herd that demanded full time attention morning through night, day after day. He wanted to see the world, "And that's why I became a soldier."

The walk over to the chapel had provided Peter with a necessary venting period, and as they entered the relative coolness of the modular tent, the young man became silent. They sat side by side without speaking for some time. Finally, Peter said in a shaky voice, "Will you pray for my Dad. I know he would appreciate that. I know my Mum and sister would too— and would you say a prayer for my soldiers and me."

Mike took a few moments to gather his thoughts, and said, "Let's say the Lord's Prayer together "Our Father…." and they prayed together. Mike placed his arm about the soldier's shoulder, and continued….

"Lord, you are with us and our loved ones every moment of every day. You are as close as our heartbeat. You know us for who we are and what we stand for. As we pass through the shadow of death, you are with us even there. We pray for the soul of Peter's Dad, John Thompson that he may rest from his labours. He toiled long and hard to provide his family with a living. We pray for Peter's mother…and sister that they might be comforted." Mike paused. "Lord, we feel your presence here in this land so alien to us, but it too is a part of Your creation. We have come as soldiers of our country to help right a wrong against a people who have suffered through generations of strife. We may wonder what good we may do when we see the task ahead of us a day at a time. But, you Gracious God, see the bigger picture. Help us to soldier on in spite of our incomplete vision, for you alone can lift us when we fall. Be with Peter and his team as they fulfill their duty toward You our Lord God, and to our Country. Amen."

* * * * *

"Mike, Padre Berry wants us to meet at his office," Steele called from outside the sleeping quarters. "He wants to hold an O Group to go over our SOP (Standard Operating Procedures.) As you know by now, he's a stickler for clarity…everything and everyone in its proper place. I like his style of organization."

"Right, I'll be with you in a second. You go ahead, I just have to go to the toilet first!"

"Still on the run, eh?" asked Steele.

"You got it. I sure hope it lets up soon."

Ten minutes later Mike entered the Senior Chaplain's office area. The other four chaplains sat on folding chairs around a small table. They had poured coffee for themselves.

"Help yourself to a cup, Mike," offered Malcolm. "Sorry to hear you're still uncomfortable. That medication should have kicked in by now!"

Mike smiled. "Seems to be improving…I'm keeping my fingers crossed anyway."

Padre Robert Morin grinned. "Better keep more than your fingers crossed, old friend,"

"OK," said Malcolm, "let's get down to business. As we have previously discussed, each of us will have a primary task. Robert with the NSE, the National Support Team; Felix as chaplain to the PRT, the Provincial Reconstruction Team; Steele and Mike with the Battle Group, and I with the Task Force Command group. You are well acquainted with your duties. Gentlemen, this is what we have been training for…the entire Task Force has set a high standard for itself. We, as chaplains, are well positioned to respond to the moral and spiritual welfare of those in our charge. We have formed well as a team, and as the brothers we are, we will in turn respond to each other's need. It has often been asked, 'If the padre looks after the troubles and concerns of all the troops…who looks after the padre.' In this day and age, it is our responsibility to look after each other. If, at any time, some concern arises or a fractious situation develops among us, let's get it out in the open and deal with it. By trusting each other, we can surmount any problem. Do any of you have anything to say before we shove off in our several directions? No? OK, we'll plan to meet at least once a week or at special instances and share what's going on in our separate bailiwicks."

* * * * *

It was late morning when Mike found himself once again in the line up for a Tim Horton coffee. This time, the waiting was brief. Just ahead of him was a group of Ghurkha soldiers from Nepal who had just been served. They were smacking their lips, as they tasted the Canadian brewed coffee for the first time. Mike walked over to their group to share in their conversation. They were all speaking English. This shouldn't have surprised him, as India is the second largest English speaking country in the world. The men were unaware that they were in the midst of one of Tim Horton's "Roll up the Rim" contests, so Mike taught them the vaunted Canadian tradition of rolling up the rim with your teeth. One man was thrilled to learn he had won a free refill.

* * * * *

Somewhere Mike had picked up an intestinal bug. It hit him with vengeance on his second day in theatre. He quickly sorted out where the nearest "blue rockets" (toilets) were located and tried to settle into a workable part time schedule.

"What's the problem, Mike," asked Steele. "You look like the boogies are after you!"

"I wish it were that simple. Just looking at you with your shaved head would scare them away. Har har! To be honest, I've got the shits, so don't look at me sideways or you might get them, too."

"Have you seen an MO? They say there's some good stuff over here to dry you up. Apparently, the condition is a common complaint. Good reason one has to be constantly aware of hygienic conditions… frequent washing of the hands is a given… whether you think they need it or not," offered Steele. "The stench from the sewage lagoon is enough to make anyone heave…thank goodness the wind doesn't prevail from that direction."

"You're right there. They gave me some meds to take. I sure hope it works quickly. Ohhhh…excuse me. Here I go again." It took a couple of days for the malady to clear up and allow Mike to broaden his scope of communicating with the troops. By the end of the second week in situ, the two padres had walked through the entire Battle Group bivouac area chatting it up with their people. Spirits seemed to run high and the troops were anxious to get on with their task, some expressing it in words, "Can't wait to kick Taliban butt."

Malcolm brought the chaplains together. "You will recall I said we would each take turn "outside the wire"…and so it begins. The drill is this: we will catch a ride in a convoy out to one of the Forward Operating Bases. I suggest we travel primarily by road…this is the way our troops do it. Air flight by helicopter is optional should it become available, but I would prefer we stick, whenever possible, to ground travel. We do not want to appear privileged. Occasionally would be OK, because that would provide you with an overview of the country.

"Once in situ, report to that site's HQ. They will book you in and suggest a spot for you to lay your head, after that you can begin making the rounds. Regardless of what some people may think or say...the troops always welcome a word with the padre. Be sensitive to their needs and concerns...some may be experiencing difficulty and it's your job to help them through any problem. Remember Colonel Walker's comments. "I expect my padres to help me keep our people focused!" If the minds of our soldiers are elsewhere, they put themselves and their buddies at risk. Assure them that you will personally do everything you can to find an answer to their situation. You will normally spend several days in a FOB area and go out to the Strong Points for an overnight. This is where you will really get to know people...and they will get to know and trust you. Shoot the breeze with them. If you get the impression they are lonely for home, let them know you are too. Towards the end of your stay have a prayer service with them...I know the Anglicans and Roman Catholics will offer the sacraments...whatever your religious denomination may be...pray with the troops. Always let the local HQ know where you are in the event of an emergency. You may have to come out in a hurry."

"To start this internal rotation, Mike, you will proceed to Patrol Base Wilson. India Company of the Battle Group is located there with the Afghan National Police."

"Padre Morin, Robert, will remain with the National Support Element as they are very active with their projects in several areas.

"Steele, visit your people in the BG compound and be sure to catch the folks retuning to KAF from a jaunt "out side the wire".

"I will hold the fort here as the Commander has asked me to be available to attend meetings for some VIP's who are visiting over the next week. Are we all clear on this? Right! Let's do it."

* * * * *

Mike travelled in a convoy of LAV's and Nyala armoured vehicles through the silent city in the black dark. Departure time from KAF was 0115hrs. It was an NSE re-supply team loaded with food, ammunition and the odds and sods of personnel in support of Patrol base Wilson. The latter included the Tactical Psychological Operations Team. In terms of service, this was one of the newer forms of conducting warfare for Canadian Troops. Their primary role was to interface with area leaders and village elders to ensure them that the ISAF Forces were only in Afghanistan to help them rescue their country from the "steel fist" of the insurgents and the drug lords. The team had to gain the trust of the local population and they did this by promising that helpful projects such as roads, bridges, schools and irrigation systems would be completed, with the commitment that these would be done in a timely fashion. This was a serious matter, for the Nalgham-Sangsar where Mike was traveling to was the birthplace of the Taliban. It was here that their charismatic leader, Mullah Omer, had begun his fanatical movement.

This was the first opportunity for Mike to meet Captain Shawn Arbing and his 2IC Sergeant Randy McCourt. These men were highly trained specialists and functioned well together supporting the PRT and elements of the Battle Group.

"This your first time "out side the wire", Padre," asked Arbing?

"Yes, I arrived with 2 RCR Battle Group and just getting my feet wet. How are things with you?" asked Mike.

"Things have been going pretty well. I take it you've been briefed on the way our team works," asked the Captain?

"I have. It sounds like a pretty demanding operation."

"It is…we have our good days and our bad ones. Sometimes it's hard to figure out whom we're dealing with. Seems the insurgents are always ready to intimidate local leaders. They're naturally concerned for their lives and fearful of reprisals…but once we gain their respect and confidence, they see that we are sincere and want to help them."

"The shuras, the meetings with the elders, are the keys to our success. We hold these in conjunction with elements of the Battle Group who see the combat teams are there to protect them. Be sure you take time to sit in on them…it can be a fascinating experience."

"I'll look forward to it," replied Mike with keen interest.

After several hours, in a blur of dust, the armoured vehicles turned into the main gate of PB Wilson. Concrete blast walls to protect the soldiers from incoming ordinance surrounded the area. The walls were topped with razor sharp concertina wire and strategically located gun towers were placed at critical points. As always, the supply force was greeted by smiling personnel who looked forward to fresh rations and a fresh water supply.

Mike reported into the PBHQ and was allocated a space to keep his gear and to bed down. Before the evening meal hour, he made arrangements with a Sergeant he knew to tour the Patrol Base area. Sgt Bill Murray was a soldier's soldier. Ruggedly built, he was a fanatical body builder, some of his mates described him as an "Indian Rubber Ball", and one could see by the size of his biceps and the obvious thickness of his leg muscles that his body was strong as steel. He was a leader and well respected by his platoon.

He greeted Mike. "Thanks for dropping by, Padre…not quite like the Afghanistan we knew back in Wainwright. I hear you're getting around a fair bit in KAF, and by the way, thanks for being there for Pete Thompson. He really appreciated your concern when his dad died."

"He's a good lad. I was happy to be of assistance. How is everything going out here," asked Mike.

"Oh, we have our ups and downs. The dust is a continuous problem…it gets into everything. I even find it gritting between my teeth! But we all get used to it…more or less."

Mike grinned. "Ya, no sense complaining, I guess, there's not a thing we can do about it that we haven't thought of already. Any enemy activity lately?"

"Last night we caught a Taliban patrol trying to sneak up on one of our Strong Points. It got a little hot for a few minutes but they turned tail and headed for the boonies. We got two of them and maybe a third as there was a blood trail that petered out in the direction they were hightailing it!"

The two men were approaching the main gate where there appeared to be some unusual commotion. Three medical personnel came rushing toward the scene. A young Afghan boy under twelve had been laid on the ground by his father who was crying for help. The lad had become the victim of an IED blast and had lost the lower portion of his right leg. The father had fabricated a rough tourniquet and this had no doubt saved the child's life.

Except for first aid, the wound was beyond the capability of India Company medics. A Medevac chopper was requested to take the boy to the hospital at KAF. The news of the sad incident spread quickly and many off duty personnel gathered in groups. Mike joined one.

"What a hell of a thing to happened to a kid," said one soldier. "War is one thing…but picking on children…that has to be the height of evil."

"You're right there, my friend. Anyone who would target helpless civilians, especially children, need to be stopped," said Mike.

"That's putting it mildly, Padre, if I get a hold of the buggers, it'll be harsh treatment, alright.

The next morning Mike was taken to Strong Point Zero by India Company's CQMS where a section size group were dug in. It was a hot and dusty day travelling across the barren land. In the distance he could see swaths of green where ancient gnarled grape vines twisted over curb-like irrigation ditches. Further in the background fruit trees were beginning to leaf out. A field of green wheat stretched out to the north and on one side four foot marijuana plants grew, the other side held a field of opium poppies. Harvest was a couple of months away. In the far distance, beyond the green belt, mountains were still snow capped and in between lay the even more barren lands of the desert. Here Bedouin tribes lived in tents as if lost in a time warp…forever on the move to scrape whatever sustenance they could find from the arid land.

Along the way Mike could see large flocks of mangy, multi-coloured sheep grazing led often by a shepherd with a stick, and straggling behind was his family. Out in fields, the average Afghan farmer still worked with a shovel and hoe from dawn, until early evening, only taking a break at high noon for a short siesta. It is as if the industrial revolution never happened. These people worked very hard and they aged fast…a ripe old age would be in the late forties. Evil factors had been at work for many millennia to keep these hard working, down to earth people in subjugation. As Mike saw it, the time for change had come, and, God willing, he was there to do his part.

* * * * *

The soldiers at SP Zero have been in position for three days. They were tired, sweat-stained, and dirty. Their body odour was sharply acrid. They dreamt of fresh rations and with the arrival of the Company CQ their hopes soared only to be dashed by a re-supply of hard rations, but thankfully large quantities of fresh bottled water. They spotted their chaplain.

They were initially concerned that the chaplain had come to this God forsaken hole in the ground with bad news for someone. A few looked anxious…wondering if there was news for them…Mike made a mental note to draw those individuals out. So, Mike smiles, even jokes as he made his way among the section.

"Hey, Padre, what's the news from home? Anything special happening? What are the latest hockey scores?" They were hungry for information. Mike was genuine in his good spirits for he knew full well that a soldier could spot a phoney a mile away. They took to him and shortly he found opportunity to have relatively private conversations. All appeared to be fine…all things taken into consideration. Canadian soldiers are flexible. Canadian soldiers can adapt. Canadian soldiers are the finest in the world. He broke bread with them. He offered prayers with them. He crawled into his sleeping bag beside them and in the pitch black of an Afghan night with the crescent moon lustrous overhead; he counted the stars with them and listened to stories of back home.

"You know, Padre, as soon as I get home the first thing I'm going to do is order the biggest fattest steak you ever saw," mused Private Riley.

"Liar," mutters his buddy, "that's probably the second item on the agenda after you toss a bag of green jelly beans on the lawn for the kids!"

On his return to KAF, Mike was tired but took time to call home to Angie. It was a cheerful conversation, but cautious on Mike's part as he was conscious of the need for security. Then, going to his computer, he sent an e-mail to his best friend, Tim Tucker, aboard HMCS Iroquois, describing his first experience "out side the wire".

Chapter Four

3 February 2007
Dearest Mike,
　Winter continues its icy blast here in Eastern Ontario, although they are calling for ease in below minus temperatures in the next few days. The cold weather doesn't seem to bother the children as they play their road hockey games whenever they can, from morning till night. Before we know it, spring will be here and they will be replacing their pucks for soccer balls.
　How I miss you, my darling! I snuggle up in front of the TV and watch endless programmes of CSI and other 'enlightening' capers. It seems such a waste of time when I could be doing something useful. I must put my thinking cap on and pull myself out of this self-pity. Sorry!
　I do so much enjoy the Ottawa Senators hockey. It's a thrilling game even when the team's not playing up to scratch. They can be very frustrating, too. But that's sports for you. I love it!
　I miss our intimate chats and the not so intimate ones where our wills are apt to meet head on, but then, those are good too because we take time to compromise and make-up, oh so deliciously.
　Needless to say I have also been thinking a great deal about our holiday together in Rome. The days are slipping by ever so slowly but I know soon we will be together again. Have you made any solid plans yet? Do you have any air bookings?
　Your grandfather has been taking good care of me. He drops in two or three times a week and we have lunch together…some times your Grandma comes over, too. They are such sweeties!

I know how busy you are over there. Knowing you so well, I can read between the lines of your email, and when we talk I can hear in your voice how tired you are. Darling, please pace yourself. I don't want to see some scarecrow of a man meet me in Roma.

You are my love and my life…keep safe and well.

Always and forever, Angie.

* * * * *

HMCS Iroquois
Somewhere in the Mediterranean Sea

Hi there old friend

Thanks for your interesting e-mail re your exploits in Afghanistan with your troops…either you have a vivid imagination or it's a pretty wild place to be.

My first full month and a half at sea has been filled with lots of incredible experiences. On leaving Halifax, I had my first official function as Chaplain to the IRO. After the Chief of Maritime Services and the Chief of Defence Staff made the official departure speeches, I had the privilege of standing in front of the families and crew to pray for them and to offer a blessing. It was a pretty amazing moment.

HMCS IROQUOIS
Departure Prayer and Blessing

> Seeing that in the course of our duties we may be set in many adversities, let us unite our prayers and praises in seeking the blessing of Almighty God, upon this ship, HMCS IROQUOIS, all souls aboard and the many friends and families who support us and face adversity with us during this time of separation:
>
> *Nous prions;*
>
> *Ô Dieu éternel, qui seul sépare les cieux et gouverne les mers déchaînées; qui a contenu les eaux dans leurs limites jusqu'à ce que le jour et la nuit s'achèvent;* Be pleased to

receive into Thy Almighty and Most Gracious protection the persons of us Thy servants, and the fleet in which we serve. Preserve us from the dangers of the sea and from the violence of the enemy, that we may be a safeguard unto our most Gracious Sovereign Lady, Queen Elizabeth, and her Dominions, *et une sécurité pour ceux qui passent sur la mer de bon droit; pour que les habitants du Commonwealth puissent Te servir Toi notre Dieu en paix et en quiétude;* and that we may return safely to enjoy the Blessing of the Land, with the Fruits of our Labours, and with a Thankful Remembrance of Thy mercies to Praise and Glorify Thy Holy Name. Amen.

"May the Lord bless you and keep you. May the Lord's face shine upon you, and be gracious unto you. May the Lord's countenance be lifted up upon you and give you peace, both now and forever more. Amen.

Leaving Halifax Harbour the reality of our departure hit home. We sailed south making a bee-line to the entrance of the Panama Canal so that we could meet up with the two other Canadian ships of our fleet, HMCS CALGARY (a frigate) and PROTECTEUR (a re-supply ship)…the IRO is a destroyer. We were blessed with great weather and although we've had up to 3m swells on rare occasions, I haven't been physically seasick. Though, like most others, I suffered from some fatigue for the first week or so, and a kind of "odd" feeling in the gut. This comes from the body constantly being in motion and your body's desire to try and stay upright; your muscles are always at work countering the affects of the sea and it is tiring physically and mentally – but it does go away.

The day after we sailed from Halifax I had a Sunday service and we had about 6 or so folks. I held the service in the Chief and Petty Officers' Mess (C&POs). It went well and since, as you know, I play guitar, we have some music during the service.

Ministry on board is primarily a ministry of presence, getting around to all the various spaces at different times of the day. I did this by going to the various messes: the Wardroom for Officers; C&PO's Mess & the Main Cave (Master Seamen and below) for meals and in the evenings, going out on the Quarter Deck, visiting the working spaces including the Bridge, doing PT with folks on the flight deck and such.

After several weeks at sea, I believe the relationship building is showing fruit. People instead of me approaching them are approaching me. I'm starting to get into more serious discussion with individuals over a multitude of issues, including their faith journey and experiences with religion. So far we've only had to deal with a few compassionate issues, but nothing too serious and thankfully nothing too sad or disheartening. It is uplifting that I am also becoming included in the good news events of our people's lives; which brings balance to the ministry. All of this is a great blessing and humbling. I have even had the chance to bring communion to some who, because of their schedule, can't make it to the service. Finally, on the request of some folks, we started a bible study group and I look forward to these sessions.

I guess that catches you up on my comings and goings…not that I have that far to travel aboard a ship, but touching on that, exercise is an important aspect of sea duty. We have fitness classes between 0800 and 0900 each morning; as well there are weights to use, treadmills, and elliptical trainers.

Now, my friend, you keep your head down when travelling "out side the wire" and don't go wandering off into ditches for whatever reason… they could be mined!

      Blessings and peace
      Tim

* * * * *

Mike stirred up the fine dust as he walked from the Nyala armoured vehicle to the Mullah's gate. His home was beside the small Mosque. Mike was in Kowal, one of the many small villages at the edge of the Zhari desert. The name was rather ironic as it had the connotation of meaning "Peaceful or peace making". The Taliban were aggressively active in the area. The houses in the village were made of dun-coloured mud baked bricks or blocks, most were covered with a type of plaster of the same hue that closely matched the overall colour of the countryside. Walls, roughly five and a half feet tall, surrounded the family compound. To Mike, everything looked the same, but this village had a special meaning for him. The temperature was approaching 38C. He was sweating. On the rutted road outside the mud walls, a group of children dressed in frayed and threadbare clothing kicked a homemade soccer ball from one child to another. They appeared cool and comfortable. The ball was made from cast off rags and bound into a more or less circular shape with a tough twine. Every time a solid kick was delivered, little pieces of fabric flew off the quivering bundle. Yet cheers would ring out amidst the children's laughter and their high spirits were contagious. Mike thought, 'Lord, how wonderful it is that in the world over, youngsters, regardless of their condition or surroundings would find time for fun and games. Bless all the children, for indeed, they will lead the way to peace and harmony.'

Mike rapped on the gate. Mullah Faizullah's young son, Hassan, opened the creaky latch and greeted the soldier whom he recognized as the Holy Man of the Canadian soldiers who patrolled the village.

"Salaam alaykum," said the boy bowing his head.

"Alaykum salaam," replied Mike. "Is your father home?"

Through the door of the flat-roofed house appeared the Mullah, his dark beard, streaked with grey, flowed down his chest. He was a short rotund man with flashing eyes. He had a reasonable command of English, although heavily accented.

"Salaam, Chaplain Mike," he affectionately greeted. "Welcome to my home. Can I offer you some refreshment… a cup of chi, tea, perhaps?"

Mike's nod and smile indicated acceptance.

Mullah Faizullah called to his wife, "Nila, bring chia for our guest."

Mike was no stranger to this household. Shortly after his arrival in theatre he had visited this village with a PRT team who were holding shuras with the village elders. They were discussing the need for a new bridge across a stream that supplied the community with water. The Taliban had destroyed it. It was at this meeting that Mike had met the Mullah and learned that he and his wife were teaching children in a tiny room in their small home. Mike was given a tour of the dwelling. The cleric taught a class of boys and his wife, Nila, instructed a group of girls in another corner. They did this at their own peril as the Taliban had issued warnings that girls were not to receive schooling. Anyone doing so would be severely punished.

The tiny teaching centre lacked everything from pencils and scribblers to a black board and chalk. Mike determined to do something about the situation, and on his return to base, he had initiated a plan to remedy the lack of supplies. In a telephone call to Angie, he had alerted her to the fact that the school supplies Lucy Kellar had gathered could now be sent to him in Afghanistan. In no time, the items were on there way.

Some weeks later, Mike arrived with two cartons that contained teaching materials … books, writing resources, a dictionary and a map of

Afghanistan and another map of a world. He had made three trips prior to this one to deliver scrounged supplies he had put together in KAF and two small blackboards that would be useful for the teachers.

Nila served tea and small cakes and promptly withdrew.

Pointing to several cardboard cartons Mike announced. "These boxes come from friends in Canada."

Nila watched shyly from her kitchen. When Mike opened the first carton, the woman's eyes grew large with excitement as she saw what the box contained. In all her dreams she could not imagine such a genuine treasure. The second carton held more school supplies, but also a new, regulation size soccer ball.

Hassan, with eyes wide, was standing in the entranceway to the outer wall and Mike turned to him.

"Hassan, would you like to take charge of this ball?"

The boy beamed with excitement and looked to his father, "May I, Father?" he asked. He knew full well he couldn't accept such a gift without his father's approval.

The Mullah grew quiet. He seemed to be pondering the situation, and then he slowly smiled. "I don't see why not. It appears to me a gift of friendship, and as our friend's Good Book says, 'It is more blessed to give than to receive.' The Prophet, may his name be blessed, has asked us also to be compassionate. So take the ball and render *tashakor*, a thank you. It will be shared by all the children…and remember, you are to 'take charge' of the ball…you are to care for its good condition. Now be off. Chaplain Mike and I have words to exchange."

The boy, holding the ball tightly to his chest, dashed through the gate and once beyond the wall, he could be heard shouting to the other children…all came rushing toward him. When they saw the ball, there was at first a roar of young voices follow a hushed silence.

"Chaplain Mike, you have been very kind and generous again. *Tashakor*, my friend," said the Mullah. "I do not know any other way to show my appreciation for these special gifts. They will be a blessing for the children."

Mike smiled. "I am rewarded already by the look on your face, and the thrill Hassan expressed when I gave him the ball. I only wish I could be more helpful. I am going to see if something can be done to make a larger classroom for your students. Would this be acceptable to you?"

The Mullah's head jerked up in surprise. "I am overwhelmed that such an offer would come about. Do you really think this could happen?"

"I will be happy to explore the possibility, but don't get your hopes up too soon. These things take time."

"Inshallah," said the cleric with head bowed. "You are a good man. But tell me why you have come to Afghanistan with soldiers. I know you to be a man of Peace. You carry no weapons. Excuse my inquisitiveness, but by nature I am curious about such things. I mean no offence"

Mike smiled. "No offence taken. I am here because my soldiers are worthy of my presence. Although they are armed and at times are required to use their weapons, they are, deep in their hearts, peace-loving people. They are often troubled by what they do and what they see. They believe they are here to help your people in your fight for freedom and decency. I am here with them to listen to their concerns, to help them to understand the impact of their actions, and to comfort them when they are injured. For that, I need no weapon of war…I need only the Good Book…the Good News that our Lord brings to the bruised soul. As your Qur'an is Holy to you, so the Bible is to our people. But this you already know. Forgive me for "preaching to the choir" as we say."

The mullah looked askance. "Preaching to the choir? What does that mean?"

"It's just an idiom that's used in Canada, meaning to tell a person something they already know. Like…let me see…like telling Hassan to say *tashakor*, thank you. He already knows how to do that as you have taught him well. His manners are excellent."

The Mullah nodded his understanding.

"Let me answer your question about my presence in a more graphic way. As I came here today, I saw a shepherd crossing the hill above the village. It was obvious by his movements that he was keeping careful watch over his flock lest they encounter problems. They are aware he is there even though they seem to rush around unconcerned. The duty of the Canadian chaplain is to be there for the troops…the flock."

"Ah, yes! I understand, the prophet Jesus was portrayed as a Good Shepherd. You are following his teachings, no?" said the Mullah nodding. "Indeed, I do understand. Again, *tashakor*, for your sharing."

"You're more than welcome," answered Mike. "I, in turn, appreciate your interest."

The Mullah proceeded. "Your soldiers are very kind indeed. My heart goes out to them when they are attacked by the lawless ones, by cowardly insurgents, the Al-Qaeda and Taliban who hide bombs along roadways to blow up your troop carriers. I have seen your people interacting with children and the refugees…how they share their rations with the starving… how they help the sick obtain medical treatment. Indeed, one of the children of our village was taken to your hospital at KAF and given life saving surgery. May Allah's blessings be with you and yours."

At that moment the Canadian armoured convoy stopped out front of the compound and Mike took his leave. Mullah Faizullah stretched out his right hand to grasp Mike's, placed his left hand over his heart to bid a fond farewell and said, "Allah be with you, my friend."

* * * * *

The convoy took off in a cloud of gritty dust that seemed to find its way into every nook and cranny of the Nyala, which was position in the middle of the five-vehicle column. The eight men inside covered their faces with neck scarves to filter out the fine particles that filled the air. Mike was grateful to have a window view. He could take in the stark scenery and contours of the passing landscape before dozing off to the hum and movement of the vehicle. He was lucky that way. If tired, his head would loll to one side and within moments he would be asleep, only waking when the Nyala would hit a bump or jerk to a sudden stop… and stop it did, suddenly and without warning the vehicle came to an unexpected halt. Ahead there was an explosion that rattled and vibrated through the convoy. An IED had been triggered a few moments prematurely in front of the lead LAV. Quick alert glances were exchanged. Personal weapons were held at the ready.

Instantaneously, the back ramp dropped and the Infanteers fanned out in tactical formation on either side of the roadway. Weapons began to fire and rounds were heard glancing off the troop carriers. Mike was required to remain inside the vehicle and automatically ducked each time a bullet struck the armoured skin.

As suddenly, the firing stopped.

"Report!" called Lieutenant George Collins, the officer-in-charge.

"All clear forward," answered Sergeant Weir. "Two contacts down… fifty meters in the forward right quadrant."

"All clear to the rear," responded Corporal Thomas. "No enemy seen."

The "all clear" was repeated by the deployed troops from their designated positions around the convoy.

The Canadian patrol had sustained no casualties. Only personnel in the lead vehicle had been severely shaken up by the explosion. Two enemy insurgents were found shot dead in a shallow scrape of ground from where they had detonated the IED using a hand held device.

Following a short discussion, Lieutenant Collins indicated that the ANP, (Afghan National Police,) would recover the enemy bodies for identification and disposal. The patrol continued on its way toward their home base at KAF. As they entered the area, the stench of human waste filled the air. Not far from the airfield was a huge sewage lagoon, more like a lake, that assailed the senses. The men groaned and covered their nostrils. It was a phenomenon people never fully adjusted to during their entire tour. The city was overburdened with a multitude of odours… unwashed bodies, rotting waste in gutters…and in the market areas, the more favourable aromas of herbs and spices.

Once through the guarded main gate, the vehicles moved to the troop dispersal area where the soldiers dismounted eagerly to seek the showers. Mike was no exception, but immediately following a good hosing down, he headed for the Team Leader's office for a debrief. The Operations Officer interviewed the remainder of the patrol. This was SOP (standard operating procedure,) for teams returning from "outside the wire."

Malcolm Berry sat at his desk, sweating profusely, his face reflected in his computer screen. "Hi there Mike, how did it go today?"

"Quite well, actually…I delivered the educational supplies to Mullah Faisullah, while the PRT, held a shura with the village elders. The Taliban were active in the village two nights ago and threatened the community with violence if they continued to talk with the unbelievers. The mullah, as I have said, is a moderate, forward-looking man, determined to free his people from the heavy-handed demands of the Taliban. Sometimes I fear for his life. He and his family are so vulnerable in that hot bed of Taliban influence," said Mike almost out of breath from the oppressive heat. Still he drew a cigarette from a package and lit up. "Hang around for a bit, I'm expecting Steele, Felix and Robert shortly for prayers and a brief meeting to bring everyone up to date, and plan for the next few weeks."

Mike nodded. "Right on! I'll just slip over to Timmy's for a coffee. I'm feeling rather dehydrated."

"You do that, I've got to finish up this monthly report and fire it off to Dave Kettle in Ottawa. As Director of Chaplain's Ops he's always keen on updates." Malcolm turned to his keyboard. "By the way, would you bring me a coffee on your return? Our perk has finally given up the ghost."

* * * * *

The Team Leader sat with his chin resting on his hands. "Gentlemen, we are now well into our tour. All of you have observed in our troops a certain lack of energy that is beginning to drag people down. It would appear that for many, issues from home have become their main concern. When you see this happening, be sure you listen closely to draw out their problems. It is vital to morale that they have someone to talk with regarding these issues, so that they don't lose focus on the mission. You should be able to relieve them of their anxieties and assure them their worries will be addressed by padres back home.

'Soldiers like to be listened to. They like to know that someone knows what its like to be in their position. Also, people want to know what has been accomplished since the tour began. It is important that they see positive signs that, indeed, we are making a difference," declared Malcolm. "Mike here has just returned from delivering school supplies to Mullah Faizullah in Kowal. It's that kind of project that soldiers like to hear about. They see the abject poverty that the children live in. It's important that they are aware of the humanitarian aspects of our role here in Afghanistan. They are well aware of the fighting phase of their deployment. They know the difference between a good outcome and a bad one…but they still need you guys to talk to…for in many cases, you are their safety net, whether they realize it at the time or not. A lot are looking for immediate results but these are few and far between…mostly seen through the efforts of the Provincial Reconstruction Teams… tangible things like bridges, roads, irrigation repairs, schools. The impact of NATO's presence here, in the area of hearts and minds, is not that self-evident. After all, many of these tribal people have been at each other's throats forever. There are blood feuds and passionate rivalries. Nationhood and democracy are foreign concepts to these people. Loyalty and honour start with the family, then the village, the tribe, the warlord and the Pashtuwali…not the Country, nor the President. These perceptions will probably only come after several generations. For this country to succeed it must do so by little steps with confidence in a brighter future. Education is a key for both the adults and the children, especially for the children, for they are the real hope for a brighter future. Perhaps this is where the Canadian effort will best succeed; helping the common people take responsibility for their country…maybe it's here where our contribution will hopefully be of some influence. Lt Col Walker, the BG Commander, has said a number of times, how much he appreciates your everyday contact with his troops, especially "outside the wire." You are his Morale Commandoes. He relies on you and so do I. So, our plan of action remains basically the same. Each of us, including myself, will rotate from our specified positions to spend up to a third of our time in forward areas. When I am away, one of you will assume the role of Team Leader. In that way, you will gain experience and come to realize the "boss's job" is not a cushy affair," Malcolm concluded. "Any questions?"

"I've been wondering about this approach ever since I came in theatre. Am I no longer considered the Regimental Chaplain to 2 RCR," asked Steele with some concern?

"You are, indeed, the Regimental Chaplain to the RCR. But don't forget that 2 RCR is a Battle Group with ancillary troops. You are their padre, too. Your role has taken on added responsibilities, which in this case, means you will continue to take your turn rotating with the other chaplains of our Canadian Task Force. Colonel Walker understands that… but you are STILL his chaplain."

"Understood," replied Steele feeling somewhat relieved, as he was devoted to the RCR.

"In a few weeks time, it will be Mike's turn for leave. I trust you have consulted about your Home Leave Travel Allowance."

"I am aware of that and will meet with a representative shortly. Angie and I plan a holiday in Italy, with Rome as our primary leave centre. It's a dream we've shared for a long time. I can hardly wait!"

"I bet," said Steele with a grin. As a bachelor, he could only imagine.

* * * * *

On the 16th of March, India Company set out for the town of Kolk. Here they established a command and observation post on the top of the Police station. The community was strategically located in the area of Nalgham – Sangsar. Foot patrols were launched to scout out potential enemy positions and to determine tank routes for the attack planned by Hotel Company on the 17th. Reports back from the patrolling platoons indicated a strong enemy presence in the area. Women and children were observed vacating the locale, while men were seen in the fields glaring at the RCR Platoons doing their recce.

Toward evening, the firefight broke out between India Company and a large force of Tier1 Taliban fighters. These were the most effective of the enemy troops; most of who were well trained insurgents from Pakistan. Tier 2 Taliban were local young men who were drafted into the ranks by threat or use of force. Their skills were poorly honed and their more determined brothers often used them as fodder.

Steele had joined India Company for their sortie "out side the wire."

"You will hang out with me on this one, Padre," declared Captain Mark Cote, acting OC of India Company when Steele had joined the team. "We can expect contact with the Taliban at any time. Stay by me and you'll be able to take everything in. Don't go off on your own and be sure to get your head down when things get hot."

'You've got it, Mark. I'll try not to get in the way."

From his vantage point on the top of the Police Station, Steele had a bird's eye view of the surrounding country. At about 1900 hrs the Taliban struck from ambush. They had effectively infiltrated between the dismounted 7 and 9 Platoons. A fierce firefight took place. The foot soldiers of 9 Platoon were close enough to their LAVs to be protected by covering fire from the 25mm canon. This allowed the soldiers on the ground to break contact with the enemy and return unscathed to their vehicles. Meanwhile Steele, with Cote, mounted up, and the LAVs 25 mm canon began to fire on observed enemy strong points.

However, it was 7 Platoon, and the sniper detachment that were caught in the open. One section sought cover in a wide-open area where no concealment was to be found. MCpl Killam, section leader, quickly took charge of the perilous situation, and had his men effectively engage the enemy positions. After a wild dash across open ground, a C-6 machine gun team was carefully sited and began firing on the flank of the Taliban positions. The fight lasted a brutal twenty minutes until 7 Platoon's LAVs could reach them. The Taliban began to withdraw...they had suffered a number of casualties, killed and wounded. The Canadians, none.

Later, back in the leaguer, Mike talked with the members of 7 Platoon. They were still wired after their experience.

"How are you guys doing?"

"Boy that was a rush, Padre. Did you see any of it?"

"I was up with CHQ and saw the whole show. You people sure know how to get the job done. Even I had to duck a couple of times when they zeroed in on our location. That's when we headed for our LAV and Cpl Jones got the 25 mm hammering. I'm just now getting over my adrenalin rush. Look at my hand shake."

"You're not the only one...comes with the territory," chortled Corporal Dingle Digby. He was a strapping good-natured lad, constantly up to mischief of one kind or another...always seen with a lop-sided ear-to-ear grin. His mother had given him his first name because her husband–to-be had bestowed upon her, his first serious kiss at the top of the Dingle Tower in Sir Sanford Flemming Park near Halifax. The boy had been teased about it all his life, with some calling him Dingle berry or Dingdong. But his friends and buddies simply referred to him as Ding.

"I see that, Ding," replied Mike, "But I'm surprised you talk about it with a grin."

"No point in cryin', Padre, just a part of the job…same as puttin' up with all this dust." For the briefest moment the soldier looked serious. "Damn dust is as fine as sandy talcum powder. It's everywhere and on everything…when the wind blows, even just slightly, it swirls around and everywhere I go I feel like I have been dusted like a crop of PEI spuds. It covers every surface and gets into my kit, books, and my teeth. If it gets windy enough in the day, the damn stuff obscures the sun, making everything appear hazy as a pea soup fog over Halifax Harbour. And to top it off its f…ing hot at mid-day. But as the veterans say…you ain't seen nothin' yet. They say it gets as high as 55 degrees soon. A fellow has to have lots of water, even at this early stage. It's the key to survival, you know."

Mike grinned. "You're quite the philosopher, Ding. I hope you guys pay attention to this wise young soldier."

"Oh, we do, we do! He's a wise guy all right…and to boot he drinks a barrel of water a day."

Ding accepted the humour for what it was. HQ Platoon was a tight bunch that looked after each other… but they had fun doing it and no one took offence.

Back in KAF three days later, Mike received a call from the PRT Commander, Lt Col Rob Chamberlain. "Padre, I've just been informed that Kowal has been hit hard by the Taliban. I understand your friend, the Mullah, was a target in the attack. I'm leaving now, would you care to join me?"

Chapter Five

21 Feb 07
Dear Michael

    Just a few lines to let you know that your parish is flourishing in your absence. What else, when your grandfather is at the helm, don't you know? Now that's your morning smile!
    In all seriousness everything is going fine. Our congregations are intrigued with the regular news of your soldierly endeavours and are delighted to get the ongoing story of your work with our Forces in Afghanistan. They are behind you 100%. Lucy Kellar keeps me updated on her Project Afghan Children. The school supplies and other useful commodities keep rolling in and the area of interest has expanded well beyond North Frontenac Township. She is receiving monetary donations as well from as far away as Kingston.
    Bishop Bruce will be in the parish for a visit in late March and I have a group of seven teens preparing for confirmation…and would you believe it, that old rascal Bert Vines has indicated he would like to become a full time Anglican…what ever he means by that. He thinks any young man like yourself, who volunteers for the Afghanistan conflict is deserving of strong support from his parish. Mind you, Bert is an old vet who saw some pretty rough times in WW2. Deep down he's made of solid stuff.
    Your grandmother and I do enjoy the times we spend with Angeline. She is a wonderful young woman. You are so lucky to have found such a helpmate. I'd like to be a little bird when the two of you meet in Rome! Well, not really.

In the meantime, be careful. Listen to your troops, especially the NCOs. Their advice is often priceless…and life saving.

God be with you, my boy

With loving affection, Gramps

* * * * *

The PRT (Emergency Response Team) was on the road within minutes. Mike rode in Lt Colonel Chamberlain's LAV. At 0720 hours, the force entered Kowal. Smoke was rising from the centre of the village and as the patrol moved in, Mike could see on the LAV's internal viewing screen that the small Mosque had been set ablaze. The Mullah's home was also burning.

"Down ramp," called the vehicle commander. "Take up defensive positions." Soldiers from the six vehicles scattered to their pre-determined positions.

"Clear," shouted Sergeant-Major O'Brien.

Mike moved quickly to take in the charred scene. Fires were still burning even though the villagers had tried frantically to douse the flames. Water from the stream that ran through Kowal was being hand carried in containers of different sizes. The effort was great, but the results were negligible. On the wall surrounding the Mullah's dwelling, a blatant sign had been painted with what appeared to be human blood. It read:

ZENDA BAD TALIBAN … Long live the Taliban.

At the base of the wall lay a blood clotted human arm, the stump covered with flies. An old clay pot lay tipped beside it, blood soaked into the ground. The arm had been used as the paintbrush. Closer to the house, the bodies of a woman and a young girl lay in the dust. It was the Mullah's wife and their teen-age daughter, Fatima. Around the corner of the building, a beheaded body was hung upside down from a small tree. It was the torso of a man with arms and one leg removed. Nearby, a head was mounted on a stick. Mike felt the gagging rise in his throat as he recognized the remains of Mullah Faizullah. About the yard were scattered household items, pots and pans, bedding. A bon fire had been lit and in the ashes were charred ends of school supplies, books and writing materials. In the air, the stench of death was insidious.

Mike felt his stomach convulse, his heart clench in anguish, and his mind reel in disbelief. The rapid charged tactical activity around him seemed to be happening as if from a distance, and for a moment or two he heard no sounds at all, as if he was in a silent movie

The ERT made a furtive search of the ruins, but found no other victims.

"Padre, how many were in the Mullah's family?" asked the CO.

"To my knowledge," Mike replied in a quiet and stunned mechanical voice, "There were four…the parents and two children…the girl over there, and a son about twelve years old. I see no sign of him."

The village elders began to congregate near the ERT vehicles. Chamberlain, with his interpreter, joined them.

The elders told of an early morning attack by a force of twenty or more Taliban fighters. The Mullah and his family were pulled from their sleeping mats. A kangaroo court condemned them as disloyal Muslims who had been previously warned neither to schoolgirls nor consort with the infidel soldiers, under the punishment of death.

"You have not heeded our warning," the leader was overheard to scream as he struck the neck of the mullah with his sword, severing the head. Two other insurgents grasped the two females, threw them to the ground and brutally raped and then shot them, all the while callously shouting obscenities. Some how, Hassan, the boy, escaped the horror. He leapt the wall, and disappeared into the maze of the village alleyways.

"He has not been seen since," announced the chief elder.

With a worried look Mike asked, "Do you have any idea where we might find him?"

"They probably caught him and took him off to molest and violate him, too," suggested one of the less optimistic elders.

A young boy named Ali standing at the fringe of the gathering said, "I know where he might be. He always went to a special place when he was upset."

"Show me where, *bechem*," requested Mike with a quavering voice.

"Come this way, Holy Man," called Ali as he quickly dodged along an alley.

"You two men and the interpreter go with them," ordered Sergeant-Major O'Brien.

The group moved down to the river and followed its bank for several hundred meters down stream to an old ruin. Ali running ahead was calling his friend's name.

"Hassan, Hassan, it's me Ali, are you in there?"

A few strides behind Ali, Mike reached the site. Kneeling down he touched Ali's shoulder and peered into the gloom of the decaying structure.

"Do you see him," he asked the boy.

"I think so. Someone is moving in there. I hope it's not Taliban," said Ali taking several steps backward.

"Hassan, are you in there. It's Chaplain Mike. Would you come to me?" Mike called a second time, and then he heard weeping. A soccer ball was hurled through the opening.

"It's all your fault! They're all dead and I should be, too! Why did you ever come here?" cried the boy.

Mike felt stunned at the accusing words as they were translated, but refused to let his feelings hamper his need to reach the boy. "*Salaam bechem*. I need to talk to you!"

One of the elders, distantly related to Hassan entered the discussion. "Hassan, it is your cousin Omer. It is not the Holy Man's fault. You know that. The Taliban are evil and have struck down your family. Come out so we can look after you!"

Several minutes passed. Slowly, dragging himself out from his hiding place under the ruins, Hassan's tear stained face appeared. Gently his cousin drew the boy into his arms to comfort him. Mike reached out his hand to touch the boy's head, but Hassan turned from the gesture and buried his head into his cousin's chest.

"It's best to leave him for awhile, Chaplain Mike, till he calms down. I will take him home with me. His father's brother lives in Kandahar… he is a doctor…and I will see to it the boy is cared for until he is notified. They are a close family," suggested Omer. "I will see you get the Uncle's address in the city."

* * * * *

The ERT finished the detail in the village by early afternoon and headed back to Kandahar. At a strategic convergence of sand dunes and washed out river beds, a Taliban attack group were waiting for them. The second LAV in the column was struck with an IED that blew three sets of tires on the vehicle and caused it to roll on its side blocking the highway. The lead armoured vehicle came under immediate assault from rocket propelled grenades and mortar fire.

The convoy, following their drills for such an event, deployed around their vehicles. The 25 mm cannon immediately began to engage the dug-in insurgent firing positions.

Mike was travelling with Sergeant Major O'Brien in the fourth LAV when the attack came. The Sergeant Major ordered the chaplain to stay put for protection. Just as the Senior NCO jumped from the tail ramp a rocket propelled grenade struck the top of the vehicle behind the gunner's position. He had fortunately been inside the LAV checking on his ammo supply.

After a quick assessment O'Brien called, "Better come with me, Padre, but stay glued to me. OK?"

"I'm with you," answered Mike as he dodged behind to listen carefully should instructions be given.

"See that little hollow beside the road? There to your left? Get in it and scrape it deeper, if you can. Keep your head down at all times unless I tell you otherwise. As you leave the tarmac keep an eye open for any disturbed ground where a land mine could be planted. I've got to take a closer look at things, but don't you move. I'll be back."

With swift sure movements O'Brien scuttled low toward Cpl Jane Barker's position under the brink of a sand dune. Sharp shards of sand flicked the area as small arms fire from insurgent positions took bead on the semi-exposed Canadians.

"What do you see, Jane?"

"Damn little. They seem well dug in."

"The lead and rear LAVs are leaving the road and appear to be outflanking the insurgents. Are you in radio contact? Mine seems screwed," enquired the Sergeant Major.

"All I get is some crackling and the odd word from Sunray. I believe you're right though; they are making a flanking manoeuvre. I can see at least that much."

An AK 47 round struck the top of the Corporal's helmet and she rolled to her side.

"Jane, are you OK?"

No response.

O'Brien worked his way up beside his corporal. He could see blood running from under the helmet. He felt for a pulse in the woman's chin and received a response.

O'Brien slid down the dune and called out to Mike. "Padre, I need a hand, but be careful. Keep low and zigzag across to me. Corporal Barker's been hit pretty bad in the head, and I want to get her down to where you have your scrape until we can get a medic to her. My radio's shot, so I can't get on the net."

The two men gingerly dragged the limp woman toward the shallow ditch. At this point, position 5 LAV, the Med Evac vehicle, saw the dilemma and moved forward to provide cover for the three exposed soldiers. As it came along side, Sergeant Brenda McLennan, jumped from the ramp of her specially configured LAV to tend the injured soldier. She was a strong but slightly built woman capable of handing patients much larger than her. Her co-ordination and handling skills were exceptional.

"Looks bad, Bren," remarked O'Brien. "I've put a sterile pad on the wound but I could see grey matter and splintered bone. The brain didn't appear to be touched, but I only had a quick glance…we were still under fire. Thank God the padre was close by…we were able to put her in a safer position and loosen her heavy gear and clothing."

"Well done, Sergeant Major. I'll take over from here." They loaded the wounded soldier into the Med Evac LAV. It was equipped with stretchers and medical supplies to attend casualties.

"Would it be all right if the padre travelled back with you? He might be able to lend a hand?" asked O'Brien.

"No problem! My corporal MA is forward tending the bumps and bruises of the people who went through the IED explosion. Thankfully, no one was seriously hurt. The armoured protection these vehicles offer is amazing…most of the time. I'd appreciate the padre's calm assistance in the event our patient becomes lucid."

Mike felt something graze his helmet and looked surprised as it slid to the side of his head.

"Damn it, Padre, I told you to keep low. I'll be in real shit if anything happens to you!"

Mike couldn't help himself and looked sheepishly into the Sergeant Major's eyes and replied with a stupid grin, "Yes, Sergeant Major."

Fortunately, the bullet had only scratched the surface. Mike pulled the covering off and examined the mark thinking; *now I have a souvenir of this crazy war.*

"What the hell are you doing…put that f…king helmet back on. Are you nuts or something?" O'Brien was getting really annoyed, fire shooting from his eyes, and pulled Mike down to ground level. "Let's get something straight, buddy…" and then he steadied and began to laugh and twirled an end of his waxed trademark sergeant major moustache. He did this often, but unconsciously. He did it most frequently when something was running through his head, but he did it every time when he was about to make some ridiculous or off the wall remark.

"You f…king Left Footers are bound to get this old Mick into trouble, aren't you. Sorry Padre that just popped out…please don't take offence. Soldiers having been using four letter words and worse for thousands of years. I bet the Roman soldiers at the crucifixion used a few choice words when they were throwing the dice at the foot of the cross. You might say it's a part of our culture. I know you're some upset when they fill the air with their occasional outbursts, especially if it's sacrilegious. Believe me, they mean no insult to you. It's mainly their way of expressing anger, frustration or disappointment."

"None taken, my friend, I was being careless," offered Mike.

This tease, Left Footers (Protestants) and Right Footers (Roman Catholic) had been going on since they met in Wainwright when Mike was assigned to O'Brien's Company for field training. The two men had become almost instant friends. The Senior NCO had led the padre through the drills in which the soldiers of India Company were training. Mike was a natural and absorbed the guidance quickly. He remembered the words of his grandfather, 'Seek out the experienced NCOs. They are the ones to instruct you in the ways of the military.'

Sergeant Major O'Brien had been a boy soldier with the famed Hastings and Prince Edward Regiment. He had joined the Reserve Unit when he was sixteen years of age. He was slightly built and on the small side for a soldier, but he had the Irish genes in him that would not allow him to quit any challenge put before him. As he grew bigger, he filled out and at age eighteen he joined the Royal Canadian Regiment where he became one of their "characters" as he progressed up the ranks to his present position. Jack was a devout Roman Catholic but he held his religious beliefs close to his chest. He was a good man with a good heart, but like many a soldier, he liked his beer a little too much, and as he aged it showed in his waist line and breathing when he exerted himself. Here in theatre, his physical condition steadily improved, as beer in the quantity he consumed was not available.

"I'll see that your kit gets back to you in KAF, Padre, just behave yourself with our 'Doc' or I'll cuff your ears." The jest brought a smile to Sergeant McLennan's face.

After the Sergeant Major left, Sgt McLennan said. "You two seem to have a pretty close relationship. How long have you known the Sergeant Major?" she asked.

"Long enough to get the cut of his jib and stay clear of his jabs," answered Mike.

"Oh, I can see you're a quick learner, Padre. We'll get along just fine." She smiled as she turned to tend her patient.

"Are you calling in a helicopter evac?" asked Mike.

"No, I think not. We're close enough to Base for a quick run in and our patient is quite stable. I have assessed the wound, and thank fully the break in the skull appears clean. The wound is serious, but I judge not a fatal blow. Thank God!"

"I second that...thank God'," said the chaplain with head bowed.

Sounds of weapons being fire became sporadic as the insurgents scuttled from their concealed positions following their pre-planned retreat route. They were, no doubt, a contingent of an elite Taliban force. There was no sense in chasing them into the remote wilderness where they had faded. They had made their point, and the Canadians had countered their ambush, killing two and wounding several others according to the blood signs left behind…sending the remaining insurgents on the run. An 'all clear' sounded over the net and the convoy, following a short on the ground de-brief, proceeded to return to Base. One LAV was left to guard the damaged vehicle until a recovery team arrive to transport it back to Kandahar.

Sergeant McLennan touched Mike's dropping shoulder. "You look bushed. Why don't you slide onto that empty stretcher and get a bit of shuteye? I gather you've had a busy day. If I need you, I'll give you a shout. OK?"

"You sure?" asked Mike stifling an unwanted yawn.

"I'm sure. Get your head down." He was asleep before his head touched the canvas of the stretcher.

* * * * *

The convoy was still 5 km from Base when the medical sergeant awoke Mike.

"Padre, will you give me a hand, our patient has become restless and is resisting her restraints. Please hold her as steady as you can while I get a drip going to relax her…talk to her. I have no doubt she will hear your voice and it might calm her."

"Do you really believe that?" questioned Mike.

"I do," she replied. "I have a very strong belief in holistic medicine. I think it's wrong just to treat a part of a patient's trauma. A human being is made up of many interconnected parts, and when one area is damaged, I'm quite sure the other parts are aware and try to respond. Now, talk to her."

Mike leaned forward to whisper into Jane Barker's ear. "Jane, can you hear me? It's Padre Mike. You're going to be all right. Your old pal, Brenda McLennan, has you in her care, and you know how good she is. I've seen you in Chapel a few times, so I know you follow God's Way. Good for you and bless you, Jane. I believe God is with you, now. How about that! I bet you'd never guess you'd be on the road with the Good Lord today… or would you?" Mike made the sign of the cross over her forehead. Jane sighed.

"I think I've got her under, Padre, thanks for your help. You're a super team member."

"Sometime I'd like to talk more with you, Brenda, about your approach to holistic care. It seems there is some of the medical staff that don't quite agree with you. Surely we must all pull together to bring about the best healing for our casualties?"

Sounding very professional and analytical, the sergeant said. "You're right. Not everyone agrees to the holistic approach…but that's science for you. Some medical people are so hide-bound to their own specialty that their vision becomes blurred. It takes skilled communication to work procedures out in theatre. The Role 3 hospital is already going full out to treat casualties. Your team of chaplains is doing a first class job. Our CO is impressed. When people are tired, it's sometimes hard to think straight. Know what I mean?"

"Indeed I do," relied Mike.

The conversation faded as the convoy entered the outskirts of Kandahar.

* * * * *

It was early evening and Malcolm was bent over the Team Leader's desk in deep concentration. He was a clear thinker who sorted through situations carefully. At the moment, he had a fair bit on his plate. He was a sensitive man who believed in a conciliatory approach to communication conflicts, but he was also determined when he made his mind up. He had high expectations for his team and was unwavering in support of his chaplains and their needs. Transport to various locations was always an ongoing problem but recently it was being managed well considering the battle conditions and the exigencies of the service.

As Malcolm pondered these thoughts, Mike entered. Looking up Malcolm noticed the exhaustion building in Mike's face. "I hear you've had a busy day, my friend...were part of a TIC (Troops in contact)! The report came in a while ago about the injury your group suffered on the way back from Kowal. How is she doing and what happened in the village, by the way?"

Mike took out a cigarillo and lit up. "I guess you could say the day was one of the worst ones of my life. When we got to Kowal, the mosque and the mullah's house were in flames. We pulled up to the gate and saw the carnage. His wife and daughter were raped and slaughtered in the yard. The mullah had been mutilated, his body desecrated, and strung upside down headless from a pole. They had cut off both legs and an arm. The other arm they used as a paint brush to announce their slogans in his blood on the enclosure wall." Mike slumped in a chair and began rubbing his bent head in distress. "I was sick to my stomach. The mullah's young son, Hassan, escaped the massacre and we found him a short distance away. A cousin has taken him into his care and will bring him to Kandahar to be with a closer relative. Much of the teaching material and books had been destroyed by fire. I was able to save two cartons. Sergeant Major O'Brien will be bring them over.' Mike stared off in the direction of the village, a blank and haunted look in his eyes. "Malcolm, I need to follow up on that. I feel some responsibility toward that child." Mike sat expelling the remainder of his pent up breath.

"Of course, we'll look into it and do what we can. You'd better get some shuteye," responded the team Leader.

"Not yet! I want to talk to you about a conversation I had with Sergeant McLennan on the way in. She's a bright, well-informed individual who is not afraid to speak her mind. She is a strong believer in the holistic approach to healing and sees the padre's role an essential part of that approach. I think it would be informative to have her share her thoughts in one of our sessions."

"I hear you. I think that's a great suggestion, but now you go and get some rest," ordered Malcolm. "We'll discuss the idea of a 'caring' symposium with the medicals later."

Mike left for his sleeping quarters in a groggy state. No sooner had he departed than Malcolm received a visitor in the person of Sergeant Major O'Brien bringing with him the rescued school materials.

"Evening, Sir," greeted O'Brien with a brisk salute.

"Good evening, Sergeant Major. Thanks for bringing that over, just put the boxes in that corner, please."

"Could I have a confidential word with you, Padre? It'll just take a moment."

"Of course, Sergeant Major, what can I do for you?" asked Malcolm.

"Well, it's about today, Sir. As we were coming back from Kowal we got into a bit of a firefight with an insurgent group. We think it was the bunch that hit the village and murdered the mullah and his family. Padre Russell was travelling with me when the bruha occurred and I had to remove him from the LAV as it was being hit with RPGs. He followed my instructions and levelled himself in a scrape at the side of the road while I went for intelligence as to what was going on. My nearest contact was one of my corporal's observing from the top of a dune. My radio was out, so I scrambled up the bank to see what she knew. I had just spoken to her when a bullet struck her in the head and I had to get help fast. I called to Padre Russell and without hesitation for his own welfare…we were under fire, Sir, he came to my assistance and we brought Corporal Barker down to relative safety until the Med Evac vehicle came forward. I just wanted you to know, Sir, without his help and calmness we may have lost her. He's a good sound man," his moustache began to twitch, urging a twirl; instead a twinkle appeared in his eyes, "considering he's an officer, that is. He relates to soldier's where they're at and that to me adds up to a top notch chaplain." O'Brien then gave his moustache a twirl.

"Thank you for that Sergeant Major, I'll see that is passed along to higher authority," replied Major Malcolm Berry concealing an inward grin.

"Thank you, Sir, goodnight, Sir." A quivering Army salute in grand style followed and O'Brien departed.

Chapter Six

E-mail from Angeline Russell
To Michael Russell
19/03/2007 10 am

My Dearest One.

How I wish the days would pass more quickly. Winter continues to hold its icy grip on these parts. The men seem to like it, and some of the women and children too, for it gives them opportunities to swarm out to the lakes for a few hours of ice fishing. They seem to thrive on the bright cold weather, where I would freeze.

Devon Lemke dropped off a four-pound lake trout and I prepared it for dinner with your parents. It was so fresh and delicious. Devon is a nice thoughtful lad and is planning to join Ontario Hydro when an opening becomes available.

I keep going through the computer sites for Rome to see if I can find something special for us to do. There are a number of excellent restaurants to choose from. I'll pick a special one and we'll splurge.

News on the Afghan front is so varied. I sometimes wonder if the media are telling the full story or simply making up details for fillers. I prefer watching CBC and CTV news channels as they both seem to be on top of the action. I also follow Christy Blatchford's column in the *Globe and Mail*. She certainly is outspoken and calls a spade a spade. I hear she's going to write a book on Afghanistan and our involvement there. I bet it will be an eye opener.

I must get this off to you so you will have it before bedtime.

You are my Love, always…

Angie

* * * * *

HMCS Iroquois
Traversing the Suez Canal

Greetings Michael

Here we are heading for the Arabian Sea. The sail through the Med was a pleasant experience. Oh, I know, a lot of people think the sailor's life is one grand sea vacation where a ship's company parties in every port. Yes, we do have good times when we reach port…after a while; being cooped up in confined spaces requires a good exercise ashore. There are diplomatic parties on board as well, where our Government officials in foreign ports entertain local dignitaries. This is primarily to foster goodwill between our Countries.

For example, we visited the Port of Aqaba, Jordan. For many of us, Aqaba was our first experience in an Islamic Country. The Ship prepared some materials for us to read to help us avoid disrespecting our hosts in this very sensitive area. Aqaba became the location for the change of command of the Task Force from the French to Canadian Command. Hospitality is a very big part of the culture in this part of the world, no change in that respect from the biblical period, and so the first thing that a shop owner would do would be to offer us some tea, hibiscus was a favourite if I remember correctly…very aromatic. The next day three busloads of us from the ship departed for an experience of a lifetime: a trip to Petra. Petra itself is only a small part of a large valley known locally as Waddi Moses, for it is part of the route taken during the Exodus. We made the hour-long drive, passing sandstone carvings strewn across what looked like a seabed without the water. Ancient waters and the winds that constantly blow through the region made these giant carvings. I found that the landscape reminded me of the area around El Paso, Texas and Las Cruces, New Mexico, with the homes and communities reminiscent of areas in Mexico. We also passed wandering camels, goats, olive farms and the occasional Bedouin tent.

From Aqaba, we did a short sail to a place that was NOT, a tourist spot. We stopped in to Djibouti for an overnight. Djibouti is a small non-industrialized country that is located on the north side of the Horn of Africa, near places like Somalia and Ethiopia. There has been no rain in the region for over two years! It is home to many refugee camps. While in Djibouti the ship's company was able to do a small good deed. We donated $1,000_to a local hospital's maternity / children's ward: a hospital that served the poorest of the poor.

I believe I forgot to mention another good deed performed by the ship's company. In Split, Croatia we went to a children's hospital with a donation of $8,600. The people on board our Canadian S(s)hips are very generous and are always ready to pitch in either monetarily or physically to help those in need. The children's wing of the local hospital could not afford much in the way of activity materials for the kids so, what started out as a fund raiser for some colouring books and crayons became a blessing to us, and to the hospital as we delivered not only the colouring books, puzzles, craft material and readers, but also four PS2 Game Systems and games, a Laptop computer, three LCD TVs and an acoustic guitar. Thirty of us that had the privilege of representing the Canadian ships and we were able to meet with the staff, parents, and most importantly the kids at the hospital. The smiles on the kid's faces are a memory that I will cherish. Even my son Daniel got in on the event; he had sent me some small stuffed animals from his collection, which I gave to the kids at the Hospital. That night the ship's band finally got a chance to play. And so we rocked the evening away as we prepared ourselves for the next portion of the journey.

During the next thirty days at sea, we patrolled various areas of the Arabian Sea and associated coastlines, continuing our mission as the command platform for the multi-national fleet that was working these waters. Our job was seen as a deterrent to the drug, alcohol and human smuggling. It is not always easy to express what it means internationally and strategically for us to be here, especially when we haven't been involved in what some would call the exciting events such as inspections of suspect dhows and big drug finds. Yet, we are but one ship in a large fleet, a fleet that can be proud of the work we have done which includes the interception of contraband that would have funded the Taliban. And with the recent addition of another Canadian ship, we have expanded our task; so while continuing maintaining a watchful eye as part of the overall war effort, we are also helping ensure safety on the waters for food shipments by the World Food Organization, into destitute areas of Africa, such as Somalia. This echoes the words of the Naval Prayer; that we may be *"a security for such as pass upon the seas upon their lawful occasions."*

Enough of my ramblings for now. It is always good hearing from you, so thanks for your e-mails. I know your time is limited for social graces such as letter writing, but always know you, and your people are in my prayers.

Take care, buddy.
Blessings and peace'
Tim

* * * * *

There is no such thing as a routine morning, noon or night on a Base like KAF. The clock is a continuum of time as it spins around the hours of a 24/7 active military establishment. Duties are fitted in a more or less orderly way, where and when they are required.

Days are punctuated with heights of drama and periods of down time…a wartime footing does not change the old Army adage 'Hurry up and wait.'

Mike tumbled out of bed at 0600 hrs, a bit woolly headed, but eager for a refreshing shower and shave. His stomach rumbled for want of nourishment, as he had only eaten a chocolate bar before crashing into his cot nine hours earlier. The morning was chilly as he made his way to the mess tent.

"Morning, Padre," offered a Sergeant cook, "You look as if you need a logger's breakfast…you know, one with a helping of everything on the menu and this morning it's all fresh from the farm. So dig in."

"Thanks, Sergeant Hall. It sure smells good." Mike loaded his plate as the sergeant looked on with a broad smile. He was an 'old timer' who took pride in his food preparation

There was a scattering of people in the dining area. Many appeared to choose to eat alone…some were lost in thought, others chatting animated with their dialogue. Mike spotted a familiar face at a corner table and wandered over to greet Master Corporal Peter Thomas who was reading a letter.

"Hi there, Padre, I heard Sergeant Major O'Brien got you into a firefight yesterday."

"Boy, news travels fast around here doesn't it?" said Mike with his iconic grin.

"I was in the Comms Centre when word came through that Jane Barker had been wounded. I knew you were with the ERT group, so I figured O'Brien would have you under his wing. What a guy! What a soldier!" answered Peter.

"A letter from home, Pete?"

"Yes, a good one! As usual, Mom has taken things in hand. Oh, she'll miss Dad, no doubt of that, but she knew what was coming and together they had everything worked out. Farm folk are like that. When you're running dairy cattle you have to be prepared for anything…like a call in the middle of the night saying your cows are blocking the road or you're bull has jumped the fence and is chasing the neighbour's stock…always something! Anyway, things appear fine at home. Thanks again for your care when the news came through about Dad," said Peter relaxing back in his chair. "Mom and my sister felt better knowing you were here for me." Peter grinned as he pulled out a chair for Mike. "But here, sit you down before all that grub gets cold. You must be real hungry."

"Matter of fact, I could eat a bear!"

Breakfast over, Mike checked in with the Team Leader. "Good morning, Malcolm."

"Morning, Mike. How did you sleep? You were pretty ragged last evening after your eventful day."

"I went out like a light…right into a deep sleep. I feel pretty good…a bit fuzzy headed to start the day, but wide-awake now. Anything special up for today?" asked Mike.

"The rest of our team will be here shortly. Would you lead our morning prayers, please?"

"I'd be happy to. I received a poem in the mail recently that will make for a good meditation. I'll slip over to my quarters and get it. Be right back," answered the younger chaplain.

Fifteen minutes later the team gathered around Malcolm's desk for their prayers with Mike leading the session. He used the prayers from his morning office out of the Anglican prayer book and for a thoughtful meditation read the poem, the author unknown, which had been sent to him from his grandfather.

Oh, how we would love
that amongst human beings
and in harmony with creation
peace would reign throughout the world,
But still today
Children cry, women are violated,
Families are torn apart
Soldiers die in combat.
So easily we wage war
Instead of conducting our discussions,
Our exchanges, and our negotiations,
With respect and understanding.
The price to pay is peace.
As difficult as it sometimes is for me,
I must dream of a world of peace
Where nations help each other and where
Human beings appreciate one another more!
When our hearts are set free from fear
We will then be able to embrace our children,
Bequeathing to them a world where they will
Grow, making way for peace and reconciliation.

After Mike had concluded with a prayer for the men and women whom they served and the Benediction, the men quietly reflected on Mike's presentation.

"Thank you, Michael," said Malcolm nodding with warm response.

Following prayers the chaplains had a rare opportunity to have fellowship with one another and unwind. Only on this occasion there was little to relax about as their discussions soon turned into a deliberation. A constant thought in the back of their minds was the theme, "What are we doing here? Are we being helpful or is this just one of those conflicts our country has asked us to become involved in as Parliament considered it an essential action in World affairs." They knew many soldiers struggled with this topic. Some were quite outspoken, others more reticent in expressing their views, never-the-less, it was an ongoing concern all along the line from the 'hot end' to the Senior Officer in command.

Robert Morin looked sceptical. "How can you expect to win hearts and minds when bodies are malnourished, children underfed and without medical care. Moderate secular schools are few and poorly supplied. The extremist madrassas schools funded by wealthy fundamentalists in Saudi Arabia teach jihad and violence. This is where the young fighters are bred and hate for the West is proliferated. People back home whine about our health system, and who gets served first, the cost of drugs, and so on. We fret about starting pre-kindergarten classes in our schools while here, schools are shamefully neglected and destroyed."

Felix, the quiet but thoughtful member of the team injected a thought. "Gentlemen, Ignorance is the Enemy!"

"Now that's profound thinking…too bad the powers that be wouldn't take that approach," added Mike. "When you think of the cost of a missile tipped with a Raytheon guidance system, think how many schools and teachers that money could support."

The padres were knee deep in the moral issues and the stand they must take in future discussions. Each man in turn shared their various recent encounters and found they were pretty much the same across the board. There were legitimate concerns that needed to be resolved deep within the soldiers' psyche and the padres had a role to play.

As the conversation wound down, Malcolm summed up the dialogue. "As Christians we believe that God's call is always toward Peace, but it is also to justice and mercy. When those latter ideals are trampled upon with force and impunity, confrontational responses become inevitable and even necessary. Unfortunately, dangerous military conflict seems to be the only strength of force we often can come up with when faced with great evil in an imperfect world. What we are faced with here in Afghanistan is a humanitarian crisis. The question, as I see it, is 'How do we respond?' This is something we must prayerfully contemplate. Perhaps from that starting point, we can help our soldiers have a clearer vision of our mission in this confused land."

Malcolm's cell phone sounded and he picked up.

"Padre Berry, here!"

"Padre, this is G1 at Joint Ops. We have both VSA (Visible Signs Absent) and multiple injuries in-coming. Report to Role 3 asp."

"Any identification yet? I have all the unit padres here at the moment."

"No, but will call you when available."

"Thanks, we are on our way."

* * * * *

The scene at Role 3 was one of organized fervour. Preparations to receive the casualties were underway as the chaplains entered the hospital area and took up positions where they could assist the medical team as required.

"Padre Berry, I suggest one of your Battle Group padres head out to the helo pad with the stretcher bearers to receive the casualties. Two can stand by to speak with the wounded as soon as we make the damage assessment, and you, sir, will be with me to determine the state of the VSA," advised Lieutenant Colonel Colin MacKay, Task Force Surgeon who was heading up the medical team.

"Steele, go with the team to meet the choppers. Mike, you and Robert, be ready to speak with the wounded when the time comes. I'll be with the Colonel in the OR. Let's do it!" directed Malcolm.

The sound of jet engines, and rotor blades increased in volume as the aircraft hovered inches above the ground. The stretcher teams, bent against the turbulence emanating from the helicopter as it landed, were ready with gurneys. Steele was poised to observe the wounded. The first casualty was inert, strapped to a striker board, his head and upper torso swathed in bandages. The chaplain could not recognize him and presumed this was the VSA. Beside this litter walked Sergeant Les Barnes of India Company. As they passed the padre, Barnes, almost imperceptibly shook his head.

"It's Corporal Jones, Padre, Davey Jones. I don't think he's made it!"

Steele could see the man's feelings on his face as his teeth bit into his lower lip and in his eyes were a glint of tears. Steele's own emotions began to rise as he recognized the second wounded man being carried down the ramp. It was Private Scotty Martin, the soldier with whom Mike earlier had shared a late night conversation. The man was semi-conscious as he was taken from "the bird", his head rolling from side to side as the stretcher-bearers lifted him onto the gurney. The last three off the aircraft were walking wounded who soon found themselves surrounded by orderlies guiding them toward the hospital tents. The padre walked with them. The casualties were still in a state of shock, but were anxious to talk about the IED occurrence. Steele listened without interrupting. Mike stood just inside the tent. As Private Martin was carried through the entrance, his eyes opened and he saw his padre gazing down at him. Feebly he attempted to speak and vainly try to raise his arm. Mike took his hand and walked beside the gurney toward the operating theatre. As they approached the surgical area, the chaplain stepped aside. Protocols had been established, and the padres followed them to the letter. There had been an earlier incident where an unwitting chaplain had interfered with a procedure that had been life threatening. With Malcolm's leadership in pre-deployment training the chaplain's position in Role 3 was validated.

Now there was no awkwardness as all worked closely together. The padres were there for the medical personnel who experienced job related stress as well as for the injured and the casualties.

The VSA had been examined first and it was confirmed that he had died from his wounds. Malcolm escorted the body to the mortuary where a brief service was held for the departed. Prayers were offered for the family who would not as yet have received the news; for the medical staff who valiantly tried their best to resuscitate the fallen, for friends and teammates of the fallen soldier, who would be eagerly awaiting information on their friend's condition.

When all the injured had been assessed medically, Mike and Steele entered the ward and visited them in turn. It was arranged that the padres would stay and assist them to call home to assure their families they had survived and that without further complications, all would be well. The chaplains had brief conversations with those at home to reassure them that their loved one was in good hands… and were receiving the best of medical care.

Also in the ward was Corporal Jane Barker…her head covered in bandages, but she was alert when Mike approached her bed.

"Looks like you've had another busy day, Padre Mike!" she remarked with a broken smile. "I haven't had a chance to thank you for being there when I was hit, and for helping the Sergeant Major to get me to safety. You chaplains amaze me…you carry no weapons to defend yourself and yet there you are in the thick of it."

"Well, Jane, you might say the Lord works in mysterious ways, great wonders to perform. I was glad to be of assistance. You're looking great. Thank God, it was only a graze with no serious damage, but then, a concussion is nothing to berate. You'll be up and around before you know it. Our med staff is the best!"

"Could I ask you to say a prayer for us?" she asked as her hand indicated the newly arrived patients. Mike bowed his head.

> "Gracious God, bad things happen to good people. Sadly it's the way of the world. I ask your blessing upon these your frail children who have pledged their all to duty and have bravely faced the horrors of war. They have

been hurt in body and perhaps in mind, but You can reach forth and give them healing. Give them trust in those who care for them in this place…the dedicated doctors, nurses and orderlies. Be with their families who worry over their condition. May they in turn return thanks to You, Loving God, for their survival? Amen.

* * * * *

Later that night, troops from all support nations, 3000 strong, gathered on the tarmac of KAF. The ramp ceremony for fallen comrades had become a tradition.

It was a solemn affair rendered with emotion. The troops were assembled on either side of the runway behind the aircraft that would carry the remains of those who had given their lives. 'No greater love.' Following a brief prayer service and Bible reading conducted by Steele, Mike offered a eulogy.

"We stand this evening to honour another fine member of the Canadian Forces, Corporal David Jones of I Company, 2 RCR Battle Group. Sadly he leaves behind his wife, Joanne and son Peter, who loaned him to us in the service of his country. Today we return his body to them with dignity and honour. While he would not have called himself a religious man, Davey Jones served with great devotion, placing his faith in his country, his unit and his family. He was a good father to Peter and had coached his minor league hockey team. Davey was an Ottawa Senators fanatic who cheered his team through good times and bad. He enjoyed the fun times with those he served, often acting the clown to the delight of his buddies. But perhaps Davey's most notable qualities were his willingness to do anything for anyone else…his sense of selflessness, his way of accepting people the way they were and his consistency of never breaking a promise. These are qualities that transform 'just another soldier' into a close-knit band of friends forever bonded. I invite you to join with me in a moment of silence in tribute to Corporal David Jones, after which I will close with a few words of remembrance."

When the brief religious ceremony concluded, the funeral cortege passed between the ranks making its way toward the C130. The bearers, friends of the deceased bore their burden with sensitivity and respect… unashamed tears rolling down their cheeks. Chaplains from all Coalition countries formed a group at the left side of the aircraft and in so doing showed their solidarity to all assembled. The Ramp Ceremony would be repeated two more times, at Camp Mirage, and at CFB Trenton where the families and friends of the fallen would suffer profound pain and congregate to receive their loved one home.

The Ramp Ceremony lasting forty-five minutes was over and the parade disbursed. The chaplains gathered in their tented office space for coffee and donuts. They were joined by two American padres, Major Jon Jankowski, a Roman Catholic priest with the Marines and Captain Agnes Roth, a Baptist minister from the US Army.

"I am impressed with your Ramp Service," stated Jankowski. "It is much more inclusive than ours. As you know, we conduct ours aboard the aircraft with the funeral party present. It makes more sense to have the microphones so everyone on parade can share in the farewell. I'm going to recommend your format to our commanders."

"I agree," added Roth, "Your liturgy is short and to the point. Everyone was tuned in, and as I watched I could tell they appreciated your words for the fallen. It's hard to say goodbye to a comrade in arms. Soldiers share such a bond that when one is lost, they all feel the emptiness that follows."

Major Jankowski nodded. "May I compliment you on the morale and team work you obviously share together as a chaplain team? It is model for all of us to follow. And thank you again for supporting us at Role 3. It seems we can always depend on the Canadian chaplains to lend a hand with our casualties. It provides a great spiritual lift, not only to the soldiers, and medical staff, but to our padres as well,"

Malcolm smiled and said, "It's good of you to join us at the Ramp service and it's always a pleasure to see you when you visit the hospital. If our team can be of any help, please let us know. It is great to have the connection with chaplains from all the supporting nations. This sense of solidarity is seldom achieved, as we tend to go our separate ways. Now, who's for another donut…more coffee?"

An alert sounded indicating incoming rocket attack on the airfield. The chaplains donned their flak jackets and doubled to the hospital area to assist the medical staff in securing protection for the patients who were taken to a ward, covered with blast blankets and a helmet placed on their heads.

"Over here, Padre," called Lieutenant Joan Miller, a nurse who was struggling with a confused patient.

Mike quickly moved to her assistance.

"She's hallucinating and needs to be held down until the spasm wears off. Can you hold her shoulders and talk to her?

Mike recognized the patient as Corporal Jane Barker. "What happened?" he asked.

"I think her head was jarred as we moved her here. I'd better get the doctor."

"Go. I've got her. Jane can you hear me?"

A moan!

"Jane, its Padre Mike. I'm here with you."

The woman began to shake uncontrollably as the neurosurgeon arrived at the bedside.

"Let's move her to the OR...rockets or no rockets, I've got to check her status. What are her vital signs, Joan?"

"Blood pressure is 80 over 40. Pulse 125. No eye opening. No verbal or motor response"

"Take the end of the bed, Padre, and let's get her into the OR. We'll have to do a CT scan."

With teamwork, the patient was quickly wheeled away. Mike helped position the bed beside the operating table and gently helped to lift her into position.

"Thanks, Padre, we'll take over from here."

In the protective ward the other chaplains were moving from bed to bed calming individuals who had become alarmed with the frenetic activity...some who had undergone recent surgery, while others had been wakened from a deep sleep.

Malcolm found himself sitting between two beds. In one was an Afghan policeman who had earlier in the day lost a leg from an IED blast. In the second bed was a child, a boy of seven, suffering from head injuries. He was just becoming conscious after his surgery and was scared and disoriented...both patients were incoherent, muttering in their own language that Malcolm could not understand. He held both their hands and in an effort to soothe them with some form of communication, he began to sing to them...any song that came into his mind in hopes the songs would bring them some comfort. Thankfully it seemed to work as both patients began to relax.

In the KAF hospital wards it was not unusual to find Coalition soldiers, Afghan civilians and policemen being treated equally...from the medical and spiritual perspective, they were valued equally as humans in need, and that was one of the reasons the Canadian Contingent was there.

An hour passed before the all clear was sounded. Fortunately, no rockets landed near the hospital site. With the help of the chaplains, patients were returned to the various wards.

The Canadian padres bid farewell to their American confreres and retired.

As he was leaving the hospital, Mike was approached by the neurosurgeon who had attended Jane Barker. "Our patient has stabilized but we're going to have to send her to Landstuhl on the next aircraft out. They are better able to handle her situation. She's conscious and is asking after you!"

"Thanks, doctor," responded Mike. "I'll see her now."

The post op area was quiet as Mike entered. He was directed to the place where Jane lay in a curtained off space. A nurse drew the screen aside. The patient turned her head and smiled up at her chaplain.

"Seems you're always coming to my aid, Padre, Sorry to be such a nuisance, but could I ask one more favour? Would you call home for me and tell them I'm all right…or at least that I will be OK?"

"Certainly, Jane, I'll phone right now. Let's see, its early morning at home."

"On second thought, perhaps I should talk to them myself…perhaps after I rest a bit."

"That's your call. Tell the nurse to give me a buzz on my cell when you're ready." As he said these words, she drifted off into a sound slumber.

Mike never got to assist her with the call, for in the late night hours she was whisked off to Germany on a medical evacuation flight.

Sleep did not come easy as minds raced with the events of the past day. Malcolm, ever the concerned and sensitive pastor got up, dressed and returned to stroll through the hospital wards, speaking comforting words and offering encouraging smiles to patients and staff.

Mike went back to his quarters to try to sleep, but tossed restlessly on his cot. His dreams spiked with wild conflicts left him heart weary upon waking… to be soothed only with thoughts of Angie. He was beginning to develop the "KAF Cough", a lung affliction that was endemic in the area. Inhaling the dust-laden air in the atmosphere caused it.

Steele stood by his hut for some time smoking his small cigar. It was becoming clear to him what this deployment was all about and the part he must play. Tomorrow he would head for one of the FOBs to visit his people in their forward position.

Robert sat by his cot reading through that portion of his breviary appropriate for the hour. Then he too dressed and headed for the hospital. He anticipated administrating the last rites to a dying American soldier whose own chaplain was in a forward area.

Felix slept for an hour. He was a tireless individual who could function well with minimal rest…a sturdy devout man whose purpose in life was to serve God's people faithfully. He prepared his kit for a return to the PRT construction site an hour's run from Base Camp.

Each chaplain was aware of the needs of the other team members. They had bonded well in their pre-deployment training and had learned each other's strengths and weakness. This was important, as stress could build suddenly, and as the soldiers said, "We must watch each other's backs." Padres were no exception.

Chapter Seven

Priority message from the Chaplain General
NDHQ Ottawa On Canada
To
Senior Task Force Chaplain
Base Kandahar
Afghanistan.

<u>Official visit of Inter Faith Committee on Canadian Military Chaplaincy</u>
Anglican Bishop Ordinary to the Forces.

Please be informed that the Rt. Rev. Peter Coffin will visit your location over the Easter period, 6 – April 2007. Commander John Wilcox will escort him from this office.

Bishop Coffin has offered to be of assistance to you in any capacity during his visit and will be prepared to preach and celebrate the Easter Sunday Eucharist.

S.G. Johnstone
Brigadier-General, the Reverend
Chaplain General

* * * * *

The Hercules aircraft descended in a wide steep spiral from Angles 25 (25,000 feet) into the Kandahar Air Field. The manoeuvre was required to counteract the threat of insurgent missile attacks on in coming flights. For the passengers on board, it was a strange sensation as their bodies adjusted to the forces exerted by the tactic.

Bishop Peter Coffin, a former CF Reserve Chaplain, spoke to his companion, Commander John Wilcox, over the roar of the engines. "Quite a ride, John," he said with a wide grin enjoying the experience. The two men had flown from Canada to Camp Mirage on an Airbus, and transferred to the Hercules C130 for the last leg into KAF.

"Our pilots certainly know how to fly in these conditions," replied Wilcox. "It's reassuring to watch them do their thing."

The aircraft rolled to a stop on the tarmac outside the terminal and deposited the passengers. Waiting nearby, the Senior Task Force Chaplain, Major Malcolm "Mac" Berry prepared to greet the visitors.

"Welcome to Afghanistan, gentlemen, I trust you had a pleasant flight?"

"A good one all the way," remarked the bishop. "Quite a thrill for the last few minutes…almost like a roller coaster ride. I'm really looking forward to this visit, Malcolm. You may not know it, but the military is in my veins. My father was Regular Force. I've heard many stories of active duty happenings. Now I'll see things first hand."

"I think you'll be pleased with the itinerary we have planned," responded Berry.

The bishop nodded. "I'm grateful for the opportunity the CF and IFCCMC (Interfaith Committee on Canadian Military Chaplaincy) has given me. As chairman, I can take back the kind of information that will help them in their deliberations. We have our annual meeting with the Minister of National Defence in May when we can discuss concerns that our chaplains may be facing, and following that gathering, we review the list of individuals who have applied to enter the Regular Force Chaplaincy."

"Your committee plays a very important role as interface between the Government of Canada and the growing multi-faith religious groups within the CF. The new chaplaincy has expanded beyond the original five member Canadian Council of Churches Chaplaincy Committee to its current position of inviting clergy from a more diverse base…a great step forward," replied Malcolm.

* * * * *

A few days earlier Malcolm had announced to his team the forthcoming visit. In his hand he held a priority message from NDHQ. "Gentlemen, this priority message in from the Chaplain General confirms the visit of our VIPs over the Easter period. I will meet them and bring them here to Fraise Chapel where we'll officially greet them and brief them on our duties. I want each one of you to outline your own area of responsibility, and be prepared for questions. Are we clear?"

"No problem for us," answered Mike, as he nodded toward Steele. "We are due back at Base from the forward area the day before. "Do you have a plan in mind for that week?"

"Yes, I'll set up a service for the Bishop and Padre Wilcox at Fraise Chapel for late Easter morning. There are a number of Coalition Anglican chaplains who have asked to join us here for the Communion Service. Steele, you will be out at FOB *Ma'sum Ghar,* and the visitors and I will join you briefly by helicopter early Saturday morning for a Eucharist. Felix will be with his PRT contingent for Easter observances, and Mike, you'll locate at FOB *Sperwan Ghar* to serve our people there. Robert will preside over an early Mass here at KAF. With that schedule in place, it will allow us to gather here in late afternoon for a social hour before going to dinner. How does that sound," asked Malcolm?

* * * * *

The planned arrangements for the visitors were firmly in place and the team looked forward to seeing them, and hearing news from home first hand. It would offer them a change in routine and an opportunity to share with the visitors their experiences "beyond the wire". A portion of the arrangements was to take the two men "outside the wire" to visit some FOBs. Toward this end, Coffin and Wilcox were issued protective clothing to wear while in theatre.

The bishop smiled from ear to ear as he observed himself in combat gear. "What do you think, Malcolm, do I pass muster?"

"Number one, Sir, but I urge you to take your dress earnestly. There are people out there who would be overjoyed to take out a person of your position, and we certainly don't want that to happen. Believe me, I'm not being facetious."

"No, I know your not, however it just struck my funny bone… quite a change from the flowing robes of a bishop to soldier's garb. I'm honoured."

"Our first item on the agenda is a visit to the Task Force commander."

*****

Holy Saturday dawned with a slight haze shielding the intense rays of the sun. This soon burnt off as the temperatures climbed into the mid thirty degree Celsius range. The Task Force Senior Chaplain and his party of visitors were greeted on the tarmac by Captain Jacob Wise, the American Marine pilot of the Blackhawk helicopter that would fly them to *Ma'sam Ghar* where they would see first hand the deployment of troops in a forward area.

"I'll take you on a short sight-seeing tour of the area as we head out to the FOB. I trust your head sets are all in working order?" asked the pilot?

"They're all checked, sir," answered Sergeant Tom Teale, the crew chief.

"Roger that! Here we go." The aircraft lifted off in a torrent of dust just as the side doors closed, not fast enough to prevent the dusty air from sweeping into the compartment occupied by the passengers. Immediately, the bishop began to cough.

"Sorry about that, Sir," remarked the crew chief, "Part of the tour, one might say. Can't avoid it in these parts."

"No problem. Even a bishop must learn to keep his mouth shut from time to time," remarked Coffin with a smile.

Down below a stark area of Kandahar Province was seen. A highway of sorts snaked through the land between bone-dry hills. The spring had produced welcome rains after a long period of drought, but this particular landscape had wicked off the moisture leaving the topography desert like.

"The Taliban like to hide out in areas like these," announced the pilot. "If you look to the right you can see the remains of a Russian tank column that was ambushed several years ago. Further on, and to the left, where what appears to be a streambed, you can spot a Bedouin encampment. I marvel how these people can eek out an existence in these desolate places."

The Blackhawk banked sharply and Wise continued his commentary. "See how the landscape changes in the distance where the sandy brown earth turns green. That's the Arghangab River valley where the UN agencies and your PRT are developing a new irrigation system for the locals. They're working on twelve major irrigation systems that service 400 kilometres of canals, and you can bet there's no media attention for that. Interesting to note, when the farmers and producers see the results of the helping agencies' improvements, they become bolder in providing information on the insurgents in the area. As roads and bridges are repaired, more farm produce can be shipped to market in the towns and cities. People back home should be given more info on these projects rather than all the doom and gloom most media like to spread.

"Remarkable the contrast between the arid and the irrigated," noted Coffin. "The lushness of the valley compared to the waterless wastes on either side."

"You can see below the acreages of old vineyards and the varied fruit orchards. Water is certainly the key means of life here. And look there, the fields of green grain and the long rows of vegetables growing. Coming up is one of your Canadian PRT teams; I believe Chaplain Berry told me it's the one where Padre Tachie is located."

"Right you are," said Malcolm.

"Over there," pointed the pilot, "equipment is widening that water containment pond and notice how the sluice ways have been re-built. That's the kind of thing that will win hearts and minds over bullets any day."

"Are you thinking bullets are not necessary?" asked Coffin.

"Not at all! With the type of enemy we face here, there will always be a need to protect those who serve the humanitarian need. God forbid that we should leave them unprotected from the terrorist elements that would stop the re-construction work. The Taliban are out to enslave the poor and unprotected…and that's not political mambo-jumbo, that's reality. They did it before, and they plan to do it again. Each day I say, Thank God for the ISAF and for the Canadian Battle Group's patrols. There's your FOB, gentlemen. Sergeant Teale, prepare to open doors on landing…not too quickly…wait for the rotors to stop… we don't want to give the bishop the wrong impression for a second time and send him off in a dust storm!"

"Thank you Captain Wise, I appreciated the overview…very interesting, and your comments are well taken. God Bless," said the Bishop, "and every good wish for a successful tour of duty."

A short distance from the helipad Steele waited with Major Bud Taylor, commander of the FOB and his Sergeant Major, scarves covered their heads and eyes to shield them against the hot blast stirred up by the landing. When the rotors became stationary, the three men approached the Blackhawk. The side door opened and Sergeant Teale jumped down to assist his passengers to alight.

Bishop Coffin's grin was sincere. "And thank you, too, Sergeant. You have given me some lasting memories to take back with me…and perhaps a little Afghan soil to digest."

"Sorry about that, sir, I guess it's just routine for us in this business."

"No need to apologize, Sergeant, I needed some toughening up as a reality check."

"Welcome to FOB *Ma'sum Ghar*," said Major Taylor extending a hand to his VIP guests. "You'll find things pretty spartan here, but we want you to feel free to mingle with our troops. Sergeant Major Lewis will be by your side to keep you on the straight and narrow. Ha ha! Pardon my sense of humour. But it is our responsibility to see that you're cared for. On the Strong Point just to our north, we had a contact with an insurgent bomb cell that was attempting to mine the road last night. You never know, those bastards may have planted a sniper nearby." Taylor blushed as he realized his language might have embarrassed the cleric.

"I will stay glued to the Sergeant Major. You can count on that Major Taylor. This is Commander Wilcox from the Chaplain General's Office. We'll both stay close to Mister Lewis. Right, John?"

"That we will! Who's going to look after you, Steele?"

"Oh, our padre knows his way around here without a guide. He's been here often enough, and he's always a welcome addition…in fact he's one of us! Now, let's grab a coffee and meet a few off duty folk. There's time before your church service. Can't tell you how many will be available to turn out as this place is on 24/7 shifts, but I have no doubt Steele will have the word out."

The group made their way to the mess tent where a dozen or more soldiers were gathered, while outside Steele covered a six foot table with a linen cloth, and from his communion kit he set out the chalice and the paten used for the administration of the sacrament.

It was 0800 hours when a congregation of twelve people shared in the Easter Eucharist; Bishop Peter Coffin gave a brief homily on the significance of the Resurrection. The temperature reached forty-one degrees Celsius by mid morning. It would be a hot, uncomfortable day.

* * * * *

Easter morning, on the main highway from KAF through the Maywand to Helmand, a 2 RCR battle Group component from Major Alex Ruff's Hotel Company, along with Major Boomer Broomfield's A Squadron of the LdSH Armoured Regiment met in a desert leaguer to hold an O Group in preparation for the day ahead. All were looking forward to their return to KAF after spending thirty-six days living on hard rations and sleeping in their vehicles among the desert dunes of Southern Afghanistan. It had been a long and tiring tasking. The soldiers were grubby from lack of clean clothing…to think of a nice hot shower was to think of heaven. However, before they could return to clean sheets and fresh rations, they had one more convoy to protect as it crossed the desert wasteland.

Commanding 5 Platoon was Lieutenant Ben Rogerson, deploying his three LAVs up front. As they approached a cross road, the lead vehicle stopped and surveyed the area for any potential threat. None was seen. For 5 Platoon it was just another guarded stop, a normal part of their convoy security SOP. The first LAV, call sign 22Bravo, preceded along the route. There was a horrific explosion and the vehicle was tossed, as if weightless into the air, the rear door flung off, and the section of soldiers inside the troop compartment killed instantly…Sgt Don Lucas, MCpl Chris Stannix, Cpl Brent Poland, Cpl Aaron Williams, Pte Kevin Kennedy, and Pte David Greenslade. One soldier, Corporal Shaun Fevens, was propelled up through the air sentry hatch and landed some fifty feet away from the site, his clothing smouldering. Blood gushed from his mangled legs and one arm. Cpl Robertson, 22Bravo gunner, shaken, but unscathed, rushed to Fevens aid. The LAV's turret commander and the driver were fortunate to survive the blast, but were battered and dazed.

Lieutenant Rogerson took immediate control of the situation. With all the composure he could muster, he reported the strike to his Company Commander, who in turn passed it through comms to the Battle Group HQ in KAF. He requested an immediate helicopter evacuation. Next, he walked forward to secure the area, and to clear a way for the Platoon medic, Cpl Rob Wickens, who rushed to the scene and immediately set to work stabilizing Fevens, then moved to examine the other survivors. At the rear of the packet, Platoon Warrant Officer Richard Yuskiw ordered his section to select a safe landing site for the Cas Evac helicopter. The area was swept and made secure and Warrant Yuskiw joined his Platoon Commander at the IED explosion site where Rogerson had the hard task of examining the bodies for any vital signs. Confirmation of the 'vital signs absent' tragedy was radioed to BGHQ with particulars on each casualty.

Within a short time, soldiers from 41 Squadron engineers and Hotel Company Commander Ruff with CSM O'Toole arrived. The CSM took on the undertaking of removing the soldiers' bodies from the wreckage and cleaning the area after the engineer's work of examining the blast had been concluded. It was heart-breaking work that was done with the sensitive touch of a well-trained professional soldier.

* * * * *

The shrill buzz of the Senior Chaplain's cell phone halted the pre-luncheon conversation in Malcolm's office.

"Padre Berry, here!"

"Sir, this is the Adjutant at BGHQ. We have been advised of incoming casualties including six VSA."

"Thank you. My team will proceed to Role 3." Malcolm slid the phone back into his pocket. "Gentlemen, we have been called to the hospital… looks like some serious contact has taken lives…Bishop Peter and Padre Wilcox, sorry to break up our gathering, but duty calls."

"Can we be of assistance," both visitors asked simultaneously

"I could certainly use your help, as you know three of the team are in the forward areas…just Father Morin and I here in KAF. This will be a very busy day. I'll brief you as we go, so take your cue from me," advised Malcolm as he prepared to leave.

With heavy hearts, the chaplains with Bishop Coffin made their way to the hospital.

Clergy are often faced with inner turmoil when they have to deal with violent, sudden death. Military Chaplains have this experience more often as they serve men and women of a younger generation. Chaplains have to reach deep within and then respond knowing that they will be guided along this unsettling, steep and painful path. They have to be confident that God is with them each step of the way, and will give them the strength to sort out their feelings in due course. Indeed, it is a journey of faith, and God will be beside them to lift their burden should it become too heavy to bear.

Preparations were well under way when the four clerics arrived. Stretcher parties were being drawn up. At the Senior Chaplain's suggestion, Bishop Coffin and Commander Wilcox offered to assist them while Malcolm conferred with the Medical staff to determine where best he and Padre Morin could help out.

* * * * *

Word of the casualties reached Steele and Mike out at the FOBs. The men were anxious to return to KAF, as they knew Malcolm and Robert would be under considerable stress as they attended to the dead and wounded. Transportation at the time of a critical incident could take up to twelve hours and it was the middle of the night before the two men "out side the wire" could return to Base, by then the chaplain involvement at the hospital was finished for the night. As they passed Malcolm's quarters a light was still burning.

"Shall we disturb him," asked Mike?

"No, he may have fallen asleep with the light on. Let's wait till breakfast. He's no doubt exhausted and we could do with a little shuteye, too. No doubt the day ahead will be a full one for all of us," remarked Steele. With that comment both men moved with tired footsteps to their respective digs for as much rest as they could manage. This was impossible as their minds were filled with the duties ahead, and the deep compassion they felt for their fallen comrades and their families back home. The padres would be present as the caskets were draped with the Canadian and Regimental flags in a designated space outside the hospital area where people could pay their last respects. The clergy would be available to any who wished to speak with them. As 2 RCR Chaplain, Steele knew that he would have to conduct the short Ramp service.

At 0700 hours, the chaplain team met in Malcolm's office. Mike was first to speak when he saw how drawn the Team Leader looked. "You don't look like you got much sleep. Let me get you a coffee."

"It was a demanding day, but by grace we made it through, with many thanks to the Bishop and Padre Wilcox for their help. I really can't thank them enough for stepping right in. They made a difference."

"Where are they, by the way," asked Steele.

"I imagine they're preparing to head out. Their plane leaves shortly for Camp Mirage," said Malcolm adjusting his glasses. "Now this morning, we all have our work cut out for us. You know what you have to do according to our SOP. Mike, you have first stand by the caskets…some of the lads' friends will come by. Be available to them. Steele, members of 5 Platoon will need to be seen. They're in unit lines now. Do you have your part planned for the Ramp Service?"

"Yes, that's in hand."

"Good. We'll meet back here before lunch to review proceedings," said Malcolm, "Now, I'd better check on our guests. They were an exhausted pair when we said goodnight! They've had an experience they'll never forget."

The chaplains' spirits were battered by the events of that Easter day, normally a day of great celebration for them, but like the professional soldiers around them they "sucked it up", and went about their solemn tasks with a prayer in their hearts. "It is you, Lord, who will see me through this difficult time and give me the words and wisdom to comfort those who mourn, and support those who feel lost in their grief."

* * * * *

Two thousand Coalition troops stood at attention on either side of the Hercules aircraft as the LAVs containing the six carrying cases rolled onto the tarmac. The parade Sergeant Major brought the gathering to attention. Pallbearers came forward to remove the bodies being repatriated.

Standing together in a group were the Canadian Chaplains ready to precede the bearing parties to the aircraft. Several chaplains from other nations offering their support stood to one side.

Steele addressed the parade.

"I am the resurrection and the life, saith the Lord: those who believeth in me, though they were dead, yet shall they live: and whosoever believeth in me shall never die.

"The eternal God is thy refuge, and underneath are the everlasting arms.

"We are gathered here today to honour six dedicated soldiers who gave their lives in the service of their country, so that the people of Afghanistan might be freed from oppression and crimes against humanity. We mourn the loss of our comrades in arms. They were aware of the dangers they faced, but heedless of the cost, they valiantly served for what they believed in. Now they join the Immortals of the Regiment…those who fell in the Boer War in South Africa; those who gave their lives on the fields of France and Belgium in the Great War; the brave souls who fought and died in the muddy gulleys and streets of Ortona in World War II.

"Our prayers are with Sergeant Don Lucas, MCpl Chris Stannix, Cpl Brent Poland, Cpl Aaron Williams, Pte Kevin Kennedy and Pte David Greenslade. We pray for their families and friends who mourn back home…that they may be comforted in their time of loss.

"Psalm 121.
I will lift up mine eyes unto the hills: O whence cometh my help?
My help cometh even from the Lord, who hath made heaven and earth.

God will not suffer thy foot to be moved: and God who keepth thee will not slumber.
Behold, God that keepth Israel shall neither slumber nor sleep.
The Lord is thy keeper: and thy defence at thy right hand;
So that the sun shall not burn thee by day, neither the moon by night.
The Lord shall preserve thee from all evil: yea, and shall keep thy soul.
The Lord shall preserve thy going out and thy coming in, from this time forth forever more.

"This is a reading from St John's gospel:
Jesus said unto them, I am the bread of life: those who come to me shall never hunger, and those who believe in me shall never thirst. All that God gives me shall come to me; and those who come to me I will in no way cast out. For I came down from heaven, not to do my own will, but the will of God who sent me. And this is God's will which has sent me, that of all that God has given me I should lose nothing, but should raise it up again at the last day. And this is the will of God who sent me, that everyone who sees the Son, and believes may have everlasting life: and I will raise them up at the last day.

"Almighty God, Giver of all mercies and comfort: Deal graciously, we pray you, with those who mourn, that casting every care on you, they may know the consolation of your love; through Jesus Christ our Lord.

"May the Lord bless you and keep you. May the Lord's face shine upon you, and be gracious unto you. May the Lord's countenance be lifted up upon you and give you peace, both now and forever more. Amen.

There was a deafening sacred silence along the line of troops as heads bowed and tears flowed openly down the faces of friends and comrades. The simple ceremony was powerful in its quiet dignity. It was a reminder to everyone of his or her own mortality. The time had come for the final salute, as the six caskets were slow marched toward the waiting aircraft that would start them on their homeward journey. In the background, a piper played a lament.

The parade was dismissed. It was the end of an exhausting two days.

*****

Across the ocean a rear party in Canada was active. Padre Greg Costen, Battle Group rear party chaplain reported to the "War Room" in 2 RCR lines. The Critical Response Team was assembled, and was chaired by Colonel Ryan Jestin. In attendance was the Adjutant of the Rear Party, a member of the Medical Staff, a Public Relations Officer, Assisting Officers, the padre, and others who served in administrative and related capacities…a total of eighteen people.

Colonel Jestin made the official announcement of the mass casualties. Padre Costen's first call was to the Base Chaplain, Major John Organ to convey that there were six soldiers killed. Four of the casualties had families in the area and two with families in other geographical locations. There would be four Notification Teams and three other padres to assist.

John Organ contacted the Area Chaplain, Padre Todd Meeker, who coordinated the Notification Teams to report to the War Room to rehearse procedures. The teams were gathered within an hour, briefed on the details and procedures, and instructed that a communications lock down was in effect until official channels cleared the release of the information for the teams to deliver.

It was an unpleasant period of time for all involved as each team member felt they held a sacred trust that was not theirs to keep, but were not yet allowed to share it with the people who needed to know it most.

Word finally came through to proceed with the notification. Before heading out on their sad mission the team shared in a prayer.

Then Padre Costen, along with the CO of the Rear Party, drove in silence to the home of Sergeant Donald Lucas. In the padre's own words this is how the news was given to Mrs. Lucas.

"Upon arrival at the home of Sgt Donald Lucas the CO and I approached the home where we saw the children doing Easter crafts at the kitchen table. I took a deep breath and rang the doorbell. This was approx 1100am. Once the news was broken by the CO, (without the children present in this case,) he departed while I stayed with Mrs. Lucas and the children. I facilitated calls to other family members, tried to answer her questions, and offered ongoing pastoral care. After approximately 30 minutes the Assisting Officer arrived with a brief explanation of his role. He began the innumerable administrative processes on behalf of Mrs. Lucas, commencing with arranging for the arrival of family from other parts of the country. Approximately one hour after notification, the Public Affairs Officer arrived to speak to Mrs. Lucas about an initial statement for the media. Shortly thereafter Col Jestin and the DCO arrived to offer condolences. I was with Mrs. Lucas for approx 4 hours until a secondary support system, some family friends, was able to come to her home.

Subsequent days were spent with Mrs. Lucas, and other family members planning services, orchestrating details with the AO for the family's transportation to CFB Trenton to meet the aircraft carrying the remains of the fallen, and trying to come up with the most effective means of breaking the news to her children, one of whom had some learning disabilities. I liaised with the Base Social workers who were able to provide me with children's books on the topic of death. These I relayed to Mrs. Lucas. She undertook the task of telling her children privately."

* * * * *

The mourning families gathered in a reserved space inside the terminal at CFB Trenton, accompanied by their Assisting Officers to await the aircraft's arrival. They were joined by VIPs from Ottawa, The Governor General Michaelle Jean, the Minister of National Defence, Gordon O'Connor, and other dignitaries who moved among the grieving families to express their condolences and share their anguish. There was palpable sadness in the room as each family dealt with their loss in their own way. Some wished to speak, others kept to themselves. As dusk fell, the Airbus carrying the six fallen soldiers came to a stop outside the CFB Trenton passenger terminal. While the aircraft shut down, the CFB Trenton Base Chief Warrant Officer briefed all in attendance on the format for the ceremony. That is when it really struck home for most of the families, and understandably they struggled with their emotions. The parties moved onto the tarmac. An informal guard of honour made up of a mix of military personnel, most from CFB Trenton, stood opposite the families creating an aisle through which the flag draped coffins were carried.

Each of the repatriated soldiers was taken from the aircraft in order of rank with the escort provided by the Regiment, Corps or unit of the fallen. A friend who would stay with the deceased until the burial was complete accompanied each fallen soldier from Afghanistan. The Assisting Officer was at the side of the family, along with a padre for this, the third Ramp Ceremony. The remains passed in front of those assembled, were saluted and the caskets placed with full honours in the hearses. The famlies then went forward and honoured their loved one, placing flowers on the caskets. This was the most trying moment for all. Once this observance was concluded, the families moved to their limos and the procession moved toward the Highway of Heroes, a stretch of Highway 401 running from Trenton to Toronto. It had received this official name in August 2007, in honour of Canadian Forces personnel killed during the war in Afghanistan. As the funeral cortège made its way west toward Toronto it passed beneath overpasses crowded with people. It was nighttime and dark by then, but that did not hinder the hundreds gathered to pay their respects to the brave fallen heroes.

* * * * *

Back in Afghanistan, KAF returned to its routine as the soldiers of H Company resumed their duties, their professionalism maintained.

In Kandahar City, a group of Coalition soldiers on stand down went shopping for gifts for their families. A man leaning with his back against a wall looked no different than the other young men idling in the *souk* or market place. The only distinction was the darting eyes that followed closely the movement of the soldiers who were looking over the handcrafted rugs and souvenirs piled high at the out door stalls.

The person following the soldiers with his shifty eyes was not Afghan. He was Pakistani and his name was Ahmed…slight of build with a wiry frame beneath his loose garments. He was a terrorist, and had been schooled and trained in an extremist *Wahhabi madrassas*, a school system that promoted Jihad against all "Unbelievers." It was financially supported by oil rich Saudi Islamic fanatics, and was the breeding ground for terrorism and insurgent recruitment.

Hidden beneath his clothing was a lethal vest binding powerful explosives tight to his body. Amed waited until the soldiers had made their purchases and began to mount their vehicle, and then he worked his way to the back of the truck, screamed in a loud fanatical voice, "*Allah-u-akbar*", and detonated his suicide charges. Mayhem followed. The mutilated bodies of Ahmed, soldiers, and civilians were flung through the air. Ahmed had secured his passport to *Jannah* or Paradise, a place where every wish is granted, for so he had been taught to believe. Sadly, the extremist fundamentalist Muslims had once again twisted the words of the *Qur'an* to promote their own heretical philosophy and had slaughtered many people in the name of Allah. Another day and another Ramp Ceremony for two American Marines and one British soldier, whose mandate was to bring freedom and a humanitarian solution to the shattered, war weary nation of Afghanistan.

* * * * *

HMCS Iroquois
Some where in the Arabian Sea

Dear Mike

We continue our sweep of the Arabian Sea. Recently we made port at Jebel Ali in Abu Dhabi for a ten day Rest and Maintenance period. There was a lot of work to be done by all the departments on the ship. This was an opportunity to work on systems that had been running constantly, and needed some regular maintenance, most of which could only be done when they were at rest. We also needed to paint the ship and clean out the bilges, most of which was done by local people hired for the job. Everyone was ready for this break, with most crewmembers getting at least one night ashore. It was nice to check into a hotel and sleep in a full sized bed and take a bath or a long shower. During our time in Dubai we were treated to one of the Show Tours that the Canadian Forces Support Agency puts together for deployed personnel. A hotel & resort facility ballroom was booked for the event, and all but a few duty people were able to attend a grand buffet and concert. Our entertainers included a couple of country singers, an R&B guitarist, a comedian / M.C., and a back-up band that did tributes to the Beatles and Rod Stewart. It was a great night and one that allowed us to take a mental break from our tour. The next day the entertainers came aboard ship to put on an "un-plugged" show for those of the crew who had been on duty the night before.

In your last e-mail you asked about routine duties on board. There are those who stand watches, and then there are those who are "day" workers. Those on watch stand a rotation of "watches" during a twenty-four hour period…these are broken down as follows: 0730-1230, 1230-1730, 1730-0030 and from 0030-0730. Those who stand watches also attend to the "Cleaning Stations" a number of times per day. They need to do all their own housekeeping like laundry and fitness; meaning that these folks work hard during our times at sea. In addition, though I am blessed with a cabin with only one cabin mate, most of these people who stand watch, the Master Seaman and below, live in "messes" that hold up to 50 people and are usually kept dark at all times to allow those off watch to sleep. The "Day" workers tend to work from 0800 till they finish their day.

Wakey-Wakey gets piped, literally a pipe blown by a Bosn's Mate over the ship's announcement system, at 0700. The weather report is announced, as is a schedule of the day's events. For me, I listen to the announcement and roll out of my upper rack around 0730, then off to my fitness program from 0800 to 0900, and then I return to my cabin. It is a 9'x 9' space with two fold down racks on the outer bulkhead (wall), a sink and a desk/storage unit. This I share with another person, and all our kit; including all my ministry stuff.

I do the Daily Office from 0900-0930. At 10:00 I head down to the C&POs for "soup"; a very civilized part of navy life, and from there I continue my day wandering the ship, going to various meetings and lectures, doing paperwork, formally sitting down with folks, preparing for services/bible study, and whatever else presents itself in a day.

Now, that about catches you up on my part. I do appreciate getting your news and find it an interesting that both of us are intensely focussed where the Ministry of Presence is concerned.

> Blessings, my friend, and May God be with you and yours...
> Tim

Chapter Eight

47 Viale Europa
00144 Rome Italy
March 20th, 2007

My dear Michael,

    I do hope this letter finds you in good health and that you are looking forward to your leave in Rome with Angeline. I am sure you will have a wonderful time. It is a delightful city with so much history in every part of it.

    As you know I have been here for work and study on Vatican papers for the past three months. Our team has moved into the east wing of the Cardinal Scorsone's palace where we will live for the month of May. This will allow us to spend more time on a pending matter that His Holiness will soon be addressing.

    This means that my delightful little flat will be vacant for that period and I invite you and Angeline to use it for your holiday. It is a second story apartment over looking a beautiful garden where the citrus trees will soon be in bloom, offering up their amazing bouquet, especially in the evenings. Would you accept this as a belated wedding gift from me? I have been in touch with Angeline recently when I had a quick visit back to the University. I'm sure she has told you of my call to her when I explained the possibility of my flat being vacant in May. She seemed delighted with the prospect, but stated firmly the decision was yours, as she wanted your needs to take precedent, and that some of the details were being co-ordinated by assistance in theatre.

Let me hear from you ASAP and I will make all the arrangements necessary for your occupancy.

As always, your friend,
Father Pat

E-mail from Angie Russell
To Michael Russell
9 May 2007

Dearest One

Only two weeks to go until we meet in Rome. Oh, I'm so excited.

My flight is all arranged and I arrive at Leonardo da Vinci airport at 9 a.m. local time. I can't wait to see you in the arrival area. Will you be in uniform or wearing civilian dress? Wave that little Canadian flag I sent over with you so I can spot you when I clear Customs.

I have made a list of the things I would love to see…with your approval, of course. I have read many books, looked up a number of Roman tour guides on the Internet and talked with our old friend from Western U, Father Kelly, who spent several years studying in Rome. He was full of ideas and quite excited for us.

You can be sure spring has sprung this way as the black flies are hatching like mad with the warm weather we've been having this past week. Your grandfather has been busy at the cottage raking the old leaves and other winter debris, and the trilliums are out on the maple ridge. Speaking of maples, there was a good run of sap starting at the end of March and tailed off by the middle of April. I'll bring a small jug of maple syrup for your sweet tooth.

Mere et Pere both send you their love and continue to wish you a safe tour. Even though I don't know when you're "outside the wire", I do pray that you are taking care of yourself. Don't do anything brave or foolish! Promise me!

If there is anything I can bring you, please let me know, I'll have lots of room in my luggage.

Hugs and kisses, my darling
I'll be with you soon.
Angie

* * * * *

It was now late April and Mike was making double sure that all his 'dots' were in place and his 'T's' crossed in anticipation of his upcoming leave. In a separate private corner of his mind, his thoughts turned more and more toward Angie and their coming time together. Warm feelings flooded him as he dreamed of looking into her beautiful eyes and seeing the love reflected there.

"How I miss her," he thought. "I feel like a half person with out her by my side."

"Hey, Padre, watch where you're going. You almost bowled me over," said a soldier dodging Mike's entrance into the Leave Centre office.

"Sorry about that, I guess I was day dreaming!"

Getting out of the war zone and returning was a complicated paper skirmish in itself. Katy Short, a woman who was working as a civilian with the Canadian Forces Personnel Support Agency, was assisting him. This dedicated team of people worked diligently to ensure that deployed personnel were given every assistance needed to plan their HLTA, a required mid-tour leave. Some personnel returned to their families in Canada, while others chose to bring their designated next-of-kin to Europe or some exotic location for a special reunion. A transportation allowance of approximately $3000.00 was allowed for service personnel choosing a non-home travel leave. They had their choice of any destination in an approved distance from other conflict theatre locations in the world to enjoy their leave in an economical way.

"Hi, Katy, I see you're busy as usual," Mike greeted.

"Always lots to do," she responded with a welcoming grin. "What can I help you with today, Padre?"

"I was just wanting to double check the arrival time of my wife's flight to Rome and to be sure my schedule is in sync with hers."

"Sure, let me check the computer for timings." Her smile was infectious and Mike enjoyed chatting with her. He knew that her father, Major the Reverend Jim Short; a Reserve Chaplain from Ladner, B.C. would be rotating through the theatre with Task Force 1-08. The Chaplain Branch was most fortunate to have several extensively trained Reserve Chaplains to accept the position as Team Leader in Afghanistan. Jim Short was one of them. He was a dedicated pastor and an ardent supporter of the military personnel in the Western Area with fifteen years service in what he termed "a call within a call."

"Looks like all is set Padre, I will check again for you a couple of days before you're due to leave. All your necessary documents are in order, your passport, leave pass signed by your Orderly Room, your insurance, your travel itinerary and contact numbers.

You asked for some general information and ideas for places to see in Rome. Here are some brochures to check out and, in addition, I made a list for your perusal. These places are highly recommended by others who have been to Rome." She passed him the list, and Mike sat to read it.

Katy's notes included: In case you have any trouble with accommodations that you have booked on your own, the following locations are quite delightful. There are convent or monastery accommodations in ancient buildings that offer excellent breakfasts, but you have to check for double occupancy. Understand, this type of location will have a "doors locked curfew", usually at 10:30 pm. There are also many B&Bs available, one I suggest you consider is the Roma, built in 800 AD. It is central to most of the popular tourist sights in Rome.

There are many activities others have suggested such as the Crypto Balbi, a small privately owned museum near the Fontana di Trevi. In it you can view layers of past civilizations that have been excavated, and you can view the digging in progress.

The Trastevere region will give you a glimpse into local Roman life. The restaurants are small and intimate and best of all, the area is centrally located so you can walk to all the major sites.

If you have to travel in Rome, it's best to take a bus, streetcar or taxi. It is not advisable to rent a car as driving in the local traffic can be quite stressful.

If you go to the Vatican have a guide take you on your 'go around'. It is worth the modest expense. Normally, there is a Papal Mass every Wednesday, but be sure to check the schedule before you go, as the Pope may be called to other duties.

A main attraction to Rome is the art. You can see a 17th Century colonnade designed by Bernini, view splendid Renaissance frescoes in a papal palace built upon the top of a Roman Emperor's tomb and the Coliseum, the Trevi Fountain, and the Piazza Navona. The Mammertine Prison can be visited, where the Apostles Peter and Paul were held in chains.

One last word of caution…be aware of pickpockets. They are everywhere and very accomplished in their art. Wear a money belt and keep your spending money in a front pocket, a vest is preferable. If you are buying gifts, mail them rather than pack them in your heavy baggage as these are frequently pilfered at the airport.

"Hey, this is great, Katy. Thank you for the ideas. You and your team are providing a super service and I have heard others say how grateful they are for your help as they are often too distracted or too tired to think straight about their HLTA details and plans. Great job! By the way, our accommodations in Rome should be no problem as an old friend has offered us the use of his flat. He'll not be using it while we are in the city… but thanks for alternates in case we need them."

As Mike got up to leave, Katy smiled and said, "Have a good day. Sir, if you have any other questions, let me know. I'll be glad to help." Then she turned to help another soldier making plans.

"What have you been up to, Mike, you look like you swallowed a canary!" greeted Steele as they met along the pathway.

"Just confirmed my leave plans. Everything's good to go. Just need a little patience to get me through the next couple of weeks."

"So that's what it's like to be an old married man, is it?"

* * * * *

The long harrowing month of April for the members of the Canadian Task Force was now behind them, but the constant work of probing patrols by the Battle Group continued pace. The grief the soldiers felt for their fallen comrades would fade to some degree, but the memory of their lost friends would always be with them. They were professionals though and the work went on. Out on the FOBs surveillance remained a 24/7 occupation. Regular TICs (troops in contact) with insurgents were encountered along the highways and byways of the Panjwayi District as spring made its appearance. IEDs were found and disarmed…occasionally some exploded causing injury to soldiers and civilians alike. There appeared to be more bomb-making cells entering the picture with foreign fighters coming into the area. There was no discrimination shown. The terrorists aimed to kill soldiers, but if area residents got in the way…men, women or children, so be it. Life was expendable and many fear mongering tactics were employed to deter people from crossing the terrorist groups or the Taliban fighters. Training for the Afghan National Police (ANP) intensified, but as yet that body had not reached sufficient standards to establish the much needed check points required to stabilize the troubled areas where the enemy seemed to infiltrate almost at will…like will-o-the wisps.

Meanwhile the countryside flourished. Farmers were busy in their fields from dawn till dusk. Produce transported by various modes, trundled along the routes into the Kandahar market places. PRT units and various humanitarian aid groups struggled long hours to ensure that projects were progressing. This kind of priority kept the local *shuras* happy, for the people could see first hand that promises made were being delivered. Rarely did the media pick up on these humanitarian advances as their antennae were tuned primarily into violence. The people back home in Canada knew little of the work that would enable the Afghan people to work free from their oppressors.

* * * * *

It was early May. Malcolm's team met to assess their various roles and to plan ahead. One of the decisions that had to be made was the placement of school supplies that had been retrieved from the wreckage of the Mullah's school in Kowal. More books, pens and pencils, and other educational related material continued to come from Canada. Lucy Keller's efforts were a great success, as not only learning tools were being collected, but also money had been contributed to help build new teaching facilities…to date $5000.00 had been donated.

"I think we should re-direct our efforts toward the Sayd Pacha School for the children of our Afghan Army partners. You know the one adjacent to Camp Shirzai. It's been operating on a shoestring for the last three years in a bombed out Russian apartment building," suggested Mike.

"Oh, yes," said Malcolm, "a Japanese non-governmental organization is building a new school for them at Camp Shirzia."

"That's the one! I know our soldiers would be keen in helping out the families of the ANA. After all, these are the people who are fighting and dying alongside our own people," remarked Steele.

"Great idea! The children are the future of this country and they want to learn. That's easy to tell from the way they scramble after note pads and pencils that are handed out by our troops. It's heart warming to see their bright faces eager for learning," added Robert.

"I will be glad to pitch in when ever I'm in from the PRT site," offered Felix.

Malcolm nodded. "Good. That's settled then. Mike, I'd like you and Steele to liaise with the school authorities. Sound OK to you?"

"Done!" both men chimed at once.

"I'd like to try and locate Hassan, if I could. They gave me his uncle's address in Kandahar. I'm anxious to see how he's doing," announced Mike.

"I think we all would like to hear," said the Team Leader. "Perhaps we could help out in some way. Poor kid was no doubt devastated…losing his family like that."

"I'll check it out tomorrow when I'm in the city. I want to go to the *souk* to buy a prayer rug for Angie and one for Lucy Keller" "That's right; you start your leave next week. I presume you have all your paper work in hand…seems like a lot of red tape, but necessary," said Malcolm with a smile. "In a way I envy you your trip to Rome…an historic and exciting city, with some edifices dating before the time of Christ. It will be a wonderful experience for the two of you. We'll miss you, but I bet you won't miss us!"

* * * * *

Doctor Haji Ali lived in an old neighbourhood of Kandahar City. High walls surrounded his home. Inside the walls, the grounds were beautifully landscaped with flower gardens and fruit trees. An extended family lived in the spacious dwelling. Grandparents and two sets of aunts and uncles shared the amenities with Doctor Ali and his immediate family. Hassan had been made welcome and treated as one of the doctor's own children. He was quickly assimilated into his new environment; so different from the one he left behind in Kowal. The doctor had wealth and influence, and had enrolled the boy in one of the few schools available to the children of the city. Mike was impressed when he was greeted and offered the generous hospitality of the household.

"Chaplain Mike, I have heard many fine things about you," said Doctor Ali. "You were praised by my brother as a gift from Allah. He was most fond of you and I thank you on behalf of my family for all that you did to support his desire to establish a school in Kowal for both girls and boys. He was a proud man and accepted very little of the financial assistance I offered to him. He had to do it his way."

"He was a fine man, sir, and I believe we became good friends in the short time I knew him."

Tea arrived and was poured for the visitor and his host.

"You have been kind to Hassan. He was quite traumatized when he was brought here, but now he seems to have accepted the will of Allah. He adds to my delight as an added member of my family. The other children have come to adore him. He is so like his father…a person of clean spirit and integrity. Look, here he comes now!"

Mike was pleased to see a smart looking, well-dressed boy enter the room. It was a pleasant surprise as the last time they were together Hassan was in sad shape, dirty and unkempt. He came right over to the chaplain, turning to bow to his uncle first, he held out his hand, which Mike grasped firmly.

"Hassan, how good to see you again."

"Thank you, Chaplain Mike. It's good to see you, too."

"I understand you are attending school. Is it a good one?"

"Yes, Sir, it is. I have fine teachers. Do you think my English speaking has improved? They tell me I'm a fast learner. My uncle says he will send me to an English school some day if I do well now. I would like that. Perhaps I might even come to Canada to attend university. I understand you have excellent ones. Do you have one near where you live," asked Hassan?

Doctor Ali looked shocked at the boy's precocious behaviour.

"Hassan, you are showing bad manners in front of our guest. What's gotten into you," asked the uncle?

"Oh, I am sorry, Uncle Haji. I do not mean to be rude. I am so glad to see Chaplain Mike. We have talked about my schooling before…father encouraged it."

"He certainly did, Doctor. I believe your brother wanted Hassan to have a far reaching education, and at one point I'm sure I said he should come to Canada some day to study. I attended a grand university where we had foreign students from all over the world. It was a marvellous experience for them," said Mike.

The doctor smiled in a benign way. "Well, who knows what the future holds, that's in Allah's hands. In the mean time, young man, you have studies to attend and high marks to obtain if you are ever going to realize your dreams. Now, pay your respects to the chaplain and get along. I'll be up to see your work later."

Hassan bowed and left the room.

"I didn't realize he was such an ambitious one. He certainly has changed in the last month since he came to us and he certainly respects you as a friend," said Ali.

"I am glad," remarked Mike, "I was afraid he might still resent me. He was very angry when I arrived at the scene where his family died. You've obviously brought him a long way since then, Doctor, and if I may be of any help in the future, please let me know. I will give you my home contact information. I would so like to keep in touch with the boy. Now I must depart as I am going on leave in a couple of days and will be joining my wife in Rome."

"Thank you for coming, Chaplain. I appreciate your interest in Hassan, and who knows, perhaps some day…"

* * * * *

It was two days before Mike was to start his leave. He was doing his final packing when Steele stopped in to see him. "Mike, let's check out Sayd Pacha School and see how we might be able to fit into their new program,"

"OK, let's do it. I've only a few things left to pack and that's last minute stuff."

Steele had made tentative arrangements to visit the Principal of the School and an older male student met the two men at the door of the school. They entered the ruins of the former Russian building where they were led to the overcrowded cubicle that was the principal's office. It was a small space with piles of books and papers on shelves, the floor, and, on the rickety desk. A pint-sized man, who appeared to be in his late sixties, sat with half glasses resting on the tip of his nose. His face was dominated with a white moustache and a beard that fell to his chest. Mike could hardly restrain himself as he winked at Steele and whispered in an aside, "By Jove, 'tis Santa!"

Sarfraz Parvi turned to see who had shadowed the light from behind. As he stood to welcome his visitors, he appeared gnome-like in stature, indeed, had he worn a red costume, he would have made an ideal St. Nick. His appearance was deceptive and belied his serious nature, and highly respected position, for he was a brilliant scholar who had trained at Cambridge University in England in the 1960's.

"Gentlemen, you must be the Canadian Chaplains I've been expecting. Welcome. He motioned for the chaplains to sit with him, and they were joined by a few more of the older male students. They all sat together in a circle on a rug, and shared tea, nuts and candies. Steele and Mike spoke honourably of the work of the school, the leadership of the Principal, acknowledging the needs of the students and teachers. This was all interpreted for the students who did not understand English. After they had tea, Sarfaz Parvi spoke; "I understand from my conversation with you, Chaplain Steele, that you may have some resources to help us with our new school. Is that correct?"

"Yes, sir, we do. Perhaps Mike will explain, as these assets come from his contacts in Canada."

"Mr. Parvi..."

"Please call me Sarfraz. Mr. Parvi was my father," the principal said with a chuckle.

"Right! Sarfraz, what we have to offer is not that much, but we hope that it might help in some small way," ventured Mike and he outlined the various school supplies and equipment that could be provided.

Sarfraz placed the palm of his right hand to his heart in a gesture of gratitude, and bowed his head gently. "But that's wonderful. It will be a benefit to our children. You know we have sixty girls enrolled and will have a special classroom for them in the new school. Your contribution will fill most of their needs."

"We also have some money to help furnish the new school building. I believe we have gathered over $5,000.00."

"How generous! And I have just the project to put it toward. I have been puzzling how to provide furniture toward the girls' classroom, as funds are so scarce. You have solved my dilemma."

Mike's cell phone beeped.

"Padre Russell, here!"

"Padre, this is Role 3 Ops. We have an urgent call for you to return to Base."

"You've got it. I'm on my way."

"Sorry, Sarfraz, but I have to leave...a hospital call. Thanks for your hospitality and we'll be in touch to go over details," said Mike.

"I look forward to seeing you again."

* * * * *

In the hospital a soldier was on the verge of extreme depression. Private Scotty Martin had talked with Mike on one of his initial visits to FOB Sperwan Ghar earlier in the tour. Mike had noted at the time that the man was a loner. Here in the hospital, he was near the breaking point, feeling suicidal, and needing reassurance. The mental health specialists were treating him for schizophrenia. They were having difficulty getting through to him. The team's head nurse had placed a call for Mike, as the soldier kept asking for him. As Mike approached the Private's bed he saw the vacant look in the young man's eyes, and furrowed lines of depression creasing his forehead.

"Hi there, Scotty, I hear you're having a hard time of it?"

"Padre, thank God you're here. I can't take this anymore." The anguish and tears began to pour out. "I wake up in the night haunted by a dream of the child who the Taliban slaughtered. He couldn't have been much more than eleven years old… a skinny kid, reminded me of my little brother. They severed his head and hung the body in the village square as a warning to others not to collaborate with the Unbelievers, or their minions at the Afghan National Police station. Padre, they put the boy's head on a stake. I can't get the image out of my mind. It was horrible."

"Take it easy, Scotty, let it come out. It's good to talk it out. I hear you."

"Oh, God, I am lost with all this. It makes no sense. Have you ever lost hope, Padre? I get so depressed. I feel I've been part of something really useless and contributed to that kid's death. I just want to end it all."

In a quiet and calm voice Mike spoke to the soldier. "Scotty, do you remember our talk that night at the Sperwan Ghar SP? How important it was to be in communication with others? You were feeling pretty down that night. When you're depressed it's easy to be discouraged and disillusioned. Look at me, Scotty! You know what I mean, 'cause you're going through it now. Would you do me a favour? Close your eyes and think of those who love you back home…think of the good things you've shared with them…those who you love. OK are you there?"

The soldier slowly nodded.

"Now, dig deep and get a tight hold of that love and know that it's hugging you back just as tightly. Love conquers all. You will find an answer there. The demons of doubt you have been chasing are phantoms, games your mind is playing on you about stuff you can't figure out…and that's where the medics can help you. For the love of God, Scotty, take a chance and trust them…give them an opening. That night on the SP… I shared with you some thoughts; on how different a world this would be if everyone strove for peace. I told you then, and I tell you now, faith and hope will guide us through these dark days, but you have to believe in this. Here, take my hand, and let's pray silently together for a few minutes."

The entire ward became soundless as the other patients became aware of the situation. After a few minutes, Mike looked up aware of the reverent atmosphere.

"Almighty God, you are everywhere, and right here with Scotty in this moment. Give us grace to acknowledge your presence in this place. We need to know in our hearts and minds that you are always with us, every minute, every hour of every day. Help us release the grip of fear in our hearts. Build in us a hope for a future free from pain and hopelessness. Bring comfort and healing to Scotty, and to each person in this ward. Bring healing to the people of this suffering nation in which we find ourselves called to serve. I ask for Your courage and blessing upon Scotty and each of us here. Amen"

After a pause, Scotty started again. "Padre, I realize I'm not a soldier like the others. Their training kicked in…mine didn't. They believe in what they are doing. I see nothing but death and destruction for no reason. I see it as a black hole with demons trying to enslave and control the people of this land. It appears to be the way it has always been…a place overrun with bandits and warlords, where tribe is against tribe, where twisted fanatical religious groups vie for power. We don't know which ANP may be corrupt or what politicians might be. So when it comes down to it, what is our purpose here? I just want to go home."

"Scotty, do you know that song, 'Let there be peace on earth, and let it begin with me'? It has a message for all of us. Peace begins with a belief in a better world. Then we must seize it, do our part, and make it happen. That's what you are doing over here…you're making it happen. You are making a difference."

A nurse came to the bedside and gave Mike a nod and a smile and said, "Its time for your medication, Scotty, and a rest. Thank you for coming, Padre Russell, your visits are appreciated by everyone." Heads around the ward nodded in agreement.

"Trust the staff, Scotty, they are here to help you. I know…they are wonderful giving people," said Mike as he rose to leave. "I'll be away on my leave over the next little while but if you need to talk with a chaplain, Padre Steele will be available. I want to leave you this copy of the Regimental prayer. It will give you something to focus your thoughts upon."

A voice was heard from a bed on the far side of the ward. "Hey, Padre, could I have a copy of that too?"

"Sorry, my friend, I've only the one with me, but I'll see that you get one."

"Would you read it for us, Sir, there are two or three of us RCR all in a row. It's a great prayer."

"Glad too! Let us pray".

"Almighty God, we humbly implore your blessing upon the Royal Canadian Regiment and all of us who serve therein. Help us to prove worthy to accept the high ideals and traditions of the past; to honour and revere the memory of those who have gone before us; to face our responsibilities in the future both in peace and war, with courage, justice, love, honesty and faithfulness. We pray especially for our comrades in the field who are at this time faced with volatile and hazardous situations. For those who have paid the supreme sacrifice and we pray for their families who mourn their loss. Remove all greed, hatred, selfishness and envy from our thoughts that we may render true service to the Regiment and for You, our God; for our fellow men and women; and for our Country. Pro Patria. Amen."

* * * * *

HMCS Iroquois
Karachi. Pakistan

How are you doing, Mike? How's your team? Seems a bit lonely for me at times to be the only one in my trade here.

We are in the port of Karachi, Pakistan, just down the road from you, you might say. No doubt the closest we will get to each other on this tour. We are the first Canadian War Ship to ever visit Pakistan since it became a country, so this was quite an event, especially for our Pakistani hosts. We arrived on a Wednesday and prepared for a formal reception with high-ranking members of the military, government and community. It was an experience to rub shoulders and share stories with these people, and it allowed all of us, both Pakistani and Canadian, to learn more about one another and move beyond some of the preconceived notions we may have had. Before the reception a few of us got the bus ride of our life to the Pakistani Naval Museum in Karachi. We drove from the port area with a full police escort through the traffic. It is hard to believe that something like 19million people live in the city. And though we didn't get a chance to explore on foot, we did pass a number of areas in town where the poorest lived along train tracks and riverbeds. It was sobering to know that so many of this city's residents live in such poverty.

The second day the ship played host to 35 children and their guardians from the SOS Children's Village in Karachi. SOS Villages is a world wide charitable organization that takes in abandoned children from the age of three to about 16, and provides a home like setting, education, health care, skill training and helps young women get married – which is very important in this particular culture. Between money that had been provided from contingency funds and $4,500 raised on board HMCS *IROQUOIS*, we were able to donate over $23,500 to the Karachi SOS Village; providing school uniforms, shoes, back-packs, school supplies, items for their group homes and a cash donation to the building of a young men's residence. During the two-hour visit, the kids had a chance to tour the ship, including an opportunity to sit on the Captain's Chair and climb aboard our helicopter. They were also treated to a variety of games, which allowed crew volunteers to interact with the children. We had snacks for the kids, with the freezies and ice cream bars making the biggest hit. It was a day of giving, and a blessing for all who were involved…crew and children alike.

Ministry at sea continues to be rewarding. I am part guidance counsellor, part individual counsellor, part interpersonal relationship counsellor, and many other "parts", but always I hope to be a witness to God's love, by offering an empathetic ear to crew members at all rank levels. We have suffered together the death of mothers, grandmothers, grandfathers and uncles; shared in the struggles of beginning and ending relationships and the joy of births and anticipated births.

You will soon be off on leave in Rome. I'll be thinking of you. Please give Angie a hug from me. Sorry, I'll have to cut this note off here as duty calls.

Every blessing, take care
Tim

Chapter Nine

Mike looked up at the Arrival Board in the concourse of Leonardo da Vinci airport in Rome and saw that Air Canada flight 890 was on time at 0900 hrs. Checking his watch, he saw that he still had an hour to wait. What to do?

He browsed the shops in the mall area and found a flower shop where he ordered a corsage of fragrant yellow roses, Angie's favourite flower. He paid the clerk and indicated that he would return in a half hour to pick up his purchase. Next, he found a coffee shop where he bought a double Cappuccino, and perched on a stool to watch crowds of smartly dressed people go by. In one group, a gorgeous Italian movie star, her agent and entourage were sweeping along. She appeared displeased with the rush, as she wanted to linger with fans that adored and recognized her.

"A coffee," she pleaded, "I need a coffee." She broke from her group and claimed a stool beside Mike.

"*Lei bada a?* Do you mind," she asked with a broad smile, and turned to the waitress, "Coffee, black, *per favour!*"

Mike blushed at her direct approach. "Not at all," he responded collecting himself, "You seem to be a celebrity of some sort?"

"You don't recognize me," she asked slightly annoyed?

"Sorry, M'am, I don't."

Her provocative smile returned, and batting her large blue eyes, she held out her hand and introduced herself as Maria Marconi, 'rising star of stage and television.' "And whom do I have the privilege of knowing."

"My name is Michael Russell."

"Well. Michael Russell, are you from America?"

"From North America…Canada to be exact."

"And what is a handsome man like you doing in Rome?" If nothing else, she was bold and to the point.

Amused, but realizing that this conversation might lead in a direction he was not prepared to go, he took the shortest route to divert the developing tête-à-tête. "I'm here on leave from Afghanistan to meet my wife coming in from Canada."

"Oh, you are a soldier. Welcome to Italy. You are meeting your wife? What a pity. I thought I might invite you to lunch," she said flashing her great beautiful eyes.

"Maria, we can't dally any longer. We are going to be late for the meeting with your new director," pressed her agent, Arnaldo.

"So let him wait! I want to talk with this young man. He's a soldier on leave from the war zone in Afghanistan. I want him to tell me about his experiences, yes?"

Mike looked at his wristwatch. "Sorry, I must head for the arrival gate. Nice meeting you."

She turned to her agent. "Arnaldo, give him my card. I am having a dinner for some friends on Saturday at Al Ceppo's. It is a delightful restaurant. I would be pleased if you and your wife could come. I know my guests would love to hear of your exploits in Afghanistan."

"Maria, please, let's go!" said Arnaldo handing Mike a calling card.

"Let me write my personal phone number on the back and you can ring me if you can come. Arnaldo, give me a pen."

Mike took the card. "Thank you…kind of you to offer, but I doubt if we will be free. We have a pretty full agenda." He waved goodbye, stopped to pick up the corsage, and half ran toward the gate, all the while thinking, now, what was that all about, and feeling in a time warp yet again from the reality of grunge and death, to opulence and fantasy. "Wait till Angie hears this line!"

* * * * *

The flight was on time…right to the minute. Mike waited outside the Customs area feeling somewhat flustered over the off-the-wall meeting with Maria Marconi. Also, he had butterflies in anticipation of seeing Angie. And then, she was there, and all else was forgotten. She dropped her suitcase, rushed to him and was wrapped in a tight hug and covered with fervent kisses.

"Darling, at last," she cried.

Breaking the long embrace, Mike presented her corsage with a flourish and another kiss, scooped up her bag, took her hand, and made for the luggage locker where his kit was secured. Then they saw an exit where they found a taxi stand.

An eager driver placed their baggage in the trunk of his cab and cheerfully announced his name as Luigi. "I am at your service if you need a taxi while you are in Rome. Where would you like to go first?"

"47 Viale Europa. Not too far from the Vatican, I believe?"

"*Si il signore. So il luogo.* I know the street, but it is some distance from the Holy See. Do I presume you are newly married?" asked the inquisitive Luigi.

"No," said Mike. "You might think so, but we have been apart for some time." And while they were driving, he told the driver just enough to satisfy his curiosity while he, Mike, concentrated on his reunion with the most beautiful woman in the world. Meanwhile Luigi gave a running dialogue of the sites they were passing along the way. Neither passenger heard a word he was saying. It was a twenty-minute ride to the villa; a beautiful, very ancient dwelling that had been in the Lombardi family for centuries. The Fascists under Benito Mussolini pillaged the family fortune and estates, and after World War 2 due to financial restraints, the upper story of their home was converted into exclusive apartments.

Father Pat's flat was spaciously laid out. The main living room was configured in atrium design with a high central glassed-in dome overhead. A balcony ran along the south side of the building and over looked a striking Mediterranean garden. Olive and citrus trees alternately lined the outer perimeter. Beds of flowers delineated the walkways, and a bubbling, venerable fountain formed the centrepiece of the grounds. The scent of orange blossoms filled the air with a delicate perfume. The bedroom had an entrance to the balcony allowing the warm scented air to circulate.

"Perhaps we should rest before lunch," suggested Mike, "You must be tired. I know I am…"

"Well," said Angie, "if its rest you need…"

* * * * *

They had a late repast from a cold plate consisting of cheese, pate, crusty bread and fruit that had been set out by the part-time housekeeper. In the late afternoon they considered plans for their stay in Rome.

"First and foremost I would like to visit the Vatican," said Angie. "Father Pat left some notes on whom to contact, and he has arranged for us to attend a general audience with His Holiness a week from today. I think it would be nice to have a tour before that."

"The Sistine Chapel is a must. Let's plan to start there," suggested Mike.

"Father Pat has given us the name and phone number of a personal guide. We'll call him and arrange a time to meet," offered Angie. "Is that OK with you?"

"Let's do it."

The call was made and the guide offered to pick them up the following morning at nine o'clock.

That evening, Mike and Angie went for a stroll and found a delightful outdoor restaurant several blocks from their accommodations, another recommendation of Father Pat's. Tables were arranged in a garden setting with lights strung between the trees. The ambiance was romantic. A lone violinist provided a variety of Italian folk music for the dinner guests. The menu offered a wide selection of local gourmet foods and a waiter hovered to take their order.

"I think I'll try the veal Parmesan," said Angie.

"A good choice, Madame, our chef is noted for this dish," said the waiter. "And may I suggest just the right wine to go with it?"

"Please do, and I'll have the same dish," said Mike.

"Would you like before dinner drinks, *Signore*?"

"I will have a draft beer and my wife will try the wine you have selected. She's our connoisseur of fine wines," answered Mike.

The dinner was served, the wine enjoyed, and the violin played on.

Later, the walk back to the flat in the balmy air was refreshing. "What a lovely evening, sweetheart, and the best part is being able to share it with you," said Mike as he squeezed her hand.

Angie squeezed back, "And now for desert, my love!"

* * * * *

Leo Amodio was a short, dark man of an indeterminate age with a wing of grey hair over each ear. His face was bright with flashing, intelligent eyes that bespoke of a person well versed in his role as a tour guide.

"Father Kelly gave me strict orders to make your visit a memorable one and that I will try to do," said the guide speaking perfect English, "And please call me Leo. Do not hesitate to ask any questions. We will go directly to the Vatican to examine the architecture of the area and view some of the treasures on display…and a few that are not open to the public, such as some precious paintings that are being restored."

Mike nodded. "Sounds intriguing, Father Kelly said he would arrange for us to take part in a Papal audience. Did he mention this to you?" "He did, and that has been set up. You will receive a formal invitation to attend next Wednesday after the Papal Mass. I will escort you there. Now, let's be off, and I will give you a commentary on the smallest State in the world," said Leo as he opened the door of his Fiat for them. It was a leisurely twenty-minute drive to Vatican City.

"The City is situated on a small hill and is completely surrounded by a wall. Within this space beats the heart of Roman Catholicism. Here we will see Saint Peter's Basilica and the square, the Sistine Chapel, and of course, the Vatican Museums. There are more than sixty-four areas of interest within the grounds, but we will concentrate on only a few of them as your time is limited and Father Kelly has indicated which ones you should see. So, I am directed by that!"

"I know we will be pleased," said Angie. "He and I discussed an itinerary in detail."

"We start our tour at St. Peter's Square. You will note that it is both round and square, redesigned by Bernini in 1656 to accommodate as many people as possible to enable them to witness the papal blessings given from the balcony of St Peter's Basilica. It was on this site that St Peter was crucified and buried, but in the First Century it was the location of the Circus of Nero. In the year 324, the Emperor Constantine ordered the construction of a basilica over St Peter's resting place.

"We now move into the basilica and you can appreciate the size of the building that until recently was the largest church in Christendom. Renaissance Masters including Bramante, Bernini, and Michelangelo rebuilt it in the16th Century. The latter designed the great dome. You will see their works, and the works of other renowned artists, throughout the church. They are regarded as treasures of untold value.

"Here, on the right, you see Michelangelo's famous Pieta, depicting Mary holding her crucified son. The artist was only twenty-four years old when he rendered this sculpture.

"Over the centuries ninety-one Popes have been entombed here, including JohnXXlll and John Paul ll.

"I'll give you time to walk through the basilica and observe on your own the architecture and the many works of art found herein. We'll meet by the entrance to the Sistine Chapel…say in a half hour."

* * * * *

"Leo, that was an amazing experience," said Angie. "The place is so vast and the artefacts are beautiful. My mind is full of new images to digest."

"You are about to see even more splendid works here in the Sistine Chapel where the masterful strokes of Michelangelo can be viewed. The structure itself is not of architectural significance, but come, and I will explain the various frescoes to you. The images are made by applying paint to a fresh plaster surface."

"It is such a bright space," Mike uttered as he took in the colourful paintings. "I have been to several ancient cathedrals and they are usually dark with age, but this is outstanding."

"Yes, that is true, but the frescoes were completely restored between 1979 and 1999…that had made a great difference in the ambient light. See there on the East wall above the altar, the person of the resurrected Christ in the fresco known as the Day of Judgement. The ceiling panels depict the nine stories of Genesis, while the south wall shows scenes from the Old Testament and the north wall portrays views from the New Testament."

"How long did it take him to finish his paintings," asked Angie?

"The ceilings alone took four years to complete. It has been said that he did this work on his back, but Vasari, the Italian biographer of the great artists, has indicated that this was not so. In his writings he recorded that Michelangelo painted from the standing position 'with his head tilted upwards.' It must have been very painful for the artist…just imagine yourself in that position for any length of time. One must remember the man was primarily with sculpture, but the Pope was adamant and insisted that Michelangelo paint the ceilings. He also created the interpretation of the Last Judgement on the east wall above the altar."

"It's hard to conceive that these paintings were done five hundred years ago!" said Mike with a shake of his head.

"They are spell binding," announced Angie.

"I'll give you a little time to venture through the chapel by yourselves so that you can concentrate on the works of the other artists as well…

Botticelli, Signorelli, Perugino, and others. I will meet you at the entrance when you are finished."

* * * * *

Following a light lunch in a small restaurant highly recommended by their guide some distance away from the Vatican, Amodio took them to the museum area where priceless antiquities were on display. The vast complex had exhibits ranging from sculptures, paintings, a lapidary gallery, jewelry collections, pottery, tapestries, statues, mosaics and ornaments made of precious metals. It was an exhausting day of exploration and the couple were tired, but pleased with their experience.

"I can't wait to get my shoes off," declared Angie. "Thank goodness I brought comfortable footwear."

"I'll run a tub for us," offered Mike. "That'll take the soreness out. Then I'll massage your feet. OK?"

"Sounds like heaven…and if you're good, I'll give you a rub down too!"

"Let's eat in tonight and turn in early. Deal?"

"You've got it."

"Tomorrow's Friday, and we've got to decide if we are going to take up Maria Marconi's invitation to dinner on Saturday. Are you sure you want to meet an Italian TV star," asked Mike?

"I think it might be fun…certainly a change of pace from the quiet existence back home. I'd like to meet the woman who tried to pick up my husband," said Angie with a twinkle, not being jealous in the least. "Let's sleep in and get well rested for the challenge. Night life in Rome is supposed to be very exciting."

"Time will tell. I'll give her a call in the morning."

"And don't forget, we are having lunch with Father Pat tomorrow. He said it would be the only time he had free while we are in Rome."

* * * * *

In the middle of the night Mike began to toss and cry out. Angie awoke with a fright. "Mike, are you alright?"

He came out of the nightmare pale, with face drawn. "Yes, I'm OK. That was a rough dream! I was on patrol in a LAV when we hit an IED. All I could see were dead bodies around and over me. I tried to help the person beside me, but my hands didn't seem to work. The man was bleeding profusely and I wanted to stop the blood. I just couldn't reach him. I was totally useless…sorry if I frightened you."

"Have you had this dream before?" Angie's training was instinctively kicking in.

"Yes, a couple of times…at least variations of it, ever since we lost the six soldiers on Easter day."

"It must have been very traumatic for you," she said reaching over to give him a reassuring touch. "Do you want to talk about it?'

"I felt guilty not being with Malcolm and the others when the bodies were brought in. I know it was hard on them. I hit a wall when I had to talk with the others in the platoon when they arrived back. I just froze up…barely able to talk…tears streaming down my face. I guess we were all crying in our own way…some inside, others visibly. It was like losing members of our family."

Angie put her arms around her husband and held him in a comforting embrace. He began to weep, and then hot tears streamed down his cheeks.

"There, there, my love. Let it out. It will help to release you of your grief."

"And yet I have to make that dark journey of faith to try to understand it all. I know that God will guide me. I just have to put my trust in Him but for some reason, I'm having difficulty taking that step. I fear it's my unworthiness stopping me. God help me!"

"And God will, beloved, give it time."

"I guess at times I'm just a doubting Thomas…but then even Thomas was forgiven. You're right! I must let go of these dark thoughts and listen to my own advice to Scotty Martin. Reach out and trust those who God gives strength and comfort through."

They lay there closely entwined, at one with each other, as a sense of peace began to flow over them…and they slept.

* * * * *

Saturday morning dawned bright. They had slept in and awakened surprisingly refreshed, considering Mike's ride on the bucking nightmare. They breakfasted on fruit and cereal washed down with hot black coffee.

In the late morning, Mike placed a call to Maria Marconi. It was answered by her maid who indicated that her mistress was still a-bed, but she would pass her the message that the Russell's would be happy to join her dinner party that evening at Al Ceppo's.

"Now, the question is…what will I wear," asked Angie? "I brought that neat little black number you like so well, or the Kelly green sheath. Tell me. What's your choice?"

"I think the latter would be a knock out dress for a dinner party. It goes so well with your green eyes and red hair. You'll have all the men drooling!"

"There's only one man I want to drool for me," said Angie as she came over to give her husband a hug and a peck on the cheek." You might even know who he is!"

Mike put his arms around her waist and pulled her into an embrace. "Let me guess. Would he do this…?"

* * * * *

"Take us to the restaurant, Sora Lella on the island of Tibartine, *per favore,* Luigi," requested Mike as he and Angie climbed into the taxi.

"I know the place. It is in an interesting part of the surviving medieval sector of the city," the driver replied.

Father Pat had preceded their arrival and met them as they entered the foyer of the restaurant.

"Greetings, you two! How lovely to see you again," said the priest, first extending his hand to Mike, then, embracing Angie in a warm fatherly hug.

"And you, Father Pat. Thank you for making time to see us. Let me say right off how delightful and accommodating we find your flat. We especially enjoy the garden from the balcony," offered Mike.

"I thought you would find it enchanting. Now, let's go in for lunch. I think I could eat a horse." Father Pat was a trencherman who loved good food, but he was diabetic, and had to watch his diet. He ate his meals at precise times.

"This place has excellent menu of Roman dishes…and the wine selection is fabulous. The dining area is on two levels. You see those steep stone stairs to our left, they lead to the upper room, but I prefer the view from here, over-looking the river and giving you an appreciation for the architecture of the area…very ancient as you can see. We see from our vantage point, the Ponte Fabricio, the oldest surviving bridge in Rome crossing the Tiber. It was constructed in 62 AD."

A waiter directed them to a window place that had been reserved.

"Thank you, Nicolo, you never forget my favourite table. These are friends from Canada, and I wanted them to savour not only the food, but also the ambiance of the location. Now, what does your chef suggest for our luncheon today?"

"Ah, Father, the *Frittata di pasta Amatriciana* tops the list of offerings today." The waiter brought the fingers of his right hand to his mouth and smacked his lips.

"And what kind of selection would that be," asked Angie.

"It's a very delicious Italian styled omelette with potatoes, bacon and onion. I highly recommend it if you wish a lighter lunch, but if you were like me I would follow it with *Brasao di Maioilino in Agrodolce*…a pork dish smothered in a sweet and sour sauce, a specialty of the house…my favourite," replied Father Pat.

"It sounds scrumptious," said Angie. "But I think I'll pass the second course…a little too heavy for me this time of day."

Over the course of the meal the discussion centred on Mike's duties and experiences in Afghanistan as their friend was eager to be fully informed.

Angie remained quiet for the most part, learning many things about her husband's role that she had only surmised from reading between the lines of his correspondence. In turn, Father Pat explained to them his work with the Cardinal's commission. All too soon, the time came for him to return to his meetings.

"What a wonderful interlude this has been for me," he acknowledged. "We get so busy in our own little spheres that we often forget the world beyond. Your work is so essential, Michael, never forget that. I will certainly continue to pray for you and your people, now more than ever, knowing the dynamics of your commitment."

"Thank you for that! It's been wonderful for us to see you again and hear of your work. We can't thank you enough for loaning us your lodgings."

The waiter presented the bill for the meals.

"Here, I've got that," said Mike. "It's the least I can do."

There was a protest, but quickly over-ruled by Angie who simply said, "No argument, Father, this is our treat and our pleasure, and a small way of showing our appreciation to you for all you have done to make our stay here a memorable one."

"So, what are your plans from here?"

"Tomorrow," Angie replied smiling, "we have been invited to a dinner party at Al Ceppo's. Mike met a film star at the airport who took a shine to him…ahem…and after a short conversation received an invitation. She…"

"She?" queried the priest with a twinkle in his eye.

Angie grinned. "She, being an Italian film star."

"Michael, what have you been up too?"

Mike blushed easily. "Well, it was all quite innocent." He went on to describe the encounter with Maria Marconi.

"You have to be careful in Rome," said Father Pat with an amused look. "There are some women around…and some men who will take advantage of good looking strangers to the City."

"Oh, it's not like that at all," replied Mike, still beet red. "I said right off that I was on leave from Afghanistan and meeting my wife coming in from Canada. It was charitable of her to offer such hospitality."

"I'm just pulling your leg, Michael; you're such a innocent candidate. I'm sure you will enjoy the occasion, but just be aware, some of these people can be pretty wild."

"Good intelligence, Father Pat, but you can be sure I'll keep him close by," said Angie.

Mike chortled. "And I her…there will be men at this party, too, you know!"

* * * * *

Saturday was spent leisurely at the flat. It was a balmy, sun-filled day. They had lunch on the balcony where they were entranced by the fragrance of the flowering citrus trees, and in the afternoon they rested in preparation for the night's entertainment. The taxi had been ordered for eight pm.

When Luigi's cab drew up in front of Al Ceppo in the Parioli area of the City, he opened the car door and said, *"Questo e un ristaurante molto esclusivo lei evenuto a!* This is a very exclusive place you have chosen."

"We are guests of one of your TV personalities, Maria Marconi," indicated Mike.

"Il Maria? Come meraviglioso. E magnifica! The Maria? How wonderful. She is magnificent."

"Can I call you when we are ready to return to the villa," asked Angie?

"By all means, Signora, at any hour. If I may be permitted, I will be most anxious to hear how your evening went."

The Russell's were greeted by a hostess who directed them to a section of the restaurant that had been reserved for the Marconi party. As they passed through the dining area they noted the splendid décor. The walls were festooned with paintings of beautiful women, and large arrangements of potted flowers were tastefully placed to advantage. The room was elegant. The tables were spread with spotless linen and laid with sliver place settings. The atmosphere was both extravagant and intriguing.

In the bar area, a group of people chatted animatedly. Maria Marconi spotted her Canadian guests immediately and crossed over to where they had made their entrance. *"Íl benvenuto, le persone care!* Welcome, dear people. I am so glad that you could join us."

"It's our pleasure," responded Mike, "This is my wife, Angeline. Angie, Maria."

Maria was glowing. She was dressed in a shimmering off the shoulder silk gown. Looking at Mike she said. "Why she's beautiful." Then turning to face Angie she smiled and greeted her. "How nice to meet you! You have no doubt heard how I chanced to meet your husband at the airport. I was in need of a coffee and he gallantly allowed me to sit beside him. In our brief conversation I learned that he was a chaplain in Afghanistan and that he was awaiting your immanent arrival."

"Yes, he told me all about the encounter and your invitation to dinner. You are very kind," said Angie with a confident smile.

"I thought it would enliven my party to have you both. It's so nice to have new people to meet other than our theatre friends. One of my guests, a producer of a new television program on the conflict in Afghanistan, is dying to meet your husband. Perhaps you are aware of our government's growing opposition to station troops in that theatre?"

Mike nodded. "That's what we've heard. It would be too bad, as we need all the support we can get, and since Italy is a part of our Alliance, it'd be a blow for them to pull out. But, I have no intention of getting into a political dialogue on the Afghan war. I'm on leave for a while to get away from the fighting. Small talk is one thing, but an in depth analysis I will not deal with!"

"But of course! Please excuse me if I have suggested otherwise. I would want you to feel relaxed and at ease. You are my special guests and I will see to it that you are not dragged into conversations that would make you feel uncomfortable. Now, come and meet my friends."

Maria asked the gathering for quiet while she introduced Angie and Mike. "I want you to meet a couple from Canada. Father Michael is a chaplain with the Canadian Forces in Afghanistan, and his wife Angeline has just joined him on his leave. Please extend to them the warmth of Roman hospitality…and remember he is on a much needed rest, so don't plague him with questions of the conflict. *La fa l'undersatnd?*"

The group crowded around to introduce themselves and lively conversations were joined. Many had visited Canada and were interested in hearing about different parts of the country.

One woman remarked on her winter holiday skiing at Whistler in British Columbia. "What a magnificent area," she said. "They have developed the resort with great taste and everyone makes you feel more than welcome. I can't wait to return."

The TV producer, Poldi Abrussi, was not entirely convinced that he should not bring up some aspect of the Afghan plight. After they had been served drinks, he took Mike by the arm and drew him into a corner. "I don't mean to be rude," he started, "but can I ask you one or two questions to clarify some things for me? As you may know, the Italian government is considering a withdrawal of out troops from Afghanistan. What exactly is Canada's position on this conflict? Why are you there?"

"I believe our commitment is clear. We are there primarily to assist with stabilization, training and for humanitarian reasons. We believe that people should be free from tyrannical oppression and slavery. Imagine where the world would be today if we hadn't challenged the Axis Powers… Hitler's and Mussolini's thugs? Likewise we can compare the rule of the Taliban and Al Qaeda with the Nazi and Fascist iron fist regimes. So, I would say, Sir, your question should not be WHY, but rather why not!"

At this point Maria gave Abrussi a sharp look, and placed her hand in the crook of Mike's arm. "Time for dinner, gentlemen, and please discontinue political conversations."

She led him over to where Angie stood talking vivaciously with a bright young couple. He was a tall, attractive actor from New York and she, no more than eighteen or nineteen, was an Italian starlet with long blonde hair and large grey eyes heightened with mascara. Angie saw Maria and Mike approaching and noted the possessive hold the actress had on him. For an instant she felt an irrational envy, and then as quickly, she smiled her radiant best. "I see you've rescued him," she said. "I must watch him more closely or he'll be approached again!" Maria smiled knowingly. "We'll both keep our eyes on him! Now, let's have dinner…Father Michael will you sit to my right with Angeline beside you. I want to learn more about Canada, as I will be travelling there to the Toronto Film Festival later this year. I have a part in one of films to be shown. They are anxious to promote me for larger screen roles and I'm looking forward trying my hand at it."

The menu at Al Ceppo's was a variety of epicurean Roman foods prepared by a renowned chef. It was totally gourmet from appetizers to desserts. As the party was examining the bill of fare, the restaurant owners came over to the table. The Milozzi sisters, Christina and Marisella, were known to dote on their customers and Maria was one of their best. They made a big fuss over her, and then moved around the table to welcome her guests. They knew most of them, but when they came to Mike and Angie, who they purposely left until last, they became even more effervescent, exclaiming their adoration of Canadians and how delighted they were to have new friends at their restaurant.

Christina addressed Mike. "Padre, would you by chance have met my nephew, Georgio Milozzi? He is an engineer serving in Afghanistan with our Italian Forces."

"No, M'am, I do not believe so. Your people are in the Sarobi district, east of Kabul, while we are deployed in the south."

"I suppose that was a silly question, but we are quite worried about him as we heard he was ill with some malady he picked up over there. Normally, he drops us a line from time to time, but recently no word."

"If you give me his particulars, I will try to get word of him through the chaplain net. We have an excellent rapport and communication with all the ISAF and NATO chaplains. Would that be of help?"

"You would do that? How very kind," chimed Marisella. "For that you will receive a special dessert that I prepare for only my most favourite people."

"Aha," cheered Maria, "You have won the heart of a Roman lady!"

Angie smiled inwardly...aha, another one!

"*Come tutto e fino ad ora. Il mio Maria?* How is everything so far?" asked the hostesses.

"*Magnifico. I miei amici, grazi.* Magnificent, my friends," responded Maria

"*Piacere il suo pasto!* Enjoy your meal!" called the sisters as they made their way to other tables.

Maria reached out and touched Mike's hand. "Can I help you understand the menu?" she asked.

"I think we would appreciate that. What do you recommend?"

"First, you must start with the *Olive Ascolane*. These are green olives stuffed with ground meat; breaded and fried…with this you will enjoy a glass of Falerio dei Colli Ascolari. For your main course, I would suggest the roast lamb. It is so succulent and tender. If you look over there you will see where they prepare it on a rotisserie in the fireplace. I will see that the meat is served with the best red wine you have ever tasted. Lastly, you will have a choice from the dessert cart. It has mouth-watering offerings to please the palate and if you have a… how you say it…*debole per I dolci*… sweet tooth, I believe… you will find it beyond description," suggested Maria. "However, I suggest you wait and see what special dessert Marisella has for you. She is a genius in that department!"

On Maria's left the Countess Conti was seated. A woman in her mid-fifties, with diamond rings on each finger, a necklace of equally fine gems, and pendant earrings of obvious enormous value. She was somewhat overweight and her corset so tight that it pushed her bust alarmingly high. Mike was concerned, yet amused. Angie gave him a nudge with her elbow knowing full well the thought going through his head.

Next to the Countess, was a genuine Roman gigolo or so Angie came to believe. His name was Alberto. He was ruggedly handsome; a good twenty years younger than his dinner partner, and obviously had roving eyes for the ladies…be they wives or sweethearts. His stare made Angie feel uncomfortable and occasionally he would stretch his foot across under the table to touch her ankle. This happened only twice, for the third time he tried she gave him a direct message and let loose with a forceful kick. The sharp toe of her shoe caught his ankle. He jerked back with a startled expression, nearly unseating himself. Instantly, Angie could hardly contain her mirth and turned to whisper in Mike's ear. His first reaction was to say something; instead he gave the man a withering look. There was no further flirtation from that quarter.

Beside Alberto sat the starlet and to her left the man from New York. He had his arm possessively around her chair and would frequently bend to caress her neck. She would respond with a shiver of delight and a blush, lightly pushing him away…at least for a moment.

At the far end of the table, opposite Maria was Arnaldo Bautista, her agent. He was her paramour and several years older than she. They had met years before when Maria was entering the world of the theatre. He had coached her, and through his connections she became star material.

Between Arnaldo and Angie a noted surgeon, Gianni Ricci and his wife Gina were placed. Gianni was a brilliant medical research scientist in the field of genetics. When he learned of Angie's background, he engaged her in conversations dealing with his current investigation into the gene that dealt with Alzheimer's disease. Their discussions were deep and immersed in medical jargon that the other guests found difficult to follow. Mike sensed his wife's interest and was content to let the two professionals delve into their topic, while he told Maria stories of his youth growing up in Canada. She was amused and laughed heartily at some of his humorous anecdotes.

The dinner lasted for three hours and afterwards Maria announced that the party would move to a small nightclub she favoured a short distance away in Traverste district.

The *Luce Dorata* or Golden Light was located in a narrow alley. Over the entrance way glittered the name of the discotheque in flashing golden neon. The doorman recognized Maria and greeted her party. She was a frequent visitor to this up-scale nightclub.

"Your table is ready, Signora," announced the Maitre'd as the group surged through the anteroom. A Blues player on a trumpet was deep into his rendition of a Caribbean tune with an African beat. Drinks were ordered as the party settled in to listen to the music and dance as the melody changed to more appropriate harmonies.

"May I have this dance, Mrs. Russell," asked Mike as he stood to pull out Angie's chair.

"I would be delighted kind Sir!"

"We haven't done this in a while," he whispered in her ear as they twirled around the postage stamp-size dance floor. "I hope my big feet remember how to do this and don't get in the way."

"You're just looking for a compliment. You have always been light on your feet…a perfect partner in every way. Hold me tight. I love you so much, my darling."

And he did.

"I don't want to be here all night, sweetheart, so let's plan to spend an hour and then head back to the flat. I'm sure our hostess would understand…after all we are on a second honeymoon. I'll invite her to dance once and explain our need to leave, OK," suggested Mike?

"Sounds like a plan to me. I'm ready whenever you are. Will you call Luigi?"

"I'll do it now and have him meet us outside at one o'clock, if he can negotiate the alley, otherwise at the top of the street."

"I'm sorry you feel you have to go so soon," pouted Maria prettily as he escorted her to the dance area. "But I understand also. The two of you have some time to make up and your leave is short."

"Thank you so much for a delightful evening. It will be one of our treasured memories of Rome."

"Let's keep in touch. It would be lovely to see you in Canada in the fall. I can just imagine the colours you have described. Your invitation to join you and Angeline at the lake sounds exciting. It will certainly be worked into my schedule, even if I have to break Arnaldo's leg…he's always rushing my timetable."

Farewells were exchanged as the Russell's departed. It had been a great change of pace for both Angie and Mike. On the way back to their lodgings, she gave Luigi, to his enjoyment, a running account of the evening.

"You have had a magnificent time. I'm so glad you have experienced true Roman hospitality. Now, what have you planned for the next while, perhaps I can be of service to you."

"Tomorrow morning we will attend services at All Saints Anglican Church. Do you know where it is," asked Mike.

"*Si, il signore,* it's on Via del Babuino. What time do you wish me to pick you up?"

"Ten o'clock would be fine."

Chapter Ten

At seven a.m., Mike slipped quietly from the bed to a chair on the balcony not wishing to disturb Angie's sleep. He had been awake for sometime with thoughts bouncing around in his head of his team and the people he served in Afghanistan. How were they making out? He felt a fleeting sense of guilt being away from his duties. He had a sensation of separation and an almost visceral need to be in touch with them. Silently, he prayed for their safety and well being. The prayer brought them into focus, and he experienced a vague sense of closeness.

After some moments of reflection, he got up and brewed a pot of coffee. Back on the balcony, he fired up his laptop computer and inhaled the scented air. The morning sun had warmed the garden allowing the perfume from the flowers and a blooming lemon tree nearby to rise. The first flight of bees droned their gathering songs as they began to harvest the waiting nectar…such contrast to the torment and aridness of Kandahar.

Mike checked his e-mail account and found a note from his grandfather indicating all was well in the parish. A second e-mail was from his friend Tim, afloat with a Canadian Task Force.

HMCS IROQUOIS
Somewhere in the Arabian Sea.

Greetings, my friend,
We have returned to our patrolling vigilance. Things have heated up along the coast of Somalia with more and more maritime security issues arising…pirates off

the cost of Somalia and the Gulf of Aiden. As you can imagine from the brazen hijackings in the area, the need for increased Maritime Security is a priority. To provide this we moved a little closer to the area where things were happening. There was an urgent need to ensure that shipments of aide were not targeted. In response to a call from the World Food Organization, HCMS VILLE DE QUEBEC, a frigate with the Standing NATO Fleet in the Mediterranean, was sent our way to escort the vessels carrying food. They were successful in their task, and we were involved in running off a few pirates ourselves. It is amazing how fast pirates clear out when there is an armed warship bearing down on them at high speed. We got some press over our assistance to an Italian vessel and a BZ (Navy, for well done) from officials of the Italian Government during our visit to Italy. During the last few weeks in "the box," of the operational area, we boarded a dhow that was suspected of carrying contraband. It was a long boarding and there was lots of cargo to move around as part of the search. For my part I made a pastoral visit to the dhow, saying a prayer for all in our RHIB (rigid hull inflatable boat) that transported our group from IRO to the dhow as part of a boarding party. It didn't seem too rough from the deck of IRO, but the five to six foot swells seemed pretty daunting when trying to climb up and down a wooden / rope ladder. I learned very quickly to trust the person on the bottom of the ladder and when they say GO or LET GO…I just do it to descend into the 20 foot RHIB or as I started my climb up the side of the other vessel. We all transferred between the ship and the dhow without incident and I spent a gruelling four hours helping to moving cargo around to allow the boarding party to do its work.

Following that experience we made our way back around to Bahrain where a change of command of Combined Task Force 150 took place from the Canadians to the Dutch. The ceremony was a signal that the main part of our mission was coming to an end.

> Thanks, again for your e-mails, keeping me company and up to date with your intense activities. Things certainly are not that extreme here at sea, although we do have our moments…
>
> God bless, Mike, as always
> Tim

Sounds like Tim is finding his way with the ships at sea and seems to be enjoying it all, thought Mike, as he took a few moments to reply to the e-mail from his friend. Interesting how the two of us are called to serve…one by land and one by sea…in the same spirit of providing a ministry of presence to our people. Canada can be rightfully proud of our personnel in uniform prepared to put their lives on the line in order to serve others. God bless 'em.

He sent a reply to his grandfather and composed one to Steele in KAF in which he sent greetings to the team. In it he gave them a brief account of his leave in Rome to date; related the hospitality of that city's citizens; described the sites and sounds, and above all applauded the epicurean feasts he and Angie had consumed. He added a note of sly humour at the last… 'Glad you're not here, for if you were, you'd want to find the right woman and escape the so-called safety of your bachelorhood! I can't wait to tell you about Maria.'

A muffled voice from the bedroom called out, "Is that fresh coffee I smell? Now, if you were a thoughtful husband, you would bring me a cup and I would be a thoughtful wife and give you a reward. What do you say, mister?"

"I am your devoted servant, Madame," said Mike as he whisked in from the kitchen with a breakfast tray that he had prepared earlier. "Now, where's my reward!"

"Put the tray down first," she said playfully, "come closer and I will give you your reward. On second thought, maybe I'd better have the coffee first."

* * * * *

Luigi was promptly on time. On the way to All Saints he was curious to learn how they found the Roman cuisine.

"It's fabulous," remarked Angie. "I've always enjoyed Italian cooking and I prepare a mean spaghetti sauce myself. Someday I'd like to learn more about the preparation techniques."

"If you want to take the time, there's a one day cooking class offered in Trevi, a short distance from Rome, or as an alternative, a three day course at The Villa, a four star hotel complex where renowned Chef Guiseppe instructs in the art of Umbrian cooking. There you would learn some secrets of Italian cuisine and collect a few recipes for your future use. I will arrange it for you should you decide to indulge," offered Luigi.

"We'll certainly think about it," said Mike. "I enjoy cooking, too! But my bent is more toward fish and game. I have fun with Chinese recipes, too. First we have to decide when we've done enough sight seeing. Perhaps next week, by then we'll want to relax our pace before our time in Rome is over. What do you think, Angie?"

"That's a good idea. I'd like that. How soon would you have to know, Luigi?"

"By the weekend would be fine. Here's All Saints. This church is such a gem and we are told it has the finest acoustical sounds in Rome. Many concerts are held here throughout the year. Shall I pick you up after the service?"

"If we need you I will call, OK?"

* * * * *

All Saints Anglican Cathedral was a Gothic structure located close to the Spanish Steps. It was built between 1882 – 87 on the site of a former convent. Previous to that date services were held in various secluded buildings in the city as Anglican worship was not permitted in the Papal regions. However, a private, practically secret congregation was initiated in 1816, and over the years grew into a vital community until permission was granted to build a church proper. At the early stage they met in a building known as 'The Granary Chapel', so-called because of its original usage.

Mike and Angie entered the west portals to the sounds of a mighty pipe organ. It's notes were pure and clear, filling the interior with ethereal music; one could almost sense it was a prelude to the arrival of a heavenly host. The Russell's made their way to a pew at the centre of the nave and knelt to offer a prayer of thanksgiving for the day and for their happiness. The service was a sung Eucharist. Mike was deeply moved. He had not attended worship in a cathedral for some time and found he was emotionally affected by the majestic choir and ceremony that was unfolding. The setting was beautiful and the liturgy had such deep meaning for him. Since coming out of a theatre of conflict, he found his feelings were close to the surface and triggered easily. Here, in this place, he felt secure, and the weight of recent responsibilities seemed to lift from his shoulders. His emotions, suddenly released from behind a dam of pent up tensions seemed safe to be expressed freely, and with Angie beside him, his spirits rose. He reached across and grasped her hand squeezing it gently as a hot tear slid down his cheek. Her response was immediate as she brushed the moisture from his face and looked lovingly into his eyes. She could read his soul.

* * * * *

Monday and Tuesday were spent viewing several ancient sites of Rome. They visited the excavations taking place at the Crypto Balbi, a small privately owned museum near the Fontana di Trevi. Here they viewed layer upon layer of former civilization and found it an educational experience. Ancient treasures such as the Coliseum, the Trevi Fountain and the Piazza Novona cast their imaginations back two thousand years. The Mammertine prison was preserved and it was here that both St Peter and St Paul had been held captive in chains.

At lunchtimes they found delightful cafes where they continued to taste delectable dishes of Roman food and sipped local wine. Evenings found them in romantic restaurants of the Trastevere region. They were developing a genuine passion for discovering new Italian dishes.

Wednesday morning dawned brightly. Angie had not slept well as she was excited at the prospect of the Papal audience. The formal invitation had been delivered the previous day while they had been out touring the city, but Leo had slipped it under their door. The event was to take place in Paul VI Hall following the Papal Mass in St Peter's Basilica.

"I will have to wear a veil," she told Mike. "I brought the black lace one that my mother sent me from Spain."

Mike twinkled at her. "How quaint. Now you will assume the role of a Spanish Prima Donna?"

"Stop your teasing. You're the last one to talk about primping. Have you decided to wear clerics? I think it would be very proper, after all in a way you're representing the chaplaincy!"

"Yes, I believe the occasion warrants appropriate dress for an Anglican priest in the midst of so many Roman confreres… I don't want to stand out in the crowd," said Mike still in a playful mood.

Leo was on time for their nine o'clock departure. "How splendid you look, *Signora*," he said as he took her arm to assist her into his car. "And you, Father Mike, are most presentable for the occasion. I have been instructed to deliver you to Cardinal Scorsone's office as he has made plans for you to sit in a reserved area. A young clergyman will escort you to the Basilica and after the Mass he will take you into the Hall where the public audience will be held. I'm sure it will be a most eventful day for both of you."

* * * * *

And so it was. St Peter's was aglow with candles and pageantry. Mike found the Papal procession an ecclesiastical spectacle with purple robed Cardinals and assistant clergy dressed in albs, while others donned colourful copes of excellent design by dedicated craftsmen. The Pope wore immaculate white vestments and nodded to the congregation while making the sign of the cross as he made his way up the central aisle.

Angie was enthralled. Her eyes glistened with sentiment as she took in the ceremonial display. Mike put his hand on the small of her back and held her close. He could feel the exhilaration radiating from her like an electrical impulse.

The Mass concluded, the priest, who was their escort, led them to the audience chamber and directed them to their reserved seats. The anticipation of the crowd and the spectacle of the event vibrated through the room. From their vantage point the Russell's were able to follow the procedures close at hand. Angie could not take her eyes off the Pontiff and once thought he had smiled directly at her.

The audience lasted forty minutes, and as it came to a conclusion, Cardinal Scorsone approached them. Reaching out, he took both their hands and said, "Dear people, how nice to finally meet you. Father Pat has told me so much about your spiritual journey together. I have spoken to his Holiness about this and mentioned that you, Padre Russell, are a Canadian Chaplain serving in Afghanistan. He would like to meet you personally and have a private conversation. Please follow me."

They made their way to a small sitting room off the main hall where they were offered refreshments. In a short time, the Pope entered, and smiling graciously raised his hand in blessing.

"Please be seated. I understand, Father Russell, you are a Canadian Chaplain serving in Afghanistan. My heart goes out to you and your people as casualties are sustained in that terrible conflict. You are there to help the poor Afghans, and yet you suffer great loss of life at the hands of the insurgents. May God be with you!"

He turned to Angie. "I can see you are a supportive spouse and I understand from the good Cardinal that you are a nurse working primarily with veterans…a most interesting calling, I'm sure. Please, may I offer you a blessing?" Angie knelt and the Pope placed his hands on her head and quietly gave his blessing.

He then addressed Mike and said, "I know you are an Anglican priest. Could I also offer a prayer for you?" Mike knelt and the Pope prayed for the selfless devotion to duty displayed by the Canadian and Allied Forces in Afghanistan; especially for the work of all chaplains called to serve.

The Pontiff went on to say in conclusion, "This conflict for the hearts and minds of the Afghan people is extremely complex. Your approach to reconstruction of the infrastructure is excellent, but your building of schools is exemplary. It is here that Afghanistan will become a free and viable nation. I cannot commend you highly enough for your perseverance. We pray, of course, for a peaceful solution to the conflict, but also understand that there are times when intervention must be taken to address the forces of evil that have been let loose in that country."

After a brief casual conversation, the Pope rose and bid the Russell's farewell. Angie was deeply moved and expressed her appreciation to the Cardinal for arranging the private audience, while Mike indicated that he would convey the Pontiff's comments to the chaplains and the troops in Afghanistan. It was a special encounter that they would always cherish.

* * * * *

The decision was made to join the three-day Umbrian cooking classes at The Villa in Trevi. The hotel complex combined the characteristics of ancient settings with modern comforts. The surrounding area was the heartland of the olive industry…one tree dated back 1700 years and is recognized as the oldest olive tree in Italy.

The Russell's were accommodated in a delightful room with wood panelled ceilings and frescoes. From their balcony they had a panoramic view of the rolling countryside. A swimming pool was only a short distance away.

"Oh, this is a cosy suite," said Angie as she looked about.

"Very nice," chimed Mike, "that pool looks inviting."

"I'm excited to take this cooking adventure. I've wanted to learn more about the way Italian cuisine is prepared for a long time. Luigi said Chef Guiseppe is a superb teacher and that some of his recipes date back to Etruscan times. It's going to be fun as well as an education," remarked Angie.

And she was right. The classes were entertaining as well as instructional. The students ate the food prepared, and local wines were offered to compliment the meals. At the end of the three days the Russell's felt gratified that they had learned valuable skills and the Chef had made flattering remarks on their progress.

"I think this experience has been a definite highlight to our holiday. What do you think?"

"I second the motion!"

* * * * *

The last days of their time together began to fly by. They decided to stay close to their flat and enjoy a leisurely pace, concentrating on each other, making thoughtful decisions as to how to meet the immediate needs of the other, and by doing so, opening up deeper levels of sharing and understanding.

It was during this time that an e-mail was received from Steele. Through the chaplains' net he had determined that Georgio, the Milozzi sisters' nephew, had been sent from the Sarobi district to the hospital at KAF in preparation for his repatriation back to Italy. He had acquired a little known disease of the immune system termed vasculitis, potentially fatal, where it shut down the small blood vessels of certain organs…in his case the lungs and kidney. Armed with this information, Mike called Al Ceppo and spoke with Marisella.

"I have been in touch with a chaplain in Afghanistan who has located your nephew. He is in hospital there and, you will be pleased to learn, he will soon be sent home."

"Oh, how can we ever thank you," she replied.

"No thanks necessary. I am glad to be able to relieve you of your anxiety."

"Will you and your wife come to us for dinner before you leave Rome," asked Marisella? "We would like you to be our special guests."

"I was planning to take her out for a romantic evening tomorrow as that will be our second last night here."

"Please, Father Michael, come to us. We will have a special table…a secluded nook for you and your lady. We will present you with a special farewell menu."

"You are very persuasive," conceded Mike. "How can I refuse?"

"*Mersviglioso! La vedremo poi.* Marvellous! We will see you then."

Luigi dropped them off at Al Ceppo for eight o'clock. Immediately on their arrival the Maitre'd sent word to the Milozzi sisters that their special guests had arrived. Christina and Marisella came to greet the Russell's enthusiastically.

"How nice to see you again. You have relieved our minds of much concern with news of Georgio. We were informed this morning that he will be home within the week. He has had a difficult time, but now we will nurse him back to full health. So, come with us and we will show you to our private alcove where you will be quite alone to enjoy the meal we have especially prepared. We call it a 'repast for lovers'."

"Thank you so much," said Angie. "This is very gracious of you."

"We could offer no less," replied Marisella. "I believe one kindness deserves another."

The niche where their table was located was in a far corner of the restaurant. The table glistened with silver wear and crystal. A bouquet of flowers and candles added to the ambience, while the couple sat side by side on a comfortable bench. Over the next two hours, course after course followed. "I don't think I can eat another morsel," confessed Angie. "I'm stuffed!"

"I think we should have a sweet," said Mike wanting to end the meal with a lighter taste in his mouth. "Maybe the fresh fruit cup with cream."

"Where are you going to put it all? I think I'll just finish up with coffee and some cheese."

They sat replete savouring the feast that had been laid before them. Christina and Marisella joined them bringing a tray with liqueurs.

"You must try this orange liqueur. It is quite delicious and will aid your digestion," suggested Christina. "It is called Filfar and is made by monks in a monastery on the Island of Cyprus."

Mike sampled it. "That is delectable…try some, Angie."

After a short visit with the sisters, the Russell's bid their hostesses good night. Mike offered to pay the bill, but was promptly scolded.

"We do not often have reason to extend our hospitality, so please accept this as our way of showing appreciation for locating our nephew. You cannot begin to know how you have lifted the worries from our hearts. If you are ever in Rome again, you must come to us…promise?"

"You can count on that," answered Mike as he took Angie's hand to lead her out. "Thank you for a remarkable meal and your kindness in inviting us. *Arrivederci!*"

* * * * *

Once back at the flat they sat out on the balcony. The moon was full and the garden was a fantasy landscape of light and shadow. The ancient fountain made a soothing sound as it burbled away. The evening air was scented with the fragrance of blooming citrus trees.

"A night to remember," said Mike as he reached over and traced the contours of Angie's face with the back of his hand.

"It has been a golden time," she responded and she wondered if it had been a conceiving time as well. They had made love often and she knew it was the right time in her cycle. "Now, let's go to bed and dream of things to come."

* * * * *

Their holiday over, Mike saw Angie off on her return flight to Canada. His return trip would take him to Camp Mirage where he would transfer to a Hercules aircraft for the hop to KAF.

Camp Mirage was a busy centre. It serviced the CF 130's, the workhorses of the Air Support Group, ferrying personnel and supplies to Afghanistan. It was also a terminal for the Airbus fleet as they made their way to and from Canada. The chaplains stationed there were a tireless team of two serving the needs of those posted to the Base. They also met personnel arriving and departing from theatre, with special interests directed toward compassionate cases. They were involved with the repatriation of those who died in theatre, and with great care and respect watched over the fallen prior to their departure for home. They held Ramp Ceremonies for them en-route from Afghanistan, and supported the escort who accompanied the remains back to Canada. On occasion, they would provide a relief chaplain for one coming out of theatre on leave. The camp Mirage chaplains proved an essential link to the outside world.

* * * * *

The Herc in which Mike flew into theatre approached KAF in what seemed to be an erratic descent. As the aircraft parked in its allotted space, Steele waited on the perimeter for Mike to de-plane. He was glad to welcome his friend back and was eager to hear of his time away.

"Hey, there, buddy. You're looking chipper. I trust all went well in Rome?"

"We had a great time, but I miss Angie already," replied Mike. All the way in from Camp Mirage he had the feeling of not really wanting to return to theatre, yet felt guilty for the thought, and wondered if he could fit in where he had left off before going on leave.

"Glad to have you back," said Steele sincerely. "The team missed you…I missed you!"

"How have things been going?"

"Not too badly, except for a ruckus in the Panjwayi between two tribal lords, but that seems to be cooling down. There is a big push to locate a couple new Taliban IED cells that have moved into the area. Those guys are acting pretty cagey and are working hard to avoid any direct contact with our people. We've upset some of their plans and caught a couple of their teams setting up their explosives."

"Any casualties recently?" asked Mike.

"Nothing too serious while you were away, thank the Good Lord!"

With that news, Mike felt much better and made his way to his quarters before joining Malcolm. He was informed that the chaplain team would meet later that afternoon to review a new schedule.

At the meeting, he was greeted with affection by all. A time for prayer and reflection was first on the agenda. Mike began to relax and the guilt he had experienced outside theatre began to slip away. These are my brothers, he thought. We are here for each other. We have a job to do, and with God's help, we will see it to the end.

"You look refreshed," said Malcolm with a grin. "No doubt your break was enjoyable. Glad to have you back."

"Thanks, wish I could say I was glad to be back. That otherworld reality out there has a pretty strong appeal. It was hard to say goodbye to Angie, but there we have it…at least we are on the downhill side of the tour now."

"Don't worry. It won't take you long to get back into the swing of things. When I was out to an FOB a few days ago, several were asking after you and wondering when you'd be back. I told them soon, and knew you would want to get out there ASP. So you will see by the new schedule you will be out at Ma'sum Ghar for services in a few days."

The team discussed their plans for the coming days. Mike was back into the routine before he knew it.

Chapter Eleven

As night fell over the airfield, and Mike finally lay down, all was not quiet. A generator droned nearby and a jet engine roared into action as an aircraft began its take off… a pair of helicopters circled in for a landing. The relentless noise did not bother him. He was used to it. It underlined the constant activity of KAF. He was tired from travelling and he missed Angie's closeness. His mind wandered back over their time together in Rome and suddenly he felt himself bleakly disconnected from her. He wondered how she had made out with her flight home…she was not the most confident person when it came to air travel. Gramps was to meet her in Ottawa. Was her flight on time? Vagrant disjointed thoughts began to bombard his mind and sleep would not come. He got up and went to the toilet, then opened his fridge and took out a bottle of water. He slipped outside to drink and was engulfed in a stifling blast of hot putrid air moving across the Base from the sewage lagoon. The thermometer beside his door read 35 degrees Celsius. He finished drinking the water and moved back into his air-conditioned quarters able to breath deeply. Thank goodness, he thought, the air conditioning is working again. Before his departure it had been producing more warm air than cold. Once again he lay on his cot and finally drifted off into an agitated restless slumber. His dreams were violent in nature as they swept him through situations he did not seem able to control. The foot patrol he had joined was under fire and he could see where the insurgents were located, but he was unable to shout out the information. No sound would come from his mouth and as the section was over-run, a blanket of guilt smothered him…at this point he awoke in a sweat with his pillow jammed between his mouth and the wall.

He sat on the edge of his bed, shook his head in an attempt to clear it. Eventually, the terror he had felt receded. Now he was wide-awake and disinclined to lay back. He reached for his Bible and turned to the twenty-third psalm… 'Yea though I walk through the valley of the shadow of death, I will fear no evil for You are always with me.' Mike mused on those last five words. He had always found a sense of calm, once he concentrated on God's loving and healing presence, and the fragments of the nightmare began to slowly dissolve. In the back of his bible he had pasted the serenity prayer composed by the great theologian, Reinhold Niebuhr …

> God, Give us the grace to accept with serenity
> the things that cannot be changed, Courage
> to change the things which should be changed,
> And the wisdom to distinguish the one from the other."

He used the prayer as a mantra and applied its significance to many aspects of his own life. Also adopting it to his pastoral ministry in the care of and the counselling of those who were troubled. He had placed a second poem inside the back cover written by Mary Stevenson entitled:

Footprints in the Sand.

> One night a man had a dream. He dreamed he was walking along the beach with the Lord. Across the sky flashed scenes from his life. For each scene he noticed two sets of footprints in the sand…one belonging to him and the other to the Lord. When the last scene of his life flashed before him, he looked back at the footprints in the sand. He noticed that many times along the path of his life there was only one set of footprints. He also noticed that it happened at the very lowest and saddest time of his life. This really bothered him and he questioned the Lord about it. Lord, you said that once I decided to follow you, you'd walk with me all the way. But I have noticed that during the most troublesome times in my life, there is only one set of footprints. I don't understand why when I needed you most you would leave me.

> The Lord replied, my precious child, I love you and I would never leave you! During your times of trial and suffering when you see only one set of footprints, it was then I carried you.

Putting his Bible aside, he reached for his Anglican prayer book and turned to the Order of Compline. This traditional service at the end of the day dated back to the 6th century and formed a part of St Benedict's Rule for monks. Mike had used it daily when he was a theological student and from time to time read it as his evening prayers before retiring. Occasionally, Angie would join him and they would go through the office responsively.

As his mind traced the collect for protection toward the end of Compline, his head began to droop forward as he began to doze. Sometime later, he did not remember when, he rose from his chair, lay on his cot and pulled a sheet over his head, and fell into a deep undisturbed sleep.

At first light, a siren sounded the alert that a rocket attack was incoming. This was the blunt awakening to reality of being in theatre. The walkways between the shacks, as the quarters were often called, began to fill. Mike joined the disciplined crowd as they hurried toward bomb shelters. An explosion erupted a hundred metres away in the area near the Tim Horton outlet.

"Dear God," blurted out the man next to Mike, "If they blow Timmy's, they may as well take away the rest of our perks."

The man beside him gave the soldier an elbow. "John, we'll have none of your puns this time of day. It's bad enough dealing with them when we're all wide awake." And so the tone for the day was set. Within a half an hour the all clear was sounded and another day at KAF got underway…not that the activity ever stopped…but there was the occasional interruption like reacting to incoming ordinance or dealing with a wry Canadian sense of humour.

Mike chuckled to himself as he admired the resilience of Canadian soldiers…their natural ability to adapt to situations beyond their control and be able to smile trough adversity…somehow this seemed to be a national trait.

The following day Mike entered Sperwan Ghar, a FOB that commanded the heights overlooking the Panjwayi Peninsula. Below was primarily cultivated farm country that lay in the forks of the Arghandab and Dowry Rivers. It was here that a great deal of re-construction work was being done on the roads, bridges, canals and irrigation systems that were so critical to the recovery of the Afghan people in this area.

Dragon Battery of 2 RCHA was located on this Base, along with other elements of the Battle Group. It was a mobile unit that could be dispatched by air or ground to locations in support of ISAF personnel in the area. At this point in time, 3 Troop of Dragon Battery was in support of American Green Berets and the ANA (Afghan National Army) who were scouring the Khakrez District for Taliban forces. The Canadian presence was an encouragement for the inhabitants to assure them they were an important part of the larger picture. The guns fired shells onto the mountaintops, driving enemy cells toward the low ground below. This strategy provided the artillery with targets in open country where no collateral damage would be inflicted upon the civilian population.

Mike visited among the gunners who received him enthusiastically. He was well known to them, and he had been of special help to several of their comrades in assisting them to deal with problems back home.

"Hi, Padre, I hear you're just back from your leave…in Rome, no less," said Sergeant Archie LeBlanc, an ardent Roman Catholic. "Did you by any chance get to see the Pope?"

"I did indeed, in fact he asked to see me personally to find out how his flock was doing here and to tell you his thoughts and prayers are with you."

"No kidding! You talked with him personally?"

"I did and I told him I would pass his message."

"Well, thank you so much. Imagine that," said LeBlanc turning to another gunner, "His Holiness sent us a personal message. Unbelievable!"

"You got it as I got it," said Mike, smiling as he moved through the 2 Troop bivouac in search of a young soldier whom the Battery Sergeant Major had asked him to see.

"Black seems to be losing it," the BSM had said in confidence to the chaplain. "He's a loner and I'm concerned for him. He's awfully quiet and hangs out by himself all the time. Ever since he saw a mutilated body hanging from a tree with his decapitated head placed on a spiked pole, he has been upset…that's when he began to turn in on himself. We learned that the Taliban murdered the child because he was working as a kitchen helper for a local ANP (Afghan National Police) unit and the insurgents wanted to make an example of him…a warning to the locals not to cooperate with their enemies."

"I'll have a talk with him and see if I can help him. Unfortunately, he's not the only one to have concerns such as this," offered Mike.

And so he had gone to look for the lad.

He found Gunner Black unloading newly arrived supplies from the convoy Mike had travelled with and spoke with the Master Bombardier in charge.

"Do you mind if I take Black aside for a bit," asked the padre?

"He's yours," came the sharp reply, "He's not much good to me the way he mopes around. Sorry, Padre, I didn't mean that the way it came out. It's just that he seems to be in a different place…you know, somewhere out there… not part of the team. Not a good thing out here where we all have to rely on each other."

"Thanks, Master Bombardier, perhaps I can help!"

"Hey, Black, go with the padre."

When they were alone Mike said, "Sorry about that. I hope I didn't embarrass you in front of your buddies?"

The young soldier's eye sockets were sunken; his eyes had that haunted look. He kept his head down as he spoke to Mike. "They're not my buddies. No one is. They don't like me 'cause I'm different."

"How do you mean…different?"

"I don't want to be here. I hate it. I want to go home! This is an evil place where terrible things happen even to children. I saw one kid, he was… " At this point the soldier broke down. His body racked with sobs and tears surged from his swollen eyes.

"Ah, I understand. You've seen horrible, horrible things. Looks like it's eating you up. Must be taking all you've got just to get through a day. You're going home in a few weeks. Do you think you could hang in there… and maybe count on your mates to understand how you feel… maybe some of them are experiencing some of what you are. Do you think kicking back in with them might help you over the hump? There's still time for you to make a difference here with the efforts the troops are trying to make."

"I have no desire to get along with anybody. I just want out. Period."

The encounter reminded Mike of a similar session he had with Scotty Martin. Dear God, he thought, I hope there's not many more like this?

Mike listened empathetically and when their time together was over he realized that he would be unable to make a difference with the soldier, and made a note to refer him to one of the mental health team. They were the people who were qualified to deal with this type of psychological disturbance, at least as he perceived it. It was obvious that the young man had a deep-rooted and potentially desperateness to his disposition.

Mike spoke to the BSM and offered his opinion. "Watch him carefully. I think you should send him to the hospital in KAF ASP. He could be a danger to himself and others as well. I'm aware that he carries a weapon with a full magazine."

"Do you think he's that far gone?"

"I'm no expert, but I think it would be wise to get him out of here."

"Thanks, Padre, I'll take it from here," replied the BSM.

* * * * *

The next day Mike arranged two worship services for the personnel at FOB Sperwan Ghar to attend. One was a prayer meeting with a short sermon, and the other was an Anglican Communion service open to all denominations. A number of people formed the two congregations including a large group of American Green Berets who had not seen their own chaplain for several weeks. He had been injured in an IED explosion and his replacement was undergoing orientation procedures. After the service an American captain expressed the appreciation of all his people. "I know that words cannot express it enough, but we are grateful that you would have us join you."

"You are more than welcome," answered Mike. "We are in this together, and I know the American padres would offer the same were the situation reversed. I don't know if you are aware of it, but the Coalition Chaplains are very supportive of each other. We do a lot of things together, not only church services, but also Ramp Ceremonies, and we often get together socially to share our concerns."

"Good to hear, Sir. God Bless!"

"And God bless you and yours."

Wherever Mike turned on that visit he was conscious of the elevated levels of conversations concerning the end of tour and the return home. It was almost endemic in proportion. He recalled the words of Lt Col Rob Walker, Battle Group Commander, when he spoke to the chaplains on the importance of preserving focus. "If our soldiers lose concentration on their task, they are apt to become careless, and that could mean trouble. I would hope that you chaplains would watch for this and attempt to counteract any lackadaisical behaviour. I would want to know if this is happening and I trust you would give me a heads up without betraying any confidence. Remember, you are my eyes and ears where morale is concerned."

Mike mulled these words over and whenever possible used encouraging language when conversing with the soldiers. "Hang in there, we've only a few more weeks to go. Keep alert and we'll keep alive." or "Stay sharp, we don't want the crazies to set in, that's when trouble starts." or "We're on the downhill slope, but remember we're not home yet." He was persuaded in his own mind that the BG Commander was right. Any carelessness placed everyone in jeopardy of losing life or limb.

* * * * *

The daytime temperatures were beginning to creep into the mid forties Celsius. It was hot and uncomfortable. The dust caught up in any breeze was choking and it was difficult for people to stay clean for any length of time. Bodies itched and sweat soaked through clothing in a matter of minutes.

By the tenth of June it became evident that the insurgents were deliberately targeting Canadian patrols and convoys. New Taliban IED cells had moved into the territory and were reported by the locals. Within a matter of hours three explosions were heard. A Nyala triggered one, but thankfully the soldiers on board suffered only minor bruises. An engineer LAV sent to assist was also blown up. Two sappers were hurt, but not seriously. A third vehicle, a wrecker, caught fire and was brewed up as their ammunition began to cook off. Fortunately in all three incidents, no one was killed.

Things were about to change. Early on the morning of June 20 as a light armoured re-supply 'Gator' was delivering much needed water, food and ammunition out to a smaller Check Point, there was a tremendous explosion that echoed all around the district. The Gator was completely disintegrated with its parts strewn over a large area. The scene was horrific as a section of 2 Platoon from Charles Company arrived to investigate. Sgt Christos Karigiannis, Cpl Stephen Bouzane, Pte Joel Wiebe, who were on the vehicle were killed instantly. The heat of the day increased. It was a grisly task for those who arrived to secure the area. When their assignment was completed the engineers struck back toward Sperwan Ghar in a 2 Platoon Nyala, and before they reached the FOB yet another IED claimed a vehicle. The wheels of a Nyala were sheared off as they were designed to do, and although the body of the vehicle was thrown into space, the people inside were not seriously injured. It had been a long, hot day in the blistering sun.

It was ironic that the press continued to file stories of casualties the Canadians suffered, but no word was published that a score of other IED sites had been disarmed with the help of local citizens, and that the PRT teams were still able to continue with the much needed reconstruction work as a part of the Afghan solution. One could only imagine what the situation would be like without the support of the troops protecting them.

"Hey, Padre, only six weeks to go," greeted Private Sam Laird as Mike was visiting through the area allotted to the Battle Group at KAF.

"You bet. We're all counting the days, but keep them safe. We all want to get home in one piece. Right?"

"Aw, don't be a wet blanket. You gotta loosen up…before you know it, we'll be climbing aboard that out bound flight on the first leg home."

"Yup, that's my plan too, and I want to make sure I have legs under me to get to the aircraft," said Mike. "Many's the slip betwixt the cup and the lip. Watch where you walk when you're out on patrol."

Three days later, Laird stepped on an anti-personnel mine and lost both his legs below the knees. He had been kibitzing with the soldier ahead of him and had lost concentration as to what he was doing. Mike saw him at Role 3 when he was brought in and spent time by his side after he came out of intensive care.

"I can't feel my legs," he cried out in a state of delirium as the painkillers began to wear off.

Mike remembered his conversation with Laird several days earlier and a sense of remorse swept over him. He knew that some people were very superstitious and wondered if the soldier would blame him for what had happened. What to do? How do I face him? What do I say? With concern and sadness in his eyes, Mike reached over and touched the shoulder of the young Private.

"Sam, can you hear me?"

The response was at first a deep moaning sound, followed by a barely discernable, "Whose there?"

"It's me, Padre Mike. I came as soon as I heard of your injury."

"What happened to me?"

"You've been wounded and we are at the hospital."

"Am I going to be alright?"

"You are receiving the best of care. I'm sure you will be fine."

"Why can't I move my legs? I want to get up, but nothing seems to move."

"That's because your legs have been injured," said Mike.

"Oh my God, will I be able to walk again?"

"The medical team will do everything they can to make it happen. In the mean time, have faith in them." Mike wanted to say, "I feel awfully bad that this has happened to you, Sam. I guess I shouldn't have said what I did to you the other day about watching where you should walk. I hope you don't think I jinxed you?" but held his own worry and regrets in check so as to focus on Sam.

"You're the best, Padre…everyone says so…oh God, I hurt."

"I'll get the nurse," responded Mike. "We'll get you something to take the pain away."

As the chaplain rose to go, the soldier appealed to him. "Don't go, Padre, stay with me awhile." And he did. Mike sat with Laird for another hour until a strong sedative settled the man into a blessed sleep.

It was late evening when Mike left the hospital in low spirits. He made his way to his Team Leaders quarters where he poured out his feelings to Malcolm. The older man listened with compassion as the story unfolded.

"Sometimes, Mike, we say the right things at the wrong time. You know and I know that your warning was given in good faith. We are all trying to get our people through this difficult time…that's part of our job. Young Laird was right when he said, 'You're the best.' You're a devoted chaplain with a big heart and now's not the time to get down on yourself. Take your own advice. It's time to keep focussed and get on with it."

"Thanks for that, Malcolm, and thanks for being there for me."

"We are there for each other, my friend, that's what our team is all about. May the Good Lord continue to guide us!"

* * * * *

The month of June was well underway when the call came in for ISAF to advance into a northern area some distance from KAF. Khakrez was a village not far from the Dhala dam. Its watershed held the key to the economic stability of Kandahar Province. It controlled the flow of water to supply the irrigation canals feeding the agricultural lands in the river valleys below. In turn, this allowed the farmers to plant and harvest a variety of crops, thus breaking the cycle of opium dependence. The dam had been severely damaged by the Soviets before their withdrawal from Afghanistan and required much needed repairs. It would take years to restore it to full operational capacity, but first the area had to be cleared of a considerable Taliban threat. The Canadian Battle Group forces that included infantry, artillery and tanks, advanced into the region in support of US Special Forces teams and the ANA Kandak. A new FOB was established at Khakrez. It was to that out station that Mike headed with a CLP (Combat Logistic Patrol) with a load of water, food and ammunition. The convoy was escorted by a troop of Recce Squadron's Coyotes. Short of their destination, the lead Coyote hit an IED and the driver, Trooper Darryl Caswell, was killed in the explosion. When the scene was secured, Mike came forward to assist with the cleanup. Solemnly, the trooper's remains were placed on a stretcher while the chaplain knelt beside the VSA awaiting the arrival of the air evac helicopter. Consideration was given for Mike to return to KAF with the body, but it was felt his presence would be more useful accompanying the personnel in the convoy, at least until they reached their destination.

"Padre," said the convoy Commander, "You can return with us to KAF tomorrow, that way you'll be able to take part in the Ramp ceremony."

"Thanks! It'll also give me a chance to talk with others along the way. This has hit them pretty hard, especially considering we're only a few weeks from heading home," answered Mike.

"You're right. One only has to look at their faces to see their hurt and frustration. I don't envy you your task."

It was long into the night after reaching Khakrez before Mike could find a place to lay his head for a few hours. He had stayed and talked with the soldiers of the convoy after their evening meal. The conversations gravitated toward thoughts of returning home. What would the transition be like? How had the families changed since the BG was deployed? What had the individual missed…birthdays, anniversaries, graduations, and other family celebrations? Was there a feeling of things unshared…being left out? At what time during the tour did the soldier begin to lose the real sense of home? These and many other questions were raised through the evening hours.

Mike felt bereft, overwhelmed and inadequate to answer them. He had these emotions too and participated in the discussions as best he could. In due course, the session broke up as the exhausted people sought rest. It had been a day that had graphically blasted the senses. For some, it became deeply rooted and at a future date would cause them and their families' problems.

Early the following morning, as the convoy formed up for the return to KAF, a Warrant Officer addressed Mike. He was an older seasoned soldier who had served with NATO in Europe, the UN in Cyprus, Bosnia and Somalia, and now on his second tour in Afghanistan. "Padre, I think you had a pretty hard time last night dealing with all the questions that were flying around. I just want you to know…you are one of us. We admire you for being with us and sharing in our concerns. As for the complex problems raised by the group, no body has any quick answers. Thank you, for being there, and giving us the opportunity to vent our frustrations. Believe me, it helped."

* * * * *

Yet another Ramp Ceremony…yet another slain Canadian soldier repatriated home. At KAF, row upon row of Coalition military personnel gathered for a brief service and a farewell salute as the casket was carried from a LAV to the waiting aircraft. As many sad times before, the unit chaplain called the assembly to prayer.

> Let our hearts and minds be gathered together in prayer: Gracious and Loving God, Our hearts speak words of thanks for the life of Trooper Darryl Caswell, a son, a friend, a stalwart member of the Armoured regiment, the Lord Strathcona Horse.
>
> We give thanks for his warrior spirit that enabled him, on and off the field, to be at the centre of the storm. We thank you for the call he felt to a life of service beyond self, for it was in this service, that his life was given in sacrifice on the field of battle. We thank you for his humble nature combined with professional skills that instilled confidence in those who knew him and served with him.
>
> For his compassion and his charisma, for the gift of humour, and his ability to hang in there until he had made you smile or laugh…we give thanks. A brother to those who serve in this area of operations and in Canada, a brother in the profession of arms, a brother of that sacred band, we few, we happy few, we band of bothers and sisters who risk shedding our blood in conflict and war.

O God, you embrace us all, may Darryl know that he is both missed and loved. We remember in prayer his family and friends. May strength and courage accompany them on this journey of loss. As too we stand a coalition of men and women in solidarity, with the people of Islamic Republic of Afghanistan, with feelings of grief and an emptiness that only Darryl could fill.

The ground beneath our feet shakes, yet the foundation, though shaken, stands firm…in life, in death, in life beyond death You are with us and we are not alone. May our actions here create a country free of fear, want and ignorance for the children of Afghanistan.

For Darryl, Eternal Rest grant unto him and may light perpetual shine upon him. May he rest in peace. Amen.

As the parade disbanded, several chaplains of the Coalition gathered in Malcolm's office space where they shared a time of companionship over coffee and donuts from Tim Horton's. In the assembly were four chaplains, three British and one American. The latter approached Mike and drew him aside.
"I understand you have just returned from Khakrez," he asked?
"Yes, it was on my way up there that we lost our trooper."
"My name is Paul Shantz. I am the replacement chaplain for the Green Berets. I was told you took a service with them recently at Sperwan Ghar. How did you find their morale? I join them tomorrow."
"They seemed to be a fine bunch of people, and yes, a good number of them turned out for the services. They're certainly looking forward to your arrival. Will you be staying with them for long," asked Mike?"
"Only a few days, I expect. We are short of chaplains and we have to spread ourselves around. I want to thank your team for including our soldiers when you visit the FOBs. It means a lot to us."
"Don't mention it. It's our pleasure to help out whenever we can. Your Forces have always been generous to us Canadians. It's the least we can do."
This was indeed a fact. The US military had provided the Canadians with a shared chapel at KAF and had been more than kind in making supplies available. Frequently the Americans loaned them a clerk to assist with the many duties associated with the chaplain's office and the

scheduling and preparation of religious services. It was another facet of mutual support found throughout the Coalition Forces.

> E-mail from Mike
> To Angie.
>
> My dearest one
>
> I have just marked my calendar to indicate another day has ended and brings me that much closer to a homecoming. I don't let others know I am doing this as it would indicate my deep desire to be out of here and that makes me feel a little guilty. I suspect, however, that Steele has seen it on my table, but has not commented on it. I guess we all have to respect each other's idiosyncrasies.
>
> Since we parted in Rome a few weeks ago I have slowly, but somehow reluctantly, worked my way back into a routine. It has been somewhat difficult, but I found if I submerged myself in my duties it eventually became easier. It is not hard to understand homesickness when it comes up from a gut feeling. I hope I'm not letting my people down by thinking this way. I have tried my best to keep focused on the task facing us in the remaining days. Indeed, this has been my resolve throughout the tour. It helps to concentrate on ministry and the spiritual care of the troops, and I've been able to accomplish this through my prayers. There are times though, when I feel discouraged…when it appears that the team isn't quite pulling together, or we seem to be receiving little encouragement from those above us…everyone needs cheering and affirmation…surely that's human nature. It may be just me putting my own needs first. Seeing something that has to be done and wanting to do it my way.
>
> I hope you don't mind me sounding off, but it does help me gain perspective. Don't worry, I'm fine and with the others, we'll see this through. Thank God, I can always feel you with me. You are my light at the end of the tunnel.
>
> All my love, as ever, Mike.

Chapter Twelve

E-mail from Angie Russell
To Michael Russell
30 June 2007

My dearest one.

Great news! I wish I were there to tell you face to face. I have taken the 'drugstore test' and it indicates that I am pregnant. I have made an appointment with Doctor Anderson to confirm the fact. I am so excited I can hardly wait to tell everyone of our good news, but I will wait for the official word from the doctor. I'll be seeing *Mere et Pere* next week and will of course let them know. I will whisper it to your grandfather on Sunday and ask him to keep it a secret until we know for sure. He can, of course, share it with Grandma Russell.

I still wake at night to reach over to you, but feel a sob come on when you're not there. How I miss you even more so now, with my emotions pretty close to the surface. Our wonderful days in Rome are a vivid memory and that helps when I feel down. But even more, the fact that you will be home in six or seven weeks gives me a real lift. Be sure to let me know as soon as you have your return dates.

I have written Father Pat with our thanks and gratitude for allowing us to use his flat. I know you sent a note, too.

He would have appreciated knowing the news of how the soldiers reacted when you told them you had met the Pope and how he sent them his greetings.

Take care, my love, take good care, and come to me...us! soon.

All my love, as ever,
Angie

* * * * *

It was July the first, and the Canadian Contingent at KAF celebrated their National holiday in a lively manner. Those who were not tasked to a specific duty were stood down at noon. As the day wore on spirited games were held between units and sub-sections...hockey using a tennis ball instead of a puck; tug-of-war competitions; horseshoes and dart challenges. Coalition partners were invited to an international barbecue. Country and Western music provided by an entertainment group brought over from Canada added to the excitement of the event. Comedians did their stand-up routines, much to the delight of everyone. Life in theatre for the Canadians was an alcohol free zone, so the 'beer call' to use two free drink tickets brought cheers. Tim Horton's supplied all the free coffee and donuts one could consume. Canadian flags were draped and flown throughout the lines. Maple leaf pins and ball caps were handed out to all. It was a relaxed, fun time, a celebration to remember, a few hours of respite from the weariness of war.

The Canadian chaplains circulated around the crowd of light-hearted soldiers, taking special interest in greeting and welcoming personnel from other nations. Steele had located a package of Maple Leaf pins and was handing them out. Mike, with several layers of ball caps perched vicariously on his head became a centre of attention as he cheerfully doled out the hats displaying the Canadian flag.

"Let's take a break, Steele," suggested Mike. "I need something wet to quell my parched throat...wonder how cold the beer is?"

"It's chilled, but I don't suppose that matters much," came Steele's ready reply.

At the beer tent they fell in line to wait their turn. Sergeant Bill Greene, a 2 RCR CQMS, was serving behind the bar and saw the chaplains. He waved them forward, but they refused to jump the line.

"We'll wait our turn, but thanks just the same," called Mike. The people ahead turned and moved aside making a path for the two chaplains.

"Hey, Padres," someone hollered out, "be our guests. You've been slaving in the hot sun passing out your wears while we've already had cold ones!"

They protested, but were ushered ahead by eager hands to where Sergeant Greene stood holding cool looking drinks. Accepting them, they turned to the others in line and raising their drinks together said, "Here's to you!"

"And here's to our Padres, " came the reply.

It was late evening before the party ended…a good day was had by all. People began to turn in, for the morning came early and the 24/7 schedules would grind on. But another day had been scratched off the calendar, for some it was only four more weeks to go and it couldn't come soon enough. People were tired.

Following breakfast the next morning, Mike made his way to Role 3. The hospital appeared to be relatively quiet. The constant smell of hand-sanitizer filled the air. From time to time, the sound of the 'Kandahar Cough' was heard in the wards…some of the medical staff was afflicted with this lung problem too, no one was exempt. Mike picked up a bottle of water from the stocked pile near the entrance. He had never drunk so much water in all his life and people helped themselves to what they needed, but by afternoon the water in these locations became quite tepid. If they had a fridge, they made sure a supply was always 'on ice'.

Mike made his way to the ICU where several soldiers and two civilians were recovering from operations. On a bed near the entrance lay a young Afghan girl. She was eight years old and had been playing in a field when an anti-personnel mine planted during the Soviet occupation had exploded. It had taken her right foot and badly fractured her left leg. The child's mother sat beside her. With the help of an interpreter, the chaplain spoke to the mother. The woman was shy at first, but when she was told that Mike was a 'Holy Man' she began to share her worries.

"My husband was in the ANA and was killed fighting against the Taliban. I am left with four children and now this. I have no man to protect my children and me. What shall I do," she cried?

"Perhaps I can help," responded Mike. "I have a friend who is a Cultural and Religious Adviser, (The Afghan equivalent to a chaplain,) at the ANA Base. He will know how to help you."

The woman gripped Mike's hand and demonstrated her appreciation with nods, bows, and a hand over her heart.

A patient was just coming from the operating room and Mike continued to marvel at the efficiency of the staff in the hospital. He was their chaplain and knew first hand of their dedication to the grim tasks that constantly faced them. He had shed tears with them when they were unable to preserve the life of a dying soldier. He rejoiced with them when they had succeeded in staunching wounds and saving lives. He listened to them when they were 'down' and prayed with them, and was accepted as an integral part of their community of healing. The Role 3 was a place of life and death, tenderness and tears, of fear, grief and loss of hope. It was a place of compassion and service.

As the gurney from the OR passed where Mike was standing, he heard a faint voice call out to him…the soldier had been wounded by flying shrapnel from a car bomb.

"Padre, will you help me call home to my wife? I've got to let my family know that I'm OK."

"Of course I will. Let me speak with your doctor first to make sure you're able to talk with them clearly enough. I'll be back in a minute."

The attending nurse shook her head no, and inclined her head toward the OR entrance from where the surgeon had just emerged.

Mike engaged him in conversation, "Corporal Mills has asked me to arrange a call to his home. Is he in any condition to do this or should we wait?"

"Definitely wait," came the reply. "We will have to operate again in a few hours as soon as his vital signs improve, then it will be straight forward. Unless there are complications, I see no problems. There's a sliver of shrapnel pressing between the femoral artery and the femoral nerve that still has to be removed. He must rest and not move needlessly or it could cause unnecessary damage."

"Thanks, I'll stay by him until he's ready to go in again," replied Mike. He pulled up a chair beside the corporal's bed and informed him gently of the doctor's decision. "The MO is pretty confident you're going to be alright, so don't worry. He just has to perform a second procedure to remove a piece of metal from your leg. Then, when you come out and the anaesthetic has worn off, we will call your wife."

It was almost noon when the surgical team took over again.

"Come back after lunch," suggested the surgeon. "He should be lucid by then."

It was three o'clock in the afternoon when Mike returned to the hospital. Corporal Mills was resting comfortably in a post op bay. He was well aware of his surroundings and immediately recognized the chaplain.

"Hi, Padre."

"Hi yourself. How do you feel?"

"A little sore, but they've given me something for that."

"Do you feel up to a call home," asked Mike?

"You bet. I want Susan to know I'm OK."

"Right! I have your home phone number and I'll place the call, but first let's get you raised a bit." A nurse, standing nearby, overheard the conversation and partially elevated the bed.

"It's ringing," said Mike. "Hello, Mrs Mills, this is Padre Russell from Kandahar. I have your husband standing by. He's anxious to talk with you." Mike passed the phone to the corporal.

"Susan. Hi dear, it's good to hear your voice. Yes, I'm fine…just a slight wound. No it's not that serious…honest." His voice was strong, but tinged with emotion.

The conversation went on for several minutes and then, passing the phone to Mike, the soldier said, "She wants to talk with you. I don't think she believes me when I tell her I will be OK."

"Yes, Mrs. Mills, this is Padre Russell. Yes, the doctor has told me your husband will be up and around in no time. Flying shrapnel wounded him and the surgeon has been able to remove all the fragments. Yes, he was lucky. No question, someone was looking after him. Yes, I will pray for him and for you, too. We'll call again in a couple of days. I'll sign off and pass you back to him. Your welcome, and rest assured he will receive the best of care."

After the call was completed, the corporal offered his thanks to the chaplain for his support and assistance. Mike tried to recall how many times he had arranged for these worrisome contacts with next-of-kin…too many he thought, but at least this one, thank God, shared good news.

* * * * *

In mid-July, a close look at action "outside the wire" gave indication that mentoring of the Afghan National Army (ANA) and the Afghan National Police (ANP) was beginning to pay dividends. In the early morning of July 17th under the cover of darkness, combined Afghan-Canadian forces infiltrated the village of Makuan where a heavily armed

Taliban unit was dug in. As dawn broke, a flight of Royal Netherland aircraft bombed the insurgent positions and artillery fire from Dragon Battery added their barrage to drive the enemy from cover. As the dust settled, Afghan and Canadian infantry charged in to finish the job. In all, sixteen Taliban fighters were killed. The remainder were captured and arrested by the ANP. The local people, who were heartened by the success of the joint task force, witnessed this impressive action. For too long, the Taliban had manipulated and stripped the villagers of the necessities of life, but now their parasitical presence had been dealt with in a visible and decisive way.

Mike visited India Company at FOB Wilson on their return from Makuan. Moral was running high with the success of the mission under their belts.

"You should have been with us, Padre," suggested Master Corporal Cheryl Pollard. "It was quite the show. The Afghan soldiers are doing a great job. Looks like our training with them has paid off."

"That's great, Cheryl, maybe now the press will start to give them credit where credit is due. The Afghan military and police have lost a lot of people killed by the insurgents. I understand there was little or no collateral damage to civilians," inquired Mike?

"True and that's so important in winning support from the villagers. It's also a difficult task in the middle of a firefight. It's hard to tell the difference between enemy and friendlies, unless they are seen carrying weapons…basically they're dressed the same."

"You're so right. It must be a hard call, at times?"

"Hard, but we do our best. Thankfully we sustained no injuries in this one…only minor stuff," reported Pollard, "and thank goodness our tour is in its last days. Can hardly wait to get back home. Seems I've missed a lot of family events in the last six months. My son graduated from Elementary School. Kids grow up so darned fast."

"And I remember the sad news when your mother passed away. There are a lot of things we miss and time marches on. One good thing tho', we have high-quality communications systems in place where we can keep in touch by phone or computer," reminded Mike. "Mind you it's not the same as being there. We still have things to catch up on when we get home, but strong families are soon back on track and we sure have a lot of those."

"Do you have your return date yet, Padre?"

"No nothing in writing yet. I have asked to stay until all our people are out of here. I'd like to be in the last chalk to leave, but time will tell.

In the meantime, let's keep our cool and finish our commitment. We don't want anyone to be careless…that always leads to trouble."

Pollard nodded her agreement. "You got it. I keep reminding my soldiers of that. They're pretty good and they know I'd kick ass if they don't listen…just as my Sergeant would haul my coals if I didn't stay sharp. By the way, thanks for helping my old buddy, Jack Mills, with his call back home. I hear he's being returned to Canada from the hospital in Germany this week. He's a fine soldier and his section really misses him."

"I was glad to be able to assist him and happy to hear he's recovering well. See you later," said Mike as he turned to continue his visit with the troops of India Company.

It was the end of a hot and dusty day when Mike took a breather. The sun was setting, closing out the day… reminding him how he was closing out his tour of duty. He sat in the partial shade outside of the mess tent and listened to the conversations inside. Many were talking of home and discussing plans they had made for their homecoming leave period.

Mike was in a reflective mood and mused on FOB positions. They appeared to be located in the middle of nowhere, much as one would recall the black and white movies of a Foreign Legion outpost, but in reality their function was to observe the roadways and the river valleys below. There, the insurgent forces lurked hidden within civilian villages and communities, masked by the everyday lives of people wanting to make a living in peace. The Forward Operating Bases and the Strong Points were pretty much the same in layout. Hesco barriers protected the perimeter of the compounds. These were collapsible wire mesh containers filled with sand, while the living areas inside the compound were surrounded with sand bags. Armoured sleeping quarters provided safe accommodation for weary soldiers. It was from these spartan locations where the troops lived for weeks at a time; from where they initiated their patrols; attended *shuras* to meet with elders in finding ways to assist the local population in reconstruction; searched for IEDs cells or buried ordinance; scoured villages for hidden arms or launched attacks on insurgent strongholds. They worked very closely with ANA and ANP personnel, not doing the work for them, rather mentoring and training them in military disciplines and skills.

The troops lived under a constant level of stress brought on by living at a vulnerable site and a busy operational tempo. They welcomed a visit from the chaplain who was able to have meaningful conversations with them, whether it was over a meal, or visiting a solitary individual on sentry duty where soldiers took shifts in a guard tower and the padre would spend time up there with them. It provided the opportunity to have a confidential one on one time with them. Often there were one-on-one incredible conversations around intimacies, fears, hopes, and dreams. The encounters frequently ended with a prayer for the soldiers and their families back home.

* * * * *

From the start of the tour until its end, the padres had to know what to bring with them on their visits "outside the wire". Mike could be away anywhere from a few days to a week, moving from point to point… sometimes by road vehicle, other times by chopper. It depended on what was available at any given time and if space could be provided for him. He had to carry all gear he brought by himself, starting with his helmet, armoured vest, tactical vest stuffed with first aid supplies, flashlight, compass, ballistic eye wear, gloves, ear plugs, anti-malaria pills, plus in his knapsack he stowed his communion kit, spare uniform, and lots of water …in other words 'one man, one kit' carefully planned. As he packed, he had to leave behind his worries about the potential danger ahead, like the possibility of being involved with an IED explosion or caught in a cross fire. Indeed, once out the gate he fortunately had the ability to leave all his personal concerns behind and focus on his mission as a chaplain. Each trip had become a little easier as he fell into a routine. His excitement and anticipation increased as he made his way into the active areas where he joined others who were confronted at some level with the same fears of death and mutilation. It was hard to explain, but he felt a special bond with these people. He was unarmed, so he didn't have to carry or deal with a weapon at all times. Regularly this became an interesting topic of discussion with people. Many soldiers, particularly Afghan troops, were perplexed by this, and considered him either very brave or stupid.

* * * * *

Returning to KAF several days later, Mike gathered his laundry together to drop off at a multinational facility. Some of the clothing was pretty pungent from the drenching sweat he had experienced beyond the wire. The laundry service was quick and efficient as items could be retrieved within 24 hours.

He arrived at his office at 7:30 a.m. to find a number of emails awaiting an answer. Several soldiers had dropped in to make confidential appointments with him. One, he noted, concerned a situation back in Canada where a wife had taken their children to an undisclosed location. Another dealt with a troubled mother whose infant child was seriously ill and was herself under a doctor's treatment for depression. In both cases, he knew he would have to make a recommendation on compassionate grounds for the soldiers to return home.

Mike made a mental note to dive into the administrative paper work that he had put off in preference to visiting the troops both inside and outside the wire. He was reminded of a meeting with several Coalition chaplains that had been scheduled for mid morning. It was a weekly gathering with American Army, Air Force and Marine chaplains, as well as British, Dutch and Australian padres who came together for support and prayer. Cooperation between the members of the group was strong and provided a base of solidarity on several levels, but most particularly in regards to the multinational hospital. As casualties came in there was an assurance that the Canadian padre who was regarded as chaplain to the hospital would see them. In turn, the soldier's unit chaplain was contacted, and if that padre was not available, the hospital chaplain would continue to see the patient until the other was located. Mike remembered such an incident when he was called by the hospital orderly room and informed that there were incoming casualties from an American unit, and that their chaplain could not be immediately located in a forward area.

Mike arrived at Role 3 and was directed to an injured officer who had been partially blinded from an IED blast. He could still see, but his head was covered with gauze and he was suffering from first-degree burns.

Bending close to the man Mike asked, "How are you doing, my friend?"

"Who's there?"

"I'm a chaplain."

"Ah, Chaplain, please tell me how my guys are doing?"

"They're being looked after. Apparently, you were the one who received the worst of the blast, but I will find out for you how they are. In the meantime, try to relax as best you can."

While the medical staff took the man into surgery, Mike visited the other six Americans in the trauma bay and ascertained that their wounds were indeed minor compared to their officer's. In the OR a surgeon worked cautiously and skilfully to remove the dead skin from the burns on the officer's face and head. He had been heavily sedated and when he was returned to recovery, Mike waited beside his bed. Slowly the man regained consciousness and in a wavering voice asked, "Is that you Chaplain?"

"It's me. I've seen your people and can assure you they are doing just fine."

"Thank you so much…that's a great relief."

Mike made a move to leave in order to allow the patient to fall asleep, but the captain seemed to panic momentarily and said, "Don't leave me. I don't want to be alone."

Mike pulled up a chair and gently touched the man's bandaged head and assured him he would stay by his side for as long as he was needed.

"Will you pray for me, Chaplain? I'm afraid I'm not going to make it."

"Certainly I'll say a prayer." And when he had finishes he said, "Don't worry, you're in good hands. I'm told your post op report is good."

Every time Mike had to change positions or stand aside to allow a nurse to tend the soldier's wounds the officer would appear concerned and begged him not to leave. It was some hours later when the American chaplain arrived at the hospital with the unit's RSM. With a nod and a brief word to the new arrivals, Mike quietly slipped away.

Sometime later he received a communication from the American Commander thanking him for his spiritual support to his wounded men. "You have proved again the valuable association we share. God bless you and your fellow chaplains for your continued support. Your deeds will be remembered."

*****

At dinner that night, Steele and Mike were discussing an up coming meeting with the Principal of the Sayd Pacha School when suddenly Steele asked, "You never told me about your meeting with Maria Macaroni."

Mike roared with laughter. "Her name is Marconi. She is a very beautiful Italian lady. She and Angie hit it off right away. I told her about you, that you were a confirmed bachelor, but willing for a challenge. 'Send him to me, she had said, I know someone who might change his mind.' So there you have it. You go on leave next week, perhaps you should consider Rome instead of Tokyo."

"No way. My plans are already made. I've always had a yen to see Japan."

"Well, don't say I didn't arrange a fantastic date for you. I think you may have missed a good chance!"

Steele chuckled. "So be it. I expect when I'm ready, the right person will come along. Thanks anyway."

The reconstruction work on the Sayd Pacha School at the ANA base, Camp Hero, was well underway when Mike and Steele made their next visit. It had been several weeks since they had met with Sarfraz Parvi, the Principal. He welcomed them heartily and offered the traditional *chi*. They sat cross-legged on colourful carpets and cushions enjoying the ritual brew and talking about the school's activities, when one of the senior students came in to inform Parvi that he had another caller. The Principal invited the man to join them.

"I want you to meet Major Abdul Samed. He is aware of your support of our School. The Major is the Cultural and Religious Advisor to the ANA here in Camp Hero. You might consider him the Muslim equivalent to a chaplain in the Canadian Forces."

Major Samed was a tall, fit man in his forties. He was a family man with a wife and seven children. The Major was a graduate of the Afghan Military College some twenty years earlier and was an experienced soldier. When introductions were made they expressed to each other what an honour it was to meet. Abdul stated his gratitude for what the Canadians were doing and his sorrow about the loss of Canadian soldiers. Mike and Steele reciprocated those feelings especially in light of the terrible casualties both the ANA and ANP suffered in the counter insurgency environment. Abdul then told them about his work as a CRA. They learned that a Chaplain and a CRA have a similar mission. A CRA may or may not be an Imam or a Mullah, but they were always someone who had a religious education as well as one who read and wrote Dari and Pashto. This was important since 90 per cent of ANA soldiers were illiterate. The CRAs took on the task of writing letters for their soldiers. Their ultimate goal was to teach their people to read and write thus enhancing their literacy and by improving their personnel life, and their ability to function effectively in the battle space.

Over the long relaxing conversation Abdul shared his other tasks. Like Canadian Chaplains, he advised his chain of command on issues of morale, as well as advocating for his soldiers over issues, like pay or leave that could not be resolved through the normal chain of command. This was especially important, as non-commissioned members in the Afghan army had not yet developed the same sense as Canadian non-commissioned members about understanding and caring for their soldiers' basic needs. Abdul listened to the problems of his soldiers, offering both compassion and advice, including working with their families. Afghan Security Forces often lived away from their homes for long periods of time. In this sense, Abdul's role was challenging since there were no Afghan social workers or psychologists. Mike and Steele were aware, as they shared experiences that Canadian chaplains were part of a larger team of support personnel both on deployment and on the home front, and although not always perfect, it was a significant sight better than resources for Afghan personnel. In that moment they felt gratitude for the system in which they ministered.

Teaching was an important function for a CRA. The Ministry of Defence sent a monthly schedule of topics to be taught. Afghan soldiers attended two teaching periods a week and officers twice a month. The topics were mostly religious. As there was no separation of church and state, as in Canada, the teachings included the history of Afghanistan, politics and the current realities of the insurgency. The CRA helped his soldiers understand that the insurgents were not following the true teachings of the Muslim faith, nor did they care about the people of Afghanistan. The random killing of civilians, especially women and children, by suicide bombers and IEDs, troubled Abdul and he advised that those violations were against the basic tenants of the Muslim faith. In the same way, Mike and Steele knew they performed similar teaching functions by helping soldiers to understand something of the Muslim faith and culture of the country in which they were guests. The CRAs were helpful to the Canadian mission and had come to the Multinational Role 3 Medical Facility to help the staff communicate with Afghan patients and to help them understand the patients spiritual needs, especially around death.

During 'Padre's hours', the Canadian chaplains' challenge was to be aware of and sensitive to the multi-cultural and religious fabric of Canadian personnel. Abdul's challenge was teaching in a country where each soldier was Muslim, but may cross the divide between different clans, tribes and families. He encouraged his soldiers by teaching them if they die in battle against the terrorism of the insurgence, they will go to heaven as *'sheed"*, or martyrs, for their faith and country.

By the end of their meeting, Mike and Steele were sore from sitting cross-legged, but their hearts were warmed by the experience they'd had; what a blessing it was for them to share Abdul's story and experiences… to know they had things in common in spite of their vast differences in customs and ethnic background.

* * * * *

Mike awoke in a dark place. Not only were his quarters pitch black, but so also were his dreams. He was shaking with apprehension and anxiety and wondered where these vivid bizarre hallucinations were coming from. *Dear God, he thought, am I losing it?* It seemed to him these nightmares were becoming more frequent. He sat on the edge of his cot and drew in several deep breaths in an attempt to clear his head. He stood up, slipped on his pants, and made his way to the latrine. On his return he lay back trying to sort out the meaning of his outlandish nightmares. *Maybe I should talk with someone…but whom? God forbid I don't want to appear to be a basket case. I wonder how others deal with these feelings? Should I discuss this with a team member or someone at the hospital? Yet I don't want to burden anyone on the team for surely they have demons of their own to contend with.* It came down to the age-old question: The soldier can take their problems to the padre, but whom does the padre take his concerns to? Suddenly, it came to him. He had established a close relationship with one of the doctors, Major Sid Joss. He was a devout Christian man who practiced what he believed. Mike had observed Sid's strict professional ethics in dealing with confidentiality and the well being of soldiers whom he had counselled. *I will talk with Sid. He knows me pretty well. In fact, when I think about it, he has already been there for me.*

Following breakfast, Mike made his way to Role 3 where Doctor Sid was making the rounds of the trauma ward. The chaplain spoke with several patients, waiting until the doctor had finished his evaluations.

"Sid, could I have a few minutes of your time?"

"Sure, let me file these notes and I'll be right with you. Come with me."

The doctor led Mike to a cubical where they could have a private conversation, but when they came to the sensitive outpouring of his state of mind, the physician suggested they take a walk where discretion could be maintained.

"I am having these persistent disturbing dreams that I can't seem to shake. I wake anxious and confused, often in a cold sweat, and find myself exhausted as if I had been in a physical wrestling match all night. I try to sort out the meaning of these nightmares, but come up short. I pray for enlightenment, but receive no answer. I pray that I'm not letting people down…that I am supporting them through their grizzly tasking…I just don't know where I'm at…and here we are in the last days of our tour."

"First of all, Mike, you've got to realize you are not alone. All of us are affected by the stress of battle and the consequent injuries to mind and body that ensue. You've seen it throughout our medical team. We've touched on this before. Do you recall a Role 3 staff meeting where this very subject was discussed? You contributed valuable information by sharing your experience in stressful situations "out side the wire", especially with the murdered Mullah and his family. You are bound to have residual feelings and concerns. Did I do the right things under pressure? Or did I add to the confusion? Did I say the right things? The mind of a good person can be bombarded with unfounded thoughts. I've come to know you quite well, not that I am playing the psychiatrist card, but by simple observation as a friend, and as my padre. It's important that you do what you're doing now, talk things out and vent your feelings. Keeping them inside leads to a poisoning of the spirit. Like you, I am a person who listens…a person you can trust without reservation, but I think you already know that."

The two caregivers took the remainder of the morning addressing Mike's distress, after which the chaplain felt the burden on his shoulders lighten. The doctor's concluding statement seemed to sum up the situation.

"You must not let a fixation on wayward thoughts detract from the good works that you have accomplished. You are a talented man, Mike, and have used your spiritual gifts wisely to the benefit of those you serve."

"Sid, thank you for your listening and wisdom. It helps tremendously. Thank you for helping me trust again what I already knew. You're a good doctor and you do make a difference. Bless you!"

"You did it yourself…you just had to let it out. Don't forget, Mike, you make a difference too…never doubt that. One has only to see you with troubled people to validate your dedication…and I bless you in turn for your assistance as a chaplain. You may not realize it, but your spiritual strength has been a Godsend to me personally. You have had a positive and significant impact on the morale, welfare and spirituality of those you have come in contact with during your tour. I thank you for that."

* * * * *

The last days in theatre came with a rush. Mike had little time to think inwardly, but concentrated on packing his bags and barrack boxes. Mike had procured a number of souvenirs for the folks back home. He found a place to transport two beautifully woven prayer rugs that he planned to place beside his and Angie's bed. As he made his rounds to say goodbye he included the Afghan merchants with whom he had bargained, the civilian personnel at KAF who supported the operation of the Base, and found a moment to slip into Kandahar City to visit Hassan, the murdered Mullah Faizullah's son, and to assure him that they would keep in touch. The boy became uncharacteristically emotional, his eyes filled with tears, and he placed his hand over his heart when Mike departed.

On returning to KAF, he checked his computer for e-mails and found one from his friend, Tim, the Naval chaplain.

> Aboard HMCS Iroquois
> The Dockyard
> Halifax NS
>
> Hello Mike
> We are finally home again!! I know you still have a few more days left in your tour. We must make plans to get together after your return and when you're ready. Is that invitation still open to visit you in Ontario at the family cottage? I'd love to get out in your bass boat and shoot the breeze.
> The day in, day out ministry onboard continued right up till our arrival home, and continues even after our return.
> Preparation for homecoming was an important part of closure. It seemed for some that the hardest part of a tour was the 6 to 12 weeks following home coming; the re-integration of families, or a single individual who then became very much 'alone,' no longer living with 50 of their closest friends was sometimes very difficult. Coming home is kind of a "time-warp" having all left home on a certain day, and from that time forward we were cut off from the daily routine of home; so we were left with memories of home as it was at that moment in time. However, for those at home, life continued, changed, and adjusted to a routine without us. The spouse/family at home carried on with all the normal events of life; school, chicken pox, struggling teenagers and such, while we at sea lived an insulated life from those realities. As such,

part of the ministry at the end of a mission was to talk to all members of the crew about the Reunion and Re-integration Process.

With help from lessons learned by chaplains who had already gone through this, I prepared a briefing that was presented over a number of days talking about the challenges that we could face upon returning home.

At dockside, the jetty was swarming with family and friends. Once the lines were secure and the brow landed, the Commanding Officer and the Coxswain went ashore, followed by the winner of the "First Across the Brow" raffle, then by a stream of crew all 'politely' rushing off the ship. It was hard not to tumble ashore over top others. Most important was that we were able to get into the arms of our family and friends. After the initial hugs and tears and with a bit of traffic control we made our way back onto the ship to gather our belongings.

There are no words to express what it means to be back home after a tour – and we thank God for the safe return of our ship and crew and care for our families and friends while we were absent one from the other.

Ministry continues now as there are follow-ups to do, but even though I will have to break from being IROQUOIS's padre officially, I will never really lose my love and care for the people I served on this mission… though we may all scatter to new opportunities.

And so, my friend, until we meet again in the near future, God willing, I will close wishing you a safe return.

Ever your friend,
Tim

Chapter Thirteen

E-mail
From Michael Russell
To Angie Russell
20 June 2007

Dearest Angie.

Our return Roto dates have just been posted. I will be returning home on July 18th, God willing and the White Knuckle Airlines fly! I can hardly wait. Some say the last weeks pass quickly, while others find it a real drag. I have no fear of that as our days are full… if one keeps busy time will go more swiftly.

I am still bathing in the afterglow of our visit to Rome. What a spectacular city, so dynamic and full of history. Wonderful that they have been able to preserve and restore the ancient buildings. The Vatican treasures are of priceless value to both the Church of Rome and all who view them.

I can still taste the food at that little restaurant we found on our last night in the Trastavere…and, of course, our 'night cap' back at our flat. You were absolutely glowing!

The days will speed by… I know it… see you soon.

Sweetheart, I love you.
Mike

* * * * *

Mike, much to his chagrin, was loaded on the first chalk back to Canada. He challenged the order, but was told since he had arrived with the first elements of TF-07, he would be required to be amongst the first to return.

"But Malcolm, I need to stay until the end of the rotation. If I don't I would feel I'd be letting the Battle Group down."

"Sorry, Mike, I spoke with Colonel Walker and he says as long as one of his chaplains remains, he is content with your return date. Orders are orders and we, as chaplains, will comply. There is enough disruption with the process to begin with, so accept the fact. I'm sure those who are going with you will be glad to have their padre to talk with…remember you're still doing a service."

In the next days that followed, Mike was busy interviewing soldiers in anticipation for the decompression stage and preparing them for their return home. On the last day, he was keen to be gone. He was tired. The vision of Angie was forefront in his mind. He wondered how his transition would go from the intense activity of a war theatre to the contrasting laid-back quiet of his parish. Would his parishioners see him in a different light? Had he changed very much, and if so, in what way?

The night before take off, the troops were moved to large transit tents. Each person was allowed to take three pieces of luggage with them on the flight…a barrack box, a kit bag and a rucksack; anything extra would be shipped directly to Canada. Morning came and the chalk was loaded aboard Hercules aircraft for the hop to Camp Mirage. It was a quiet flight except for the hum of the engines. Very few people were talking. Most appeared lost in their own thoughts or listened to music on their ipods… some dozed with heads hung forward over their chests. Seating on a Herc was not comfortable, to say the least.

As the troops disembarked from the aircraft, a Movements team met them and directed them to an area where they could shower and freshen up. Civilian clothes that they were allowed to wear onward were removed from baggage and uniforms packed in there place.

Padre Anna Brooks was aware of Mike's immanent arrival and was waiting for him.

"Welcome to Camp Mirage," she greeted as he made his way across the tarmac.

"Hello Anna, good to see you again."

"You look tired. I suppose your last few days have been hectic? Well, you can begin to unwind now. Come with me and let me offer you some hospitality. You can change and shower in the chaplain's quarters."

"Thank you so much, and yes I do feel draggy. How are things with you?"

"Much the same as usual. It's always a busy place with the comings and goings, but one gets into a routine after a while."

"By the way, Anna, thanks again for your kindness when I came through after my leave. You do a wonderful piece of work here at CM meeting the flights coming in. Your care of compassionate situations is recognized as a great service and morale booster for our troops in theatre. Personally speaking, our conversation at the time I returned from leave gave me pause to prepare for the return to duty. It was kind of hard leaving Angie, almost like going back for a second tour."

Major the Reverend Anna Brooks, an Air force Chaplain, was the senior Canadian chaplain at Camp Mirage. In the past several weeks she had met people who were coming into theatre as handover personnel. The new arrivals were eager to get on their way, as they wanted to become firmly established at KAF before their main body of troops arrived. Occasionally there were delays in transferring from Camp Mirage to Afghanistan due to a shortage of Hercules aircraft that required minor repairs or servicing. Only four of these planes were allowed into this transient point at any given time. This restriction was part of the agreement the Canadian Government was required to comply with to obtain landing rights. Other assets of the Air Force were held in reserve at KAF.

Camp Mirage, (CM) because of its transient nature, was a high-pressure location that operated on a 24/7 basis. At any given time it was staffed mainly by Air Force personnel.

Earlier in the day Padre Brooks, as was her custom, looked over the dining facility to find an individual or a group she could join for breakfast. She possessed a keen intuition that zeroed in on the atmosphere of any given scene where people gathered…alert to any unusual signs of some one acting isolated or miserable. Brooks was a good judge of character and her 'flock' knew her as a straight shooter who called a spade a spade. It would be a Frosty Friday when a person could pull the wool over her eyes. On the other hand, there was no one at Camp Mirage with a bigger heart. Frequently compassionate cases were referred to her from KAF and she would meet the aircraft and take the person aside, talk with them to ease their stress, and in the case of death or some kind of other tragedy, listen with sincere empathy to the party to comfort them through their pain.

Padre Brooks was well supported by the Command staff that viewed her function as indispensable for the morale of CM, both those who served there, and the many who passed through on their way in and out of theatre.

She was as caring as always in her response to Mike's gratitude about her pastoral care, expressed as they stood on the tarmac at Mirage. "A lot of people feel like you did Mike, in returning to theatre after leave, and going back in for the second part of your tour. I'm glad I was helpful to you as you returned after leaving your wife. But now…you're on your way home via Cyprus and I hope you find the transition time there helpful. It's such a beautiful location. I'm told you can physically feel the tension drain away, so be prepared to relax and try to remember not to get involved in chaplain duties. People there will fill that role. You're there to de-compress too!"

* * * * *

After showers and a meal, the troops, now in civilian dress, boarded an Airbus for the trip to Cyprus. It was a smoother flight on a quieter plane and conversations were livelier. Many talked of their expectations when arriving home, some worried about the kind of reception they would receive, knowing that problems existed on the home front that would have to be resolved.

The interval in Cyprus was deemed essential to allow the troops this kind of breathing space, a time to let off steam, before returning to their families and communities back in Canada. Mike knew the Canadian chaplain, Major Laurelle Callaghan who had developed the decompression concept. It stemmed from her own experience when she returned from duty in Kosovo…she had left a war torn country only to be thrust suddenly back home into a different time zone and a different atmosphere. It was disconcerting and a distinct jolt to both her and her family. Callaghan worked diligently on a plan for a more humanizing approach to repatriation. In consultation with her Commanding Officer and other chaplains, she developed the idea of holding interviews with returning troops where an assessment could be made of their state of mind. Realistic conversations could be held to investigate workplace re-integration back in Canada, home-front situations, anger management, and potential posttraumatic stress situations.

As it developed into a working plan, the first interviews were held in theatre where the soldier was asked: 1) What was the best part of the tour? 2) What was the worst part of the tour? 3) What are you going to tell people when you get home?

The third question was significant as it brought out most of their concerns and fears. Individuals knew they would become the centre of attention and would be grilled on their experiences and came to understand that they needed 'a good and honest story' to tell.

Going home from modern war zones was different from when WW2 troops came home by long journeys on ships and had time, for the most part, to detach physically from action and more deliberately talk things out. In the current time of war, people could go from hell to home in a matter of hours. The insertion of a decompression layover with counselling would go a long way to lessen or identify problems.

It was this decompression process that allowed the personnel on the flight with Mike to begin to let their guard down as they headed to Cyprus. The stress of combat was beginning to ebb and some of the older soldiers told tales of their exploits while serving as UN Peacekeepers on Cyprus.

"Wait till you taste the Brandy sours they make there. Just don't knock too many down or you'll have to be carried back to the hotel. Why I knew a fellow"…and the tall tales began to flow much to the merriment of those inclined to listen.

As the Airbus descended into the Cypriot airport, Mike was in a window seat, and had a bird's eye view of the surrounding territory. He was fascinated by the environmental and geographical change below. The countryside was green and lush, cultivated fields and citrus groves dotted the landscape.

Buses gathered at the airport to transfer the chalk of 80 soldiers to a luxurious beach side resort where a Canadian cadre support team lined the entrance walkway and clapped their hands in greeting. It was a greeting unexpected by the troops and triggered their emotions so that more than a few cried openly. It was like the first expression of welcome back home for those who had been away for many arduous months.

After check-ins, the group was briefed on the various facilities and recreation possibilities that were available, as well as a schedule of events that would take place as part of the decompression program. A lecture series known as 'Battlemind' was given by one of the chaplains deployed with the Decompression Team. This was a plan of procedure that had been developed by the Americans following their deployment in Iraq that allowed the now veteran soldiers a chance to look inward through another person's eyes. The purpose of the agenda was to provide intervention therapy between the battlefield experience and the onset of Post Traumatic symptoms. It was delivered by means of classes using both lecture and video techniques geared to prevent behaviour learned while deployed from manifesting as maladaptive behaviour once the soldier returned home.

A great deal of free time was built into the agenda and a favourite place to head for was the swimming pool with adjoining hot tubs and spa. A number of young females and males dressed in revealing beach ware added to the attraction of the site. A full 'free day' allowed people to take tours to a variety of places such as historical monasteries, old towns and villages where they could shop, or to a scuba diving location in the Mediterranean. Several found transportation to Nicosia where they had been stationed years before on UN duty and searched out old haunts where they had dined on Turkish or Greek foods. Each soldier was given an allowance of money for meals, transportation and tours. The Town of Paphos is a delightful centre with many places of interest and a wide variety of shops and restaurants. Cypriot linens for dinner tables were a popular purchase.

Mike spent much time on that sunny day, wandering the area. He was thankful for his issued sunglasses to shade his eyes from the bright sun, relieved there was no KAF dust to protect his eyes from anymore. He stopped for a drink at Starbucks, just a familiar reminder of home. Finishing his cold drink, Mike headed back out into the bright light of day. He visited the local stores for family souvenirs and found one shop that offered a tablecloth and napkins at an excellent price. The storeowner indicated that an eighty-year old lady high up in the hills north of Paphos crafted the fine detailed needlework. It had taken her many painstaking months to complete her work.

"Thank you for that information," said Mike. "My wife will be thrilled with this gift."

"Are you a Canadian, by any chance," asked the shopkeeper?

"I am," relied Mike.

"I thought I recognized your way of speaking. My name is Andreas and I used to have a shop in Nicosia before the Turks invaded the northern regions. It was very close to the Canadian Headquarters. Your people were my best patrons. Are you just visiting Cyprus?"

"Just passing through, actually, I've been serving in Afghanistan."

"I thought you looked like a soldier. Did you see much action?"

"I am a chaplain, so I was a non-combatant."

"I knew several Canadian chaplains...wonderful people. Can I buy you a soft drink or perhaps a coffee, Sir? Let me show you a few more items. I will give you a very good price."

"Thank you, Andreas, you are a good salesman, but I must move on. I'm meeting a friend at the Top Town Restaurant in a few minutes and I'm already a late. I believe the proprietor's name is Tony Apostolakos. I was told he had a restaurant by the same name in Kyrenia before the Turkish invasion."

"Yes, that is the one. He lost everything including the shirt off his back...barely got out with his life. His wife was a British citizen and they allowed her go back to England, but she returned to Cyprus and they re-settled here in Paphos."

"I have an old friend back in Canada who used to dine at Tony's place in the seventies. He was a chaplain, too. In fact, he shared some recipes with Tony that became a part of the restaurant menu. It will be interesting to meet him."

Sergeant Major Jack O'Brien was enjoying a cold local beer in the small bar at Top Town and waved a welcome hand as Mike entered the restaurant. It was an old one-story building with a garden roof where meals were served on pleasant days. Container plants with small palms were selectively located to provide an outdoors ambience and the outside half-walls were covered with a fuchsia flowered bougainvillea vine. The bar was immediately inside the entranceway with the main dining room through a set of double doors and the motif was Mediterranean in style with rounded arches over the windows.

Jack looked at his watch and grinned. "And here I thought padres were never late! Come sit over here. I'll give the waiter a high sign. What'll you have to drink?"

"My mouth is watering for one of those Brandy sours I've been hearing about...supposed to be the best drink in the world, according to the old sweats, that is, those who don't nuzzle beer all day," answered Mike with a chuckle.

When the waiter brought them their drinks, Mike asked him if he could speak with the owner.

"Sorry, Sir, Tony is up in Nicosia and not expected back until later. Is there a message I could pass?"

"No, that's alright, I'll write a note for you to give to him...it's about an old friend of his from Kyrenia days."

At dinner, Mike and Jack were served a full Greek meal of humus, grilled calamari, roast lamb and a crunchy, sweet, honey soaked baklava for desert. They had Filfar, the Cypriot orange liqueur, with Turkish coffee to end the sumptuous dinner and returned to their hotel well sated. Mike went through the evening alternating from focusing on the visit with Jack, and finding himself feeling the experience to be a bit surreal, pinching himself mentally to ensure that he really wasn't at KAF anymore, and really in Cyprus and on his way home.

It was not until the next morning that Mike realized he was missing his expensive sunglasses. He tried to think where he might have left them and decided to retrace his steps while shopping the previous day. At the Starbuck's coffee shop, he enquired if a pair of sunglasses had been found and was told none had been handed in. He proceeded to an old church supply store that he had previously browsed with the intention of returning to purchase some religious items. The owner of the store waited on him and offered him a Turkish coffee, that he accepted and soon they were having a great visit. When the merchant learned that Mike was a chaplain, he asked if he could give him a gift from his shop and indicated a wall where a group of icon paintings were on display.

"Please choose one, Father,"

"Why thank you, but you select one for me," said Mike.

"How about this one," suggested the proprietor pointing to a picture, and said. "This is a painting of Saint Anthony of Padua, Saint of lost things." He went on to share a few stories of how he had lost some items and Saint Anthony had helped him find them.

The remark seemed unusual to Mike as he thought immediately of his lost sunglasses and it occurred to him to check back at Starbuck's ... perhaps it was a sign from the Saint. And indeed it was. At the coffee shop the server, whom he had spoken to earlier, told him the glasses had been located just after his last visit. So, thought Mike, the Saint has blessed me.

The four days of relaxation and decompression sessions on Cyprus passed in the twinkling of an eye. Before boarding the Airbus for the trans-Atlantic crossing, the soldiers changed from civilian dress back into their cad pat uniforms for their return to Canada. As they approached the Canadian coast, a pair of Air force F-18s from CFB Bagotville fell into formation beside them and one of the fighter pilots hooked up with the Airbus radio to welcome the troops back home and to thank them for their service. It was another moving and emotional moment for those onboard.

It was late afternoon when the plane dropped into the Fredericton airport where a crowd of people awaited the arrival and in the midst was Angie waving wildly as the passengers descended. The crowd was told to proceed to the Base as the troops were taken directly by bus to CFB Gagetown for their return documentation before being released to join their families. It was a heart-warming reunion and another dam of emotions was opened.

Chapter Fourteen

Homecoming. There is a time for celebration and a time for sombre reflection; a time to remember and a time to forget; a time for thanksgiving and a time to withhold thanks; a time to re-integrate and sort those things out that might obsess the mind.

In the 2 RCR drill hall, the families were united with their loved ones returning from Afghanistan. Spouses dodged about trying to get a glimpse of their partner. Before the troops were dismissed, the CFB Gagetown Base Commander addressed them and then presented several awards. To his surprise, Mike was called forward to receive a commendation that read:

CANADIAN EXPEDITIONARY FORCE COMMANDER'S COMMENDATION

"Captain Michael Russell deployed to Afghanistan as one of the 2nd Battalion, The Royal Canadian Regiment Battle Group Chaplains from February to August 2007. With unwavering devotion and concern for the welfare of soldiers, he provided compassionate counselling that assisted them in coming to terms with grief, thereby being instrumental in their return to operations. Trusted and highly respected by all members of the Battle Group, he was duly regarded as a "soldiers padre" and greatly contributed to the overall mission success."

Mike blushed at the applause that followed. He spotted where Angie waited with the other dependants and saw her raise a handkerchief to her eyes. On the order to dismiss, the scene was one of near pandemonium.

Children ran about screaming with joy when their parent appeared, then dashed into waiting arms to be hugged, kissed and reassured. Some though hid behind a parent's leg, unsure who this person was who had been gone so long. There were tears of happiness and jubilation.

"Oh, Michael, never leave me again," Angie beseeched, tears streaming, as he enveloped her in a bear hug. But, within moments there were tugs on Michael's arm as some soldiers brought their family members to meet 'their Padre' who had been with them through good times and painful moments. And others came over to meet Angie, the spouse lucky enough to have this caring and gentle man as her husband.

The day was one of celebration, but in the late afternoon, Mike and Angie slipped over to St Luke's Chapel where they knelt side by side to give thanks for his safe return, the life of their baby growing within Angie, and to remember those who had lost their lives and those who had received grievous injury to body and mind. Mike prayed for vision and guidance, as he was well aware that he still had things to sort out. His nightmares had abated, but he continued to have vivid dreams of his tour, some good, and a few disturbing. He knew, that with time, these would begin to fade, especially with Angie by his side to comfort him. He trusted that in faith, he could face the future fearlessly.

Two days later, they were homeward bound. Their car was loaded with Mike's personal gear and the gifts he had brought back with him. Mike felt he was also getting gifts…Angie in the car by his side, and the loveliness of reaching over during the drive to touch her abdomen where their child nestled. They stopped for a night in Quebec City with Angie's parents who enthusiastically welcomed him. Henri LeClaire was determined to take Mike aside and question him thoroughly on his experiences. He was anxious to compare notes from his own time in the service during WW2, but his wife, Colleen, cautioned him.

"Leave the boy alone, Henri, give him some space to recover from his travels and his tour. We'll drive up and see them in a couple of weeks and then you and his grandfather 'can have at him' after he's had a time to rest and recuperate."

"Thanks, Mom," said Angie. "He is still in his coming-down phase. Re-integration should be a slow process where the person is no longer under pressure to perform."

"*Aw Oui!*" I should be more considerate knowing what I went through. *S'il vous plait me pardoner.*"

"No forgiveness necessary," relied Mike. "And we will have a good chat when you come to Plevna."

* * * * *

It was as six-hour drive from the LeClaire home to the rectory in Plevna. They arrived in mid afternoon on a hot summer day. The air conditioning in the car had afforded them a pleasant trip, but as soon as the Buick's doors were open the stifling air and humidity hit them.

"Some contrast from KAF," snickered Mike. "There the heat is less humid. I hope the house is cooler." And it was. Canon Russell had set the thermostat to seventy-two degrees F. The neighbours that had been alerted to the couple's immanent arrival came outside and cheered a welcome to the homecoming soldier.

"I hope you're ready for this," remarked the Canon. "The whole village wanted to know when you were due home…so I told them. And I also said, 'Let's wait till Sunday for any community get together', but they were adamant and insisted that we gather at the Community Hall Saturday evening. So, be prepared for the day after tomorrow!"

"It's so good to have you home, Michael, you have been in my prayers every day," said Grandma Russell with heart felt emotion showing on her face. Mike hugged her and she clung to him not wanting to let him go.

"Come on, Mother, let's get out of here and head for the cottage. These two need to unwind and settle in."

"I've left the fridge stocked, Angie," said Grandma. "I don't think you'll need anything for a couple of days."

"And I put a bottle of champagne there to chill. So enjoy," added the Canon.

* * * * *

"I don't know what I missed more, this bed or having you in it. Do you think when that wee one comes there will be room for three of us?" teased Mike stroking Angie's still flat tummy.

Angie mocked him right back. "We'll if it's a tight squeeze, you can always move into the spare room."

"That'll be the day! You and I will guard the edges and the babe can sleep between us."

"Think you have it sorted out, do you? Time will tell, but for now let's just curl up together."

Saturday morning, there were many vehicles parked by the Community Hall. The 'decoration brigade' was in action. Canadian flags were hung outside the entranceway and people scurried around carrying embellishments into the building. The entire district seemed to be pitching in for the celebration, for as Lucy Kellar was heard to say, "It's not just a party for the parish, and everyone wants to join in. After all, look how many responded to help the Afghan kids…it was the whole neighbourhood and beyond."

By seven in the evening, the parking spaces around the hall were filled and an overflow of cars lined the street. A piper entertained the crowd as they arrived and the skirl of the bagpipes set toes a-tapping. Inside the building walls and windows were grandly decorated for the occasion, while on the stage a group of local musicians played folk and country tunes. It was a merry gathering. A bar had been set up in a corner with a sign overhead, "IF YOU DRINK, DON"T DRIVE." And in case some didn't heed the warning, there were four Provincial Police Officers in attendance keeping an eye on things, but their primary task was to act as an honour guard for Mike on his arrival

Hand in hand, Angie and Mike walked down the street along with his grandparents. As they approached the hall, people began to pour out and cheer. The OPP Officers stood either side of the doorway at attention while the 'official' party entered. The shindig was formally underway and before long the chant went up, "Mike. Mike. Mike."

Grinning ear-to-ear, and a little overwhelmed, Mike took a deep breath, then mounted the platform. A great cheer went up.

"Thank you everybody for this fantastic welcome. I am almost lost for words, but not quite." Much laughter. "How can I ever tell you how much your support has meant to me while I was in Afghanistan. I received letters and care packages from friends, and from people I barely knew. These I shared with my soldiers in the lonely outposts where treats and messages from home were very precious. I felt your care and good will for the troops, myself, and the hurting people of Afghanistan. Many of you, through Lucy Kellar, pitched in to send much needed school supplies and equipment to the poor and deserving children of Afghanistan. I could spend an hour telling you of their desperate situations, but I'll leave that to another time as I plan to give a series of talks on my experiences over there. If you want to hear more, you'll have ample notification as to where and when. I also know from my grandfather, whose excellent care you were in, that there have been changes, concerns, and events in many of your lives, and I am eager to hear from you as we reacquaint ourselves with each other.

"Before I step down, I want Lucy to join me on the platform." A way was made for her and as she reached the stage, Mike reached down and took her hand. "This young lady is, and should be, an inspiration to everyone. I was almost going to say that she single-handedly took on a project that people older than her would have found trying. But, of course, she didn't do it by herself. She did it with your backing…and her dad and his company saw to it that the goods were delivered.

"When I left the Pasha Sayd School, I was given this picture, signed by a group of girls in their own class room where your gifts from Canada provided the furniture." Mike held up the picture for viewing. "Girls in Afghanistan are rarely given the opportunity for an education. Things are changing over there and we as Canadians should be justly proud of our contribution toward a people who have endured years of warfare and abject poverty under a ruthless regime. But there I go, sounding off when I had just finished saying I would relate the story at a later date."

"Lucy," said Mike, "That picture is a gift from the girls you have helped. Now, here is my present to you. Angie, please pass me that parcel. Lucy, I had this prayer rug made especially for you. I told the craftsman the story of your project to help Afghan children. He was impressed and as a special token to you he has woven your name into the carpet. Please accept it with my gratitude for your unfailing devotion."

The hall erupted in loud cheers. Lucy was overcome and could only say, 'Thank you to Mike', and then she reached up and kissed his cheek.

Angie laughed and said in an aside to her husband, "Oh my, looks like I've got more competition?"

The party went on until late in the evening with dancing and merry making. In generic terms, a good time was had by all.

Many months had gone by. In the fall, Maria did enjoy a visit with Angie and Mike. In return she invited them to join her at the Toronto Film Festival. When February rolled around, Angie presented Mike with a beautiful baby girl on Valentine's Day. There was a little worry during the birthing, as the child seemed hesitant to make her way into world. Mike was heard to say after the safe delivery. "Just like her mother…a mind of her own!"

Mike experienced a busy first year home. He'd had some apprehension concerning his re-integration into his role in parish ministry. This worry soon dissipated as his flock greeted him with open arms. Indeed, they fretted for fear the Bishop was going to offer him a larger parish 'out front', but Mike had foreseen this possibility and had asked the Bishop to allow him to stay in the Land of Lakes Parish for at least one more year until he was re-settled after his wartime experiences.

Mike kept his promise and delivered a series of talks and lectures on the chaplain's role in Afghanistan, and his reflections on the plight of Afghans. Many had difficulty comprehending the complexity of Canada's commitment to the people of Afghanistan, but Mike simply summed things up by saying, "We are needed there. As a freedom loving people, it's the least we can do!" He addressed churches of other denominations and was frequently called upon to speak at Service Club meetings and schools. Occasionally he received an honorarium for his participation and these sums he turned over to Lucy Keller's ongoing project for Afghan children. Chaplains in succeeding rotations after Mike's had accepted the responsibility for delivering supplies and monitoring the developments at the school where funds received were donated toward other school projects. A healthy dialogue was established between Lucy and the girls at the Syad Pasha School. Pictures were exchanged and Lucy could see in their letters how well the students were learning and improving their status as future leaders for their country.

As for Mike and his inner journey, he put it this way: "People sometimes ask me if I am more impatient with other's peoples seemingly small problems, in fact I feel the opposite. I believe that I have more patience and a better understanding of where people are coming from.

In terms of God, I believe that my faith is stronger…my sense of thankfulness for life and the small things feels deeper. My anxiety about the future and how it might increase seem not as strong…I am more able to take each day on its own and live in it…I can very quickly in my mind and imagination go back to the tour…things like newspaper articles, things I see around my life…such as carpets, souvenirs and photographs can take me back and I will find myself reliving or re-looking at things as if they were a movie. They are not tormenting memories, nor do they scare me or upset me. They are often good and warm…the Afghan sky at night from a FOB with no other light obscuring the stars…riding in a LAV or a Nyala… seeing the faces of the other soldiers. Then there are ones of watching the blood being mopped up after a mass casualty in the hospital; standing waiting for the helicopters to come in, wondering who the casualties were and what kind of condition they were in; standing beside the remains of a soldier's body in prayer with the hospital or morgue staff; waiting with wounded soldiers - either to call home or to try to determine what next might unfold; wondering how the families of our dead soldiers were doing after their loved ones died and how they felt about the loss and whether they could live with it being necessary; wondering what they had missed in their lives, feeling sad that they were in the news because of their deaths... and in the eye of the country for a week or two and then too soon forgotten; thinking about the good people I worked for and with, and what they meant and still mean to me; re-walking the road sweeps, going into combat, walking through fields wondering about stepping on the mines, being shot at, riding in vehicles and keeping the possibility of a IED blast far, far away at the recess of my mind; all the ways I looked for and created to serve people, care for them, listen to them, to give them hope.

Despite all these memories - I have at times felt reluctance to contact various people I was on tour with not really knowing what to say or what to talk about. I do have contact with some people, but it is intermittent. As much as I miss people I was deployed with, I think I also knew that something had ended when the Roto ended and if we spoke or crossed each other's path again, we'd talk and be like old friends.

So it is like I am still there in some ways - and I like those memories -but also that I have moved on...

Epilogue

There are three kinds of homecoming from a war zone. The happy kind, the suspense filled kind of returning to concerning or uncertain circumstances, and the gut wrenchingly sad kind, experienced by those who attend a Repatriation Ramp ceremony at CFB Trenton. The latter is a sombre ritual with the immediate family in attendance along with selected Government officials including the Governor General and the Minister of National Defence. The Colonel of the Regiment is present with representatives of all ranks. The Colour Party stands formally at attention with Regimental flags waving as the uniformed pallbearers march out to the aircraft to receive the fallen heroes. The coffin is lowered and the slow march begins toward the awaiting next-of-kin.

Sometime earlier the families would have arrived and directed to a closed-off section of the terminal. The VIPs greet them there. Sadness is palpable in the room with the families, magnified if there is more than one soldier repatriated. Families gather in tight groups supporting each other… some are open and wishing to speak, others keep to themselves. The VIPs circulate to talk with each group expressing condolences.

When the aircraft sets down, the Base Warrant Officer briefs people on the format for the reception ceremony. This is when the horrible reality hits home for most of the families and they begin to struggle with their emotions. When the BWO concludes his remarks, everyone files out onto the tarmac in front to the terminal. An informal guard of honour of mixed military personnel is formed to create an aisle through which the draped coffin is passed. A close friend of the deceased accompanies the body, starting in Afghanistan, and remains with the fallen during repatriation rituals and until burial is complete. An Assisting Officer assigned to care for the family from the time of notification stands with them on the tarmac. A chaplain is there to offer assistance that may be required, and lead a brief service of prayers and pastoral words). The assembled military component comes to attention and salutes as the casket is placed in the hearse. The time has come for the family to receive their loved one home. It is a trying moment for all around the hearse. After a few minutes the family and close friends move to their limos to begin the journey from CFB Trenton to Toronto along the section of Highway 401 that is now designated as the Highway of Heroes. Every overpass along the route is crowded with people paying their respects. Uniformed police officer and firefighters stand at attention and salute as the vehicles pass beneath the spans. Canadian flags are draped over the railings and young children watch with wise solemnity as the procession makes its way westward. The people of Canada are witnesses as they monitor their television sets. The Nation is hushed, and joins with the wind around the motorcade in lamenting sighs of prayer as the procession disappears in the distance.

Sleep well, my kindred spirits, we mourn your loss and pledge always to remember your valiant sacrifice.

The Final Inspection

The soldier stood and faced God,
Which must always come to pass.
He hoped his shoes were shining,
Just a brightly as his brass.

"Step forward now, you soldier,
How shall I deal with you?
Have you always turned the other cheek?
To My Church have you been true?"

The soldier squared his shoulders and said,
"No, Lord, I guess I ain't.
Because those of us who carry guns,
Can't always be a saint.

*I've had to work most Sundays,
And at times my talk was tough.
And sometimes I've been violent,
Because the world is awfully rough.*

*But, I never took a penny.
That wasn't mine to keep...
Though I worked a lot of overtime,
When the bills just got to steep.*

*And I never passed a cry for help,
Though at times I shook with fear,
And, sometimes, God forgive me,
I wept unmanly tears.*

*I know I don't deserve a place,
Among the people here.
They never wanted me around,
Except to calm their fears*

*If you've a place for me here, Lord,
It needn't be so grand.
I never expected nor had too much,
But if you don't, I'll understand."*

*There was silence all around the throne,
Where the saints had often trod.
As the soldier waited quietly,
For judgement from his God.*

*"Step forward now, you soldier,
You've borne your burdens well.
Walk peacefully on heaven's streets,
You've done your time in Hell."*

*Author
Sgt Joshua Helterbran
224th Engineer Battalion USA*